"A kiss?"

Jess was astonished. "You quit your job on the basis of one kiss?"

"It's not as idiotic as you're making it sound," Alison said irritably. Her blue eyes were stormy as they glared at Jess. "Not unless you kiss every woman like that."

"But it was only a kiss," he muttered hoarsely.

She beamed. "Not 'only.' It was *quite* a kiss."

He made an inarticulate sound deep in his throat.

"So," she went on guilelessly, "I thought we ought to see where it might lead."

It was his turn to stare. "You wanted to see where it might lead?" he rasped finally. He reached out and took hold of her, pulling her to her feet, hauling her against him.

"Here," he said, his mouth on hers. "Here's where it'll lead."

Dear Reader,

I am not one of those people who can plot a book ahead of time—just ask my editor. I am as interested in what's going to happen next as, I hope, you are. And while I am writing, I don't so much speed down four-lane highways of logic as I do clamber over rocky precipices and fall into the occasional gorge.

But though I write each book primarily by groping, there is, I find after I've finished, a logical inevitability to each story. If there isn't, I've done something wrong—I haven't been true to the characters, or perhaps I simply don't know them well enough yet, and I need to know them better before I can write the logically inevitable stuff. (This is called rewriting. My editor and I know a lot about this, too.) In any case, when I get to the end, if I've done it right, I find myself saying, "Yes, this is what I meant."

A Cowboy for Christmas grew out of a childhood preoccupation with cowboy heroes, a healthy respect for unforeseen possibilities, a belief in the virtue of dreaming impossible dreams and a serendipitous encounter with a friend who shared them all. "What if...?" I asked myself. And Jess and Alison came to life.

When I was writing this book, all those notions were inarticulate mutterings in the distance, leading me on. Now that I've finished and can sit back and see where I've been—where Alison and Jess have been and where, I hope, they are going—I understand all this much better.

I understand that Christmas is a time of belief in the unexpected. It is a time when dreams are possible, when love is within reach—for all of us, cowboys included. It is a holiday of both joy and promise, and, as such, it asks us for courage, for hope, for faith.

I hope as you read *A Cowboy for Christmas* you'll see what I mean.

Merry Christmas,

Anne

A Cowboy for Christmas

ANNE McALLISTER

SILHOUETTE

Sensation

First published in Great Britain in 1994
by Silhouette Books, Eton House, 18-24 Paradise Road,
Richmond, Surrey TW9 1SR

ISBN 0 373 59277 9

95-9411

Made and printed in Great Britain

Chapter One

If there was any animal stupider than a cow, Jess Cooper didn't know what it was. Unless, he thought grimly, it was the cowboy who had been trying unsuccessfully for the past hour to outthink one.

He scowled at the empty meadow, the untouched salt lick, the grassy slope edged by oak brush where he'd expected to find the half dozen black Angus cattle that Mike Gonzales had said he'd seen over that way yesterday.

He should've known better.

He sighed and reached up to remove his hat, then rubbed his fingers through his hair. Settling the hat back on his head, he reined his horse around and headed up the valley the other way. His bones ached and his stomach growled. He'd been too far from the ranch house to go back for dinner, and the couple of sandwiches and thermos of coffee he'd brought along had disappeared hours ago.

But these few cattle were all that was left up this way. He'd brought the rest down over the past two days so they'd be available to be checked over and sorted before shipping. If he didn't get them today, it would just mean coming back tomorrow.

He straightened, ready to head down when a gleam, sudden and unexpected, caught his eye.

He blinked. There, glistening against the velvet green backdrop far across the valley, the wide front window of the ranch house reflected the fiery brilliance of the setting sun. It stopped him mid-movement, made him settle back in the saddle and smile.

"Like a diamond," he said aloud, though if he'd been able to think of anything more precious than diamonds to compare it to, he would have. Because, had Jess Cooper seen mere jewels, he could easily have turned away.

Diamonds were just sparkly stones. Distant and unreal. Meaningless.

Not like the ranch.

The Rocking R Ranch was real. It was almost four thousand acres of southwestern Colorado: mountains and valleys, meadows of timothy and clover, forests of aspen and spruce. It was Nathan Richards, forthright and stubborn, Jess's boss. It was half a dozen horses, a couple of dogs and just over three hundred head of black Angus cattle, some stupider than others.

It was "home." He said the word softly, barely breathing life into it. He felt funny saying it, as if not only the word but its implications were alien to him.

And if he was honest, they were.

He'd been Nathan's right-hand man at the Rocking R for nearly three years, the longest he'd been any one place in his thirty-four-year life. Until now he'd never thought of any place as home. He wasn't exactly sure when he'd started thinking that way about the Rocking R.

It wasn't *House Beautiful,* that was for sure.

"House Functional," Nathan called the two-story log house he'd built twenty years ago when the first frame house on the land had burnt to the ground.

It was functional, Jess conceded. But it was something more. There was something special about it that drew him back whenever he was down in Texas at a cattle auction, up in Denver selling their own beef, or even spending a Saturday night in town.

Used to be he didn't care where he laid his head or where he woke up in the morning. Now the Rocking R was in his blood. Now he wanted to be here.

He'd even begun having hopes of owning the spread someday, making the old man an offer, putting his name on the dotted line.

But to dare to call it *home*—to actually say the word out loud—still seemed to be tempting fate.

"Presumptuous," his eighth-grade English teacher, Mrs. Peck, would have called him.

And about this Jess was afraid she would have been right.

Nathan disagreed.

Nathan Richards had had his share of dreams in seventy-nine hard-living years. "Gotta have 'em," he'd told Jess the day he'd hired him.

They'd stood facing each other in the coffee stall at the cattle auction, the old man and the young one, the dreamer and the cynic, and Nathan had taken a deep swallow of the lukewarm brew and nailed Jess with his pale blue stare.

"Gotta have dreams," Nathan repeated. "A man ain't alive without 'em."

Jess wasn't sure about that. Dreams had done more damage than good to his own father. Les Cooper could never let go of the notion that he was destined to be the world's champion steer wrestler. And he'd wrecked his marriages, all three of them, and his family in the pursuit of that dream.

Jess wanted nothing so grandiose. Generally he tried not to think about what he wanted in life. It seemed like asking for trouble.

"Don't got any dreams?" Nathan had challenged him. "Young feller like yourself?"

"Not really," Jess had replied at last.

"Damn shame, not to have hope," Nathan said. His pale eyes had regarded Jess thoughtfully. "What's it like to be hopeless?"

Jess's chin had come up. "I'm not hopeless," he said, a rough edge to his voice.

"No?" Nathan shrugged. "'Pears so to me. What's your future then? What do you want?"

Jess wrapped his hands around the coffee mug, clenching it really, not daring to think about his future, his dreams. It was like wishing on a star. Childish. Foolish.

It was enough, he reckoned, to get from day to day.

But when Nathan continued to wait for his response, he ventured gruffly, "Own me a few head of cattle. Have a place to graze 'em."

"Come work for me and you got it."

Jess simply stared. It was too simple. Too impossible to be that simple, he told himself.

Jobs—especially jobs like the one Nathan seemed to be offering—didn't just drop like roast ducks into the mouths of cowboys drinking coffee at a café. Least of all to washed-up rodeo cowboys on the mend from four cracked ribs and a broke-in-three-places leg.

But Nathan Richards meant what he said. And he had a habit of making things happen.

"'Sa matter? Don'tcha think you can do it?" he'd challenged.

And Jess, never proof against a dare, had replied, "Damn right I can."

And over the past three years, with Nathan's blustering encouragement and continual needling insistence on the necessity of looking with hope toward the future, Jess had dredged up a few dreams of his own.

Small ones to start with. That'd been hard enough.

But by the end of that first day's auction, Jess had had the start of his herd. Seven yearling heifers. Black Angus, like Nathan's.

"Put your own brand on 'em," Nathan said to him. "Got a brand figured out?"

What young boy hadn't? Jess wondered. He'd doodled his own on more schoolbook covers and carved it into more trees than he could remember.

"You bet," he replied. Now there were seventeen of them branded with his JC.

Yeah, Nathan had a way of making things work, of inspiring a guy to look ahead, to plan, to figure, to hope.

Jess still wasn't comfortable with it. But now and then he dared.

But he was still surprised when Nathan hadn't thought he was crazy, when he'd broached the subject of the ranch last week.

"Buy me out?"

Jess had been afraid the old man would laugh and tell him that some dreams really were too big, especially for men like him.

"Not right away, I don't mean," he'd protested quickly. "I know you got a lotta years left."

But Nathan's blue eyes had got that faraway look in them, the one that Jess had learned to wait on, to sit quietly and expectantly while Nathan thought things through. So he shut his mouth and waited.

The old man stretched and stuck his sock-clad feet out toward the fire, then folded his hands on top of his flat belly. His blue eyes met Jess's. "Don't see why not."

Don't see why not.

The rest of the world would have had a million objections: Jess's past, Jess's present, Jess's prospects.

God bless old Nathan Richards, Jess thought. He didn't have a one.

"Mine," he said softly now, trying out the word as he looked around him. "My ranch."

He looked over his shoulder, almost expecting to see the ghost of Mrs. Peck scowling at him. But all he saw was the empty meadow behind him. That was comeuppance enough.

"And I gotta find *my* cattle," he said to Dodger, for they were in fact his, the ones up in this pasture. And with shipping day barely two weeks away, he needed to bring them down and look them over, get them shaped up and ready to sell. Putting his heels lightly to the horse, he rode on.

If he hadn't passed them on the way up, they'd headed round the hill toward Sutter's place. It'd take him another hour before they reached a fence so he could round them up and herd them home. Provided they'd stayed together, of course. And what were the odds on that?

His stomach growled, reminding him of the time. It was getting close on toward supper. He hoped Nathan wasn't cooking anything that would burn.

The old man was a surprisingly good cook when he wanted to be.

"Course I am," he'd said, offended, when Jess had first commented on it. "What'dya think? Was your grandmother taught me."

Jess smiled now as the horse threaded his way through the aspen and down the slope. His grandmother, Ella, had cooked and kept house for Nathan until her death eight years ago. Jess had been surprised to find out that Nathan had never replaced her.

"Couldn't," the old man said simply. "She ran the show."

Jess didn't believe that, but he admired Nathan's loyalty. He'd learned in the meantime that Nathan was a better cook than Ella had ever been. He'd never said so.

Wouldn't do to give the old man a swelled head.

He was luckier this time. He'd gone scarcely more than a mile before he spotted the cattle—five in all, with four of them standing there looking at the fifth who'd got her head stuck between two strands of the barbed wire and couldn't pull back out.

"Damn fool cow."

It wasn't the first time. It wouldn't be the last, unless he made some sort of rough contraption that would prevent her from poking her head in where it didn't belong. He could sell her, of course. Serve her right to wind up on somebody's Sunday platter. But she was a damned fine-looking cow, sleek and fat. Hers had been the best of this year's calves.

"Beautiful but dumb," he told her. She couldn't even turn her head to look at him.

He dismounted and slipped between two bovine bystanders. "Think the grass is greener over there, do you?" he asked as he eased the barbed wire over her ears.

She chewed stolidly on, stepping back when he nudged her with his shoulder. "C'mon. Move it."

Freed now, she did, giving her head a little shake, then turning and ambling up toward the creek, her companions following.

"Not that way!" Jess swung back into the saddle and headed after them, cutting them off and herding them downstream, Scout the dog helping. They balked, then moved, disgruntled, going at last the way he wanted them to go.

It was another forty minutes before he'd brought them down into the hay meadow with the rest of the herd.

The wind came with just a little nip now that the sun was gone. September days were warm, but the nights cooled off quick. A guy could feel winter coming, but it was still a ways off. No snow in the air for a while yet.

He shut the gate, then took his time, enjoying the peacefulness, the sense of belonging he felt every evening now as he headed back toward the house, prolonging the anticipation.

There would be warmth there, a fire, a meal and Nathan.

After supper, while Jess leaned back and propped his feet on the hassock, Nathan would grumble about the events of the day. Later, while they played checkers, he would tell Jess what letters had come in the mail, where his far-flung family was and what they were up to now. Nathan talked about them so much that sometimes Jess felt as if they were his family, too.

The best kind of family. One that you could enjoy secondhand without having to be responsible for.

He smiled, thinking about them as he led Dodger into the barn and took off his saddle. Hell of a family Nathan had—only son in the foreign service in Sri Lanka or some damned place, grandsons in London, in Florida and L.A. His only granddaughter was a librarian in New York. Nathan had gone to visit her in July.

"What's the matter? Can't she bear to leave the big city and come out here?" Jess had asked him the day he'd taken Nathan to the airport in Durango.

He'd worried about the old man making the trip on the little plane to Denver, then having to go miles in the airport to get the jet to New York.

"I reckon she could, but she's pretty busy. I'm not."

"She oughta come here," Jess insisted. "She used to when she was a kid."

"You remember her?" Nathan lifted one white brow.

Jess shrugged. "Seen her once or twice."

"Pretty little thing, wasn't she?"

Another shrug. "Don't remember."

"Ayuh." Nathan's scepticism was obvious, but Jess ignored it.

Yes, he remembered Alison Richards. And yes, she had been pretty, with her long shiny dark hair, her wide grin and her deep blue eyes.

But she'd been no more than fifteen the last time he'd seen her. And far above his touch besides. A diplomat's daughter had little in common with a cowboy. Even if the age differential hadn't existed, he'd never have approached her. They were from different worlds.

She'd had a bit of a crush on him that summer, and he'd done his share of daydreaming about her. But he was smart enough to know nothing would come of it. Intelligent, worldly girls like Alison Richards never got serious about men like him.

In any case, getting serious about a woman wasn't something Jess ever intended to do. He'd seen enough of marriage in his childhood to know that.

He wondered, though, as he coped by himself during the weeks Nathan was gone, if the old man had mentioned to his granddaughter who his hired hand was.

He wondered if Alison Richards would remember him, if Nathan had.

He hoped not, since the last time she'd seen him, he'd been sprawled in the dust and bleeding. The mere memory of that could still make Jess squirm.

He'd waited for Nathan to say something about his visit, about Alison after he got back. The old man never did.

"So, did you have a good time?" Jess was finally forced to ask several days later when Nathan didn't volunteer anything.

"Informative," Nathan said. "Good thing I went."

Jess waited for him to elaborate, but he never did, just started talking about a bull he'd heard was for sale down El Paso way.

Jess sighed, but didn't ask anymore. A guy didn't pry. Nathan's granddaughter wasn't his business. He didn't care about her at all.

But if Nathan's granddaughter didn't come up in the conversation again, the bull did. Just this morning the old man had brought it up again. "Maybe we oughta go down after shipping this fall, take a look at 'im."

"What do we want another bull for?" Jess wanted to know.

"Always gotta look to the future, Jess. We might give it some thought."

Maybe they would, Jess thought now, unbridling Dodger and rubbing him down. Maybe they'd buy the bull and bring him home. Maybe they'd find a few head that Jess could use as well, if he could afford it.

But maybe, he thought, smiling and flexing his shoulders, he'd have all his money tied up by then.

Just as he was going out the door this morning Nathan had said they'd have to talk about putting together a land contract, too.

He gave Dodger one last stroke, filled his bin, then headed for the house, Scout at his heels.

The reflected brilliance of the sun was gone now, but in its place he saw the warm glow of light from the kitchen. His pace quickened as his stomach growled again, anticipating one of Nathan's thick stews or a slab of beef and potatoes.

He stamped up the steps, one last cue for Nathan to put the meat on, just in case he hadn't seen Jess ride in. Then he opened the door to the porch, took off his boots and rolled up his sleeves. He ran hot water in the sink, splashing it over his face and arms, then ducked his head under the faucet. Groping for a towel, he rubbed his hair briskly and mopped his face, scowling at himself in the splotchy old mirror as he did so.

His hair needed cutting again. Used to be he got it done regular. On the rodeo circuit he'd had an image of sorts and a desire to impress the ladies. Now, with only Nathan to impress, he didn't bother.

But Nathan could cut it. Better than playing checkers again and losing. He had a snowball's chance in hell of ever winning a game against the wily old fox. Nathan always had something up his sleeve, and even when you thought you had him cornered, he'd distract you.

"Got a letter from Ali today," he'd say and pat his pockets futilely. "Now what'd I do with it?" Or, with a glance at the kitchen, "Cathy Lee baked us an apple pie. Sure would like a piece. How 'bout you?"

And so Jess would ferret out the letter or cut each of them a piece of pie, and when finally he could get his mind on the game again, damned if he hadn't forgotten his well-planned move.

It was only a matter of time until Nathan captured the last of his pieces and chuckled with satisfaction.

Letting the old man hack at his head seemed a better bet all around.

Jess stuffed his feet into a pair of old moccasins, ran a comb through his hair, and, whistling softly under his breath, opened the door to the kitchen, sniffing hopefully, trying to guess what dinner would be. He didn't smell anything.

"Nate?"

He could hear the television in the living room. Nathan didn't like television. He swore he never watched it, but Jess had his suspicions.

"Thought you didn't like TV," Jess had chided him just last week after Nathan had treated him to a long discourse on Peter Jennings's story about the latest situation in the Middle East while he washed up after supper.

"Don't," Nathan huffed. "Infernal idiot box."

"So where'd you hear all this stuff you're tellin' me?"

"National Public Radio, of course."

"Of course," Jess said diplomatically, then gave Nathan a bland smile. "When did Peter Jennings go to work for National Public Radio?"

"G'wan, get out of here," Nathan grumbled. "'Less you wanta dry these dishes."

Laughing, Jess had left. Now he grinned. It would be hard for Nathan to claim National Public Radio was on the idiot box tonight.

He crept quietly into the living room, spotting Nathan's thinning white hair just visible over the top of the lounger that faced the set.

Peter Jennings had long since gone home. Whatever was on now had a laugh track and a very silly girl in a tutu doing pirouettes across a kitchen floor.

Jess shook his head. Boy, would he give Nathan a hard time about this!

He advanced stealthily until he stood directly behind Nathan's chair, then cleared his throat. "What's this? A rerun of 'All Things Considered'?"

Nathan didn't reply.

"Come on, Nate. 'Fess up. I caught you."

Nathan didn't move.

Jess frowned. "Nate?" He moved around the side of the chair, touched Nathan's shoulder. *"Nathan?"*

But Nathan didn't hear him. He didn't see Jess or the girl in the tutu who pirouetted right out the door and into a commercial for laundry detergent. He didn't feel Scout's cold wet nose nudge his hand or Jess's trembling fingers touch his cheek, then frantically grope for a pulse.

Nathan Richards was dead.

JESS COOPER could rope a steer with the best of them. He could brand a calf, ride a bull, break a horse.

He couldn't talk on the telephone worth a damn at the best of times, and he sure as hell couldn't call up Nathan's family and tell them something like that.

"You tell 'em, Charley," he pleaded with the doctor who'd met the ambulance at the hospital, examined Nathan's lifeless body, then had shaken his head sadly and told Jess what he already knew.

Charley Moran clapped a hand on Jess's shoulder. "Better coming from somebody who knows them."

"I don't!"

"Never even met them?"

"Yeah, well, once or twice, years ago. But I—"

"I've never met them at all. People don't want to hear about the death of a loved one from a stranger. Believe me, Jess."

People didn't want to hear about the death of a loved one from anyone. Jess knew that.

He twisted the brim of his hat in his fingers, damning Charley silently with his eyes. A nurse bustled past with a patient in a wheelchair. Charley squeezed his shoulder sympathetically.

"He was a swell old man. The best."

Jess nodded miserably.

"We'll all miss him."

Another nod.

Charley's hand gave one more squeeze. "No one more than you."

"Ain't that the truth." Jess looked away. He still couldn't swallow the awful lump in his throat.

"Dr. Moran?" The nurse beckoned to Charley, and the other man gave him one last sympathetic look and hurried away.

Jess stayed right where he was. He still couldn't believe it. Less than two hours ago he'd been whistling and contemplating a haircut as an alternative to letting Nathan scalp him in checkers. It hadn't been more than an hour and a half since he'd called the ambulance.

There had been no hurry by that time, of course, and he'd known it.

Jess had seen death before. His mother. His father. The old lady at the boarding house in Grand Junction. Pete Cummins, gored by that bull down Gallup way. Countless cattle and horses.

A guy ought to be used to it by now, oughtn't he? Be able to accept the inevitability?

But, God Almighty, *Nathan?*

He'd never known a man more alive than Nathan, with his guileless blue eyes that belied his devilish grin. It was Nathan, not Jess, who always talked about the future, for crying out loud. It was Nathan who had always insisted on dreams, hopes, plans.

Jess had just gone along with them, echoed them. He tried again to swallow, rubbed a hand across his eyes.

"Damn you, Nathan," he muttered. "How could you go and do something so stupid as die?"

He found a phone booth near the door of the hospital, went in, leaned against the wall and picked up the receiver.

He didn't dial. Couldn't.

He walked back out again. Charley was just coming down the corridor.

"Ah, good. You called?"

Jess shook his head. "Don't have the number," he mumbled, heading toward the door.

"Directory assistance," Charley suggested to his back.

But directory assistance was beyond Jess right now. Talking rationally to a bunch of Nathan's far-flung relatives was impossible. He got into the pickup and flicked on the ignition.

"Boleyns' will be calling you. Got to get things started," Charley said from the doorway.

Boleyns' was the undertaker, efficient as hell. Jess had no doubt but that they could get Nathan buried without the advice and consent of any relatives at all. He shoved the gearshift into reverse and whipped out of the lot.

"You can't stall around on this," Charley called after him.

But Jess was already gunning down the highway, throat tight, eyes blurred. He had some grieving to do and, as far as he was concerned, grieving came first.

HE CALLED Sri Lanka at three in the morning. It was as soon as he felt he could say the words. It also seemed a safer bet than calling anyplace in the States—more likely to be daytime for one thing, and more likely to have a bad connection for another.

Jess knew he couldn't tell anyone without his voice breaking. Nathan's son half a world away didn't have to know that.

The connection was better than he'd hoped it would be.

David Richards was shocked. His own voice broke, his pain apparent. "I'll come as soon as I can," he said. "I won't get there in time to make the arrangements. Ali can do that."

Jess hoped to God he wouldn't be expected to call her. He was vastly relieved when David said he'd take care of it.

"She'll be devastated," he told Jess. "No one loved him like Ali did."

I did, Jess thought, but he didn't say so.

"No, sir," he said quietly. He stood barefoot in the darkened living room and stared unseeing out the window into the night.

"She'll take care of everything. I'll let you know when we'll be arriving," David went on.

"I'll be expecting to hear from you."

The connection crackled. "You can...handle everything on the ranch?" David asked worriedly.

The ranch.

Jess had tried not to think about the ranch.

More than Nathan had died last night. Jess's dream had died as well. But it didn't seem fair to think of that now.

It seemed selfish, rotten. He felt guilty the instant the thought crossed his mind. His dreams didn't matter. Never had. It was Nathan who mattered, Nathan who'd been like a father and grandfather to him, Nathan who'd been for the past three years virtually all the family Jess had.

"I've never been much of a rancher," David went on shakily, his voice still ragged. "I guess you know that."

Jess struggled to keep his own emotions out of his. "Don't let it worry you, Mr. Richards. I can handle the ranch."

YOU CAN'T go home again.

Alison Richards, like any good librarian, was familiar with Thomas Wolfe's sentiment. And she believed he was right. Which was why she hadn't been back to the Rocking R Ranch in twelve long years.

She knew her father would be surprised to know she thought of the Rocking R as home. After all, she'd only spent a few summers there while she was growing up. She'd spent far more time in Beirut, Mexico City, Hong Kong and Athens.

But it was in southwestern Colorado that she'd invested her soul.

It was here in these mountains that she'd first given her heart.

Foolishness, she thought now, as she turned the rental car onto the narrow gravel road that led off the county highway and up into the hills where her grandfather had his land.

The foolish act of a foolish child. And no one save herself had ever known she'd done it.

"Just as well," she said aloud. She shook her head at the folly of the fanciful young girl she had been. She'd read too many fairy tales.

"And too many Westerns," she told herself, smiling wryly now.

She obviously hadn't watched enough television. Everyone knew that cowboys never hung around. Most of them made their careers out of riding off into the sunset at the end of the show. Why should reality be any different?

Besides, Alison had grown up now and made a career of her own. She'd made hers by going to library school. A prosaic, if fitting, end.

She'd wanted to bring to other children the same enthusiasm for reading, for learning, for understanding and enchantment, that she had known.

She was a good librarian, too. She kept up on new titles. She tried to remember her patrons' tastes in reading. She encouraged the young, sympathized with the old and stayed late to shelve books if the pages hadn't got it done by the time the library closed.

And if her life wasn't exactly what she'd dreamed it would be when she was five or ten or fifteen, well, whose was?

She was happy enough. She had a good job, a steady boyfriend, a neurotic cat. She was a grown-up now. And she'd do well to remember it, she thought, coming back, as she was, to the scene of her youthful dreams.

She'd never imagined she'd come back like this.

She'd just seen Nathan two months ago. He'd been hale and hearty, as opinionated as ever, poking his nose in every aspect of her life, looking down it at her boyfriend, Gary, scratching it at the antics of her cat.

She'd taken a week's vacation to be with him. They'd gone to Ellis Island, to a Yankees game, to lunch in the open-air pavilion at Rockefeller Center. In the daytime they'd enjoyed New York. At night they'd talked about the ranch—not the way it was now, but the way it had been.

"You oughta come back for a visit," Nathan had told her, smiling, his feet stretched out and crossed at the ankle, one toe wiggling to tease the cat.

But Alison had shaken her head. "No." She didn't want to. It was perfect just the way it was, a memory to be taken out and cherished, not a reality to be faced as an adult.

But reality had a way of intruding, no matter what. She'd just been going off to work yesterday morning when her father had rung her with the news.

"I'll get there as soon as I can," he'd said. "But if you can make the arrangements, I'd appreciate it."

"Of course."

There was only one funeral home in town. It hadn't been hard to track it down. She'd done as much arranging as she could over the phone. Nathan had, she discovered, done a lot of it himself.

"A great planner, your grandfather," Horace Boleyn had said. "Had the format of his funeral all figured out. And, of course, he'll be buried at the ranch in the family ground next to your grandmama."

"Of course."

"So, visitation Friday noon to nine. Funeral at St. Francis Church Saturday at ten? How's that suit you?"

"I think that should work."

"Call with your flight time and Cooper can pick you up at the airport."

"Cooper?" Just for a moment Alison stopped breathing.

"Jess Cooper. Your granddad's man."

Alison couldn't have said how long the silence lasted. Boleyn broke it finally, saying, "Shall I tell him to pick you up?"

"I'll rent a car. We all will. Th-thank you, Mr. Boleyn. I'll see you Friday."

She hung up and stared unseeing out the window. Jess Cooper.

Not *her* Jess Cooper.

It couldn't be. Of course it wasn't.

There were bound to be a dozen Jess Coopers in the west, maybe more. Nathan had never mentioned him, for heaven's sake! Surely if his hired man were the same cowboy who'd worked for them all those years ago, Nathan would have said.

No, she thought now as she shut the last gate and climbed back into the car to head up the narrow track toward the ranch house, it couldn't be the same Jess Cooper.

A minute later she found out it was.

Chapter Two

She was taller than he remembered. More slender.

Prettier, too, damn it.

He'd seen pictures of her since she was fifteen, of course. Nathan had taken a couple of rolls of snapshots in July. He'd caught her laughing at an outdoor café. He'd taken one of her cooking spaghetti in her apartment and another playing with some flea-bitten cat. But they hadn't done her justice.

They hadn't caught the red highlights of her long brown hair as it drifted in the breeze or her casual grace as she got out of the car or her shapely bottom as she opened the trunk.

Jess stood inside the barn and watched as she brushed her hair back from her face and looked around slowly. She wore sunglasses, so he could only guess when her gaze rested for a moment on the barn. But he felt a flicker of discomfort, wondering if she might be able to pick him out in the shadows watching her, even as he was sure she could not.

She turned then and faced the house, squared her shoulders, lifted her suitcase and headed for the door.

It was unlocked. She could get in without him. He wouldn't have to follow her, talk to her. Not yet.

But to avoid it was just postponing the inevitable. And there wasn't much point in that.

Odds were she wouldn't even remember him. And if she did, well, so what?

He rubbed his hand through his hair and settled his hat back on, jerking the brim down a bit more than usual. Then, taking a breath, feeling sort of like he felt when he was just letting himself down on an unknown bronc, he set off toward the house.

She had already disappeared into the kitchen by the time he got to the porch. He hesitated a moment on the steps, then pushed open the screen and went in.

She was standing by the table, one hand clenched on the red gingham oilcloth that covered it. In the other she held a photo that Nate had tacked up on the bulletin board—one of him and Jess, laughing together at the barbecue after the branding in the spring.

His steps made the floorboards squeak, and he stopped just inside the door.

She heard him, of course. But she took her time turning, and even when she had, he felt off balance because she was still wearing her sunglasses, and he couldn't see her eyes as her head lifted from looking at the photo to looking at him.

"Jess Cooper," she said at last.

And he knew she remembered him. He felt a tide of hot blood creep up his neck and hoped she wouldn't notice. Her voice was different than he remembered it, deeper, smokier. Of course, he told himself. It would be. She'd been a girl then. She was every bit a woman now.

He cleared his throat and bent his head acknowledging their acquaintance. "Ma'am. I just... I want to say... I'm... really sorry about... about Nathan."

He saw her swallow, then she managed a small smile. "Yes. So am I."

And then neither of them said a word.

Up the valley Jess could hear the mooing of the cattle. A jay was racketing in the branches of the pine just outside the window. He could even hear the refrigerator hum. He shifted his weight from one foot to the other. "Shall I...take your bag up...ma'am?" he asked at last.

"I'll do it."

"The bedroom—"

He started to gesture, but she said, "I thought I'd use the one I used to have. If that's all right?"

"Of course. I mean, it's not my house."

But it had been his bedroom, the one she was talking about. Yesterday evening he'd moved his gear back out to the old bunkhouse that hadn't been used since his grandmother had died, maybe before. From the first Nathan had invited him into the house, and he hadn't argued. Maybe that was what had made it seem like home to him, made him feel as if he belonged.

But Nathan's family wouldn't expect to find him there. He was only the hired hand, after all.

"You suit yourself, ma'am. I'd best be getting back to work. It's a busy time of year." He backed toward the door. "If you need anything, you let me know." He pivoted on his heel to make his escape.

"Jess?"

He turned. She had taken off her sunglasses and he felt trapped in the brilliant sea blue of her gaze. "Ma'am?"

Her lips quirked. "I know I'm older than the last time you saw me, but I didn't think I'd aged that much."

He blinked.

"You used to call me Alison."

He shrugged, feeling foolish. It wasn't her age he was stressing, for heaven's sake. It was the distance between them. But he could see she didn't understand.

"Sorry. Alison," he muttered.

"Thank you." Then as he started to leave again, she stopped him again. "How long have you been here, working for my grandfather?"

"Close on to three years."

Her eyes widened slightly as if she found it hard to believe. "He never said. Never mentioned you."

God bless Nathan Richards, Jess thought. "Prob'ly didn't think it was important." He hesitated. "Is that all, ma'am?"

She just looked at him, one brow lifted.

He scowled. "Alison," he amended at last.

She smiled. "That's all. My father should be here by suppertime. So should Doug and Peter. Chris can't get here until late. I'll have supper ready by seven. I know it's kind of late, but Dad's plane doesn't get in until late afternoon. Will that be all right?"

"You don't have to fix me supper, ma . . . er, Alison."

"But it's expected. We'd like you to come and—"

"No, thank you. I'll eat on my own." And he was down the steps and heading toward the barn before she could say any more.

It was all right to sit at the table and eat with Nathan, to listen to Nathan's plans and dreams. Nathan was his sort of person. Nathan took a man as he came, didn't expect dazzling conversation or informed world views, wouldn't think a guy was an idiot if he couldn't direct dial Sri Lanka on the first try.

But he wasn't about to eat with David Richards, hotshot diplomat, and his sophisticated offspring. Jess didn't need people looking down their noses at him.

And even if they were polite enough not to, even if they kept their conversation limited to what they had in common with him, he wouldn't be able to do that, either. What they had in common was Nathan, and there was no way in hell that he was ready to talk about Nathan Richards.

Anyway, he thought angrily, as he led his horse out of the barn and swung into the saddle, he didn't have time to talk about anyone or anything.

He had the ranch to see to.

The ranch was both Jess's pain and his salvation. He tried not to think about it as his any longer. There was no point. He didn't expect he'd have a chance to buy it now. Those who would be able to "see why not" would undoubtedly scotch it.

But he'd told David he could manage, so he did, caring for it, doing whatever needed to be done.

God knew David was right: there was a lot of work. But doing it was better than sitting around feeling sorry for himself, feeling miserable about Nathan.

Nathan couldn't have picked a worse time to die. For most of the year, he stayed at the house, planned and dreamed, did the cooking for the two of them, doctored whatever cattle Jess brought down, kept the barn mucked out.

But in fall he made decisions.

Nathan spent most of the year listening to Jess tell him about the cattle, noting which ones had good calves, which ones were sickly, which ones gained well. He would sit for hours asking questions, scratching his nose, nodding his head.

Then, in October, Nathan put everything he heard together with what he could see and decided which cattle were going to be shipped for sale in Denver and which were staying on.

In two weeks, the big trucks would be pulling in, expecting Jess to have a hundred head of cattle ready to go to the sale barn in Denver.

So he couldn't be bothered with David Richards or his clever professional sons or his beautiful grown-up daughter, Alison. This year the decisions were going to be up to him.

Surely David wouldn't sell the ranch before then.

Would he?

ALISON WAITED until he was gone, till she heard the sound of his boots hit the dirt, and then she breathed again. Slowly, tentatively, as if she wasn't quite sure she remembered how.

The second breath came easier and then the third.

It was the shock, she told herself, that made something as simple as breathing so hard. It was her astonishment at encountering Jess Cooper again face-to-face.

As a teenager she had dreamed about him nightly. A young hired man on her grandfather's ranch, he was the man on whom she'd hung her fantasy of the perfect hero.

Six feet of lean, whipcord strength, with dark shaggy hair, tanned, work-hardened hands and mysterious dark brown eyes, Jess Cooper had attracted her from the moment she'd first seen him.

Maybe it was the way he sat a horse, or maybe it was the way he wore his hat. Maybe it was his cool, quick competence in the saddle and his slightly shy awkwardness when she'd met him later in the kitchen. Maybe it was simply the physical Jess Cooper with his lean, rangy, hard-muscled body and his soul-melting eyes. Heaven knew, just that would have been enough.

But whatever it was, he was the one she thought of whenever she read about knights in shining armor. He was the one she dreamed of whenever romantic heroes were mentioned.

In all the books she'd read, Alison had never had another fantasy hero affect her the way Jess had. She hadn't been able to look at him without her heartbeat quickening and her palms becoming damp.

It had been twelve years since she'd seen him, and she had never completely forgotten.

He must think she was a total idiot, she fumed now, her cheeks warming at the memory of the past few moments. She had acted almost as tongue-tied and foolish this time as she had whenever she'd been around him all those years ago.

Except that last time...

The last time had been different.

It had been the day before she was to leave Colorado and go back to Mexico City. She had been out for a ride, hoping against hope that she would run into Jess.

She wanted to give him one last chance to say all those things she'd dreamed of him saying, to tell her he cared, to ask her to write to him and to promise that he would write to her.

She had headed up toward the north meadow because she'd overheard the foreman telling her grandfather that there was a break in the fence up there. But, though she rode for two hours, Alison had never found the fence break, and at last she gave up, convinced that she'd missed him.

She'd been following the creek down through the woods toward the lower meadow near the road when she'd heard voices, hard and angry, and the sounds of scuffling. Curious, she'd urged the horse forward.

Coming into the clearing, she'd halted only for an instant to take in the scene. She'd found Jess, all right.

He was lying on the ground, fighting for all his worth against the three men who were pounding him into the dirt.

Alison didn't even stop to think. She just kicked her heels into the horse's sides, riding right towards the men, yelling,

"Quit that! Stop! Leave him alone! What do you think you're doing?"

The men glanced up, took one look at her on horseback bearing down on them and stepped back. One of them reached out to try to grab the reins of her horse, but she evaded him, hurtling past, relieved that Jess had rolled out of the way.

"Get out of here! Leave him alone!" She wheeled the horse around, heading back toward them.

"Another one of your women?" the tallest one spat at Jess. He went after him again, taking one last swing, connecting full force. Jess fell back sprawling in the dirt, blood streaming down his face.

"Come on, Wes," said the fat one. "I think he got the point."

The tall one turned to Jess. "If you don't, we can make it again." He smiled. "It'd be a pleasure."

"Get out!" Alison yelled at him, heading the horse in his direction.

He aimed a kick at Jess, then jammed his hat onto his head and followed the other two through the trees to where Alison could see a truck parked by the side of the road.

She waited only long enough to see them get in before she slid off her horse and ran to Jess's side. "My God, are you all right? What happened?"

He swiped at the blood on his face, spitting into the dirt. "Nothing. It's all right."

"*Nothing?* Why were they—?" She couldn't even find the words to express the horror she felt. She pulled out a handkerchief and used it to stanch the blood still coming from his nose.

He tried to get up, winced at the pain and tried again.

"Maybe you've broken something." Alison slipped her arm around his back, helping him to his feet. "Are you sure you should be doing this?"

He shook her off. "I'm okay." He looked around, then muttered under his breath. "My horse ran off."

"You can take mine. We can ride together," she said quickly. "You should see a doctor."

"I don't need a doctor!"

"But—"

"I'll be all right." He limped over to a fallen log and lowered himself gingerly, grimacing as he did so. Alison followed. He looked awful. One of his eyes was almost swollen shut. His nose looked broken. There was an ugly abrasion along the line of his jaw.

"Give me your shirt. I'll get it wet in the creek and you can wash."

He'd looked as if he would protest, then apparently thought better of it. When he shrugged carefully out of his shirt, she saw that his ribs had taken a beating, too. She hurried to the creek and came back with the shirt dripping. He reached out to take it from her, but she wouldn't let him.

"I'll do it. I can see."

"And I can't?" he'd said gruffly.

Alison smiled slightly, lifting her hand to brush a lock of hair away from his swollen eye. "Not very well."

She knelt between his knees and began dabbing carefully at the cuts on his face. He tensed, trying to hold still. She worked slowly and efficiently, marveling at the steadiness of her hand.

Every other time this summer that she'd come within two feet of him, she had nearly had heart palpitations. Now she was kneeling only inches from his bare chest, while she gently washed his face. She licked her lips, trying to think of him as no more than a collection of cuts and bruises. Yet at every moment she was aware, always aware, of the physical Jess Cooper.

Jess sat stoically waiting until she was finished and sat back on her heels. The moment she did so, their eyes met and Alison's breath caught. She licked her lips nervously.

Would he kiss her?

The thought came unbidden, and, without even realizing it, she leaned almost imperceptibly toward him.

He hesitated, then, "Come on," Jess said, straightening and trying to get up so that Alison had to scramble backward to avoid being knocked on her rear. "It's getting late. You need to get back." He stepped past her, brushing at the dust on his jeans, then limped toward Alison's horse.

"Wait a minute." She hurried after him. "Why were those guys beating on you?"

He shrugged, holding out the reins to her horse for her. Alison didn't take them.

"What was going on, Jess? Pops will want to know."

"Nathan doesn't need to know anything," Jess said sharply.

"He's going to have a hard time not knowing," Alison pointed out, "with you looking like you've been dragged through a thicket backward."

"I'll tell him I fell off my horse."

"You think he'll believe that?"

"I don't give a damn what he believes, it's not his problem!" Jess dropped the reins and stalked off toward the woods.

But Alison followed him. "What happened, Jess? Tell me. Tell me or... or I'll tell Pops exactly what I saw."

He turned and glared at her. "Why?"

"Because...because they shouldn't be allowed to get away with it."

He grimaced. "Doesn't make any difference. It smartened me up, that's all."

"What do you mean?"

"Damn, but you're a nosy little kid."

"I'm not nosy. And I'm not a kid! Am I?" she challenged him, slapping her hands on her hips. The act made her breasts strain against her shirt.

Jess scowled at her, then shrugged. "I guess you're not," he muttered, looking away.

"So tell me."

He gave her an exasperated look. "Why should I?"

"Because . . . because I care . . . about you."

"Don't bother. I'm not worth it. Ask Cindy Brinkmiller." He started to turn away again.

Alison caught his arm. "Who's Cindy Brinkmiller?"

He pulled his arm out of her grasp. "Oh hell, leave it, will you? She's the reason her brother and cousins were beating me up."

Another woman? She'd never thought about Jess with another woman. He belonged to her. "Why?" Her voice sounded hollow.

"Because she's pregnant, damn it, and she told them the baby's mine."

Now Alison did feel like the child she'd just denied being. She felt out of her depth, floundering. Sex was something she fantasized about. Babies were part of another world. And to think of Jess . . .

"Is it?" she whispered. "Yours?"

He gave a scornful laugh. "As if I'd ever got close enough to do more than kiss her."

Alison felt almost giddy with relief. She beamed. "Thank heavens."

Jess gave a hard look. "What's that supposed to mean?"

"I just meant . . . I meant . . . you're a little young to have children."

"I'm not having children," he told her gruffly. "Ever."

"But when you marry—"

"And I'm not getting married, either."

"But surely when you—" *When you know how much I love you,* she'd been going to say. But even Alison knew better than that. "But when you meet the right person," she began hesitantly.

"I'm not lookin'." He took the reins out of her hands. "Come on. Get moving. The old man'll be sending out the posse soon."

"But you—"

"I've got to find my damned horse."

"I'll take you."

"No." He jerked his head toward the sorrel. "Get on. And when you get home forget all about this."

She wanted to argue with him, but he was looking at her impatiently, and she knew words wouldn't do any good. She touched his arm, felt it tense under her fingers.

"Jess?" She spoke his name. It was a question, but even she wasn't certain what she was asking.

He shut his eyes. A muscle in his jaw ticked. When he opened his eyes again Alison read torment in them. She waited. And finally his control broke.

His hand came up and touched her hair, stroked her cheek. And then his lips touched hers.

The kiss couldn't have lasted more than a few seconds before he jerked back, some rational part of him regaining control. His teeth snapped together. He rubbed a hand over his face, then winced.

"I shouldn't have done that."

But Alison didn't agree. Rationality hadn't regained any control over her. She'd dreamed about those lips touching hers every night all summer long. She'd fantasized about those rough fingers caressing her skin. She looked at him lovingly.

"Thank you, Jess," she whispered. She raised her hand and touched her lips lightly, then touched his.

He pulled away. "Damn it, Ali. Quit that. I told you, I shouldn't have done it. Get on your horse and get outa here. And forget everything that happened this afternoon."

She hadn't, of course.

That kiss had given her a year's worth of daydreaming. The husky way he'd called her "Ali" had provided many marvelous nights.

She loved him. And she was sure, from his kiss, that he loved her, too. She'd gone back the following summer, confident that things would develop between them.

He'd been long gone.

She'd felt betrayed. And foolish.

She felt foolish now. She was twenty-seven, not seven. It was time to grow up.

It was nothing she hadn't been telling herself for years. And nothing that her father and brothers hadn't told her as well.

Just two weeks ago her brother, Peter, had flown in from L.A., and had introduced her to three eligible lawyer friends in the space of three days.

"You're not by any chance matchmaking, are you?" Alison had asked him, a wicked glint in her eye.

Peter grinned just as wickedly. "Just helping nature out a bit."

"You'd hit the roof if I did the same for you."

"You know any eligible women? Bring 'em on," Peter had challenged her.

But Alison didn't know anyone she thought was good enough for her favorite brother, and she said so. "But you seem quite willing to fob just any old man off on me,'' she complained.

''They're not old,'' Peter said, still smiling. Then he sobered. ''No, I know what you're saying, Ali. But maybe your standards are too high. You might be sitting here till you're eighty if you're waiting for Prince Charming.''

''I'm not waiting for Prince Charming,'' Ali had protested. In fact, she was seriously considering marrying Gary. He hadn't asked, but she suspected he would.

Gary was a middle management man for a computer software firm. She'd met him playing softball in June. He'd asked her out. She'd gone. She liked Gary. He was comfortable, stable, friendly. Not a dream man.

But Alison was beginning to think that dream men were just that, ephemeral, insubstantial figments of her imagination. She wanted a home and a family. She wanted a man to love and children to cherish. But at this rate she wondered if she would ever find them. Maybe it was time to stop telling herself that the right man was out there, and that she'd know him when she saw him.

The way, all those years ago, she'd known Jess Cooper.

''And that was such an enormous success,'' she mocked herself.

She should have forgotten him. It was her own folly that she never had.

Actually, she thought now as she picked up her bag and headed for the stairs, it was probably a very good thing she'd run into him again.

It would be a salutary experience, meeting up with her childhood dream lover as an adult.

If she was ever going to get on with things and meet the real man who was out there waiting for her, she would have to come to terms with Jess Cooper as he really was, not the way her youthful fantasies had imagined him.

She would see him the way an adult would see him...and be cured.

HE ATE baked beans out of a can, sitting on his bunk and pretending he was reading *Livestock Weekly.* There was another rental car parked next to Alison's when he'd come back from bringing down more cattle that afternoon. He'd seen a light on in the kitchen, people moving around. He'd turned his back and walked to the bunkhouse, a confused but willing Scout at his heels.

"You don't need to follow me," Jess told him gruffly. "Your grub is up at the house."

But Scout wasn't going unless he did, and he ended up sharing the beans with the dog. Before he finished them off, he heard another car growling its way up the hill.

He got to his feet and peered out the corner of the window, watching as it stopped next to the others and two men got out. Alison's father and brother, undoubtedly. They took suitcases out of the trunk and started across the dirt toward the house. Jess saw the door open and Alison standing there silhouetted in the light.

He turned away and flung himself down on the bunk, staring down at a fascinating article on new vaccines.

It didn't hold his interest any more than the one on the relative merits of feeding alfalfa hay or clover. He flipped to the back, scanning the ads. That was what he should be reading—the Help Wanted section.

Lord knew there was a good bet he'd be needing a job before long. There wasn't a chance in hell that David Richards would hang on to the ranch and let him run it. And sure as shooting, when he sold it, whoever bought it would either run it himself or bring in his own man.

So much for his dreams.

It didn't do to get tied to a place, that was certain. It only made it harder to leave.

THE BEDROOM was almost exactly the way Alison remembered it. The same narrow bed, same chifforobe of bird's-eye maple, same desk with a bookcase above that she'd used all those years ago. It felt lived-in, too, as if she'd slept here last night and the night before.

She ran her hand lightly over the old log-cabin quilt. That was the only change she could see: its blues and grays were more faded than she remembered.

She stood quietly listening as her brothers and father settled in for the night, remembering other similar nights, thinking how much the same everything was.

And how different.

She had, as her kindergarten teacher friend, Donna, would say, stayed "on task" all evening. She hadn't let her thoughts stray to Jess at all. She had talked with her father about his trip from Sri Lanka, she had listened to Peter describe the gorgeous redhead he was dating now. She had tried to make sense of Douglas's careful evaluation of the worth of ranch land and had even been able to report coherently the call from Nathan's lawyer, Mr. Kirby, which had precipitated it.

After dinner she had sat in front of the fire Peter had made and reminisced with them all about Nathan, and when Jess's name had come up, she'd talked easily and sensibly about Nathan's ranch manager.

There, she told herself as she climbed the stairs to get ready for bed. See? You can handle it. You were just spooked when you saw him this afternoon. It was just shock.

The next time she saw him, it would be fine—like seeing Kenny Loggia, who worked with her in the library, or Dan Hernandez, the CPA she used to date. No big deal.

She put on her nightgown, brushed her teeth and slipped beneath the covers. And couldn't sleep.

Gradually the rest of the family quieted down. She heard her father close the door to Nathan's room where he was sleeping. She heard Peter and Chris go up to the loft, heard the soft murmur of their voices for a while, then silence. Down the hall she could hear the rhythmic squeak that was undoubtedly Doug doing his nightly regimen of sit-ups on the old wooden floor. And then, nothing.

She should be exhausted. She should have gone out like a light the moment her head hit the pillow. She hadn't.

She tossed and turned, sighed and punched her pillow. Finally, despairing, she got up and started back downstairs.

She heard a soft creak. She froze for a moment, then moved on. She must've been wrong about Doug. He was sometimes wakeful, too. And now that she was down she could see a small light on in the kitchen. He must be making some warm milk. She pushed open the door.

"Can I have some, too?" she began. Then, "Oh, it's you."

It wasn't Doug at all, but Jess who stood in the middle of the kitchen.

Alison was suddenly acutely conscious of her thin nightgown, of her rapidly reddening face. "I saw the light. I thought it was my brother. I didn't know—"

"I—I'm sorry I disturbed you. I just came to get...that." Jess pointed past her at a shabby looking blanket on a bench in the corner.

"You should have stayed in the house," Alison said. "You must be freezing out there. There's plenty of room."

"No. It's not for me. It's...it belongs to Scout. He was...restless." Was it her imagination or was his color deepening, too?

"He can come in, too."

"He's all right," Jess said gruffly. "We both are." He moved past her to get the blanket. His sleeve touched her bare arm. She quivered.

"Sorry," he muttered, grabbing the blanket and edging past her again. "Night." And he was out the door without another word.

Standing there barefoot and shivering on the cold linoleum, Alison knotted her fingers against her breasts and watched him go, watched with rapt attention as his lean-hipped, broad-shouldered silhouette vanished into the darkness.

And she knew for a certainty that she wasn't as immune as she'd hoped.

Chapter Three

Jess talked to David Richards at the wake. They talked about cattle and land prices and prospects and such like. It had to be done, Jess knew, and it was easier than talking about Nathan.

David didn't seem to mind. He had to get back to Sri Lanka as quickly as he could, which meant leaving late on the afternoon of the funeral.

"I met with the lawyer today and got everything taken care of that concerns me. I know Dad would have understood. He believed in taking care of one's obligations to the living." David paused and ran a hand over his face. "He was a wonderful father."

Jess nodded. "I reckon he was."

"He thought very highly of you. I'm glad you were here to be with him. You'll sit with us tomorrow at the funeral."

"I—"

"He'd want you there. We do, too. He's left something for you, too. Kirby will talk to you about it." He gave Jess's arm one last squeeze, then turned to speak to another mourner.

Jess, feeling dismissed, still couldn't leave. He needed to ask one more thing, the thing he'd been leading up to from the start, the thing he was almost afraid to put into words because the answer meant he would have to start making other plans. "Mr. Richards. I was just...wondering... what...what about the ranch?"

David turned back to Jess, blinked, then smiled, his blue eyes gentle and uncannily like Nathan's for just a moment. "Don't worry about the ranch, Jess. The ranch will take care of itself."

NATHAN'S FUNERAL was short and sweet. The minister spoke briefly about the inspiration Nathan had provided for his family and friends, for all those whose lives he had touched. Then, while the morning sunlight streamed in the narrow stained-glass windows, everyone listened while Jimmy Rodriguez, the town's musical pride and joy, played a haunting English folk tune, Nathan's favorite, on his guitar.

Afterward David got up to speak. He shared a couple of family memories that communicated once more the openness with which Nathan Richards had faced the world, the enthusiasm that he'd brought to it, the joy with which he encouraged his only son to embrace it as well.

"He could have kept me tied to the ranch," David said. "But he believed that every man has to choose his own destiny. Despite the fact that it has taken me away from him for most of my adult life, I will always be grateful that my father had the generosity to allow me to choose mine."

Jess, listening, shut his eyes, felt an ache in his throat.

He was startled into opening them a few moments later when he heard Alison's hesitant voice.

She stood at the podium, her face pale, her eyes bright, as she looked out over the full church.

"My brothers," she said slowly, "who have never been shy about grabbing the limelight in the past, have been more than willing to allow me my share on this occasion." Her expression became fondly wry as she went on, "In fact they have generously allowed me to speak for all of us. I suspect it's because they don't mind if I cry in public, but they're embarrassed to."

She spoke haltingly about her first memories of the ranch, about how no matter where her father's job took them, that it was the place she held in her heart as home, and that even more than the ranch, home meant her grandfather.

"I always knew, in the back of my mind, that he was here." She smiled a watery smile. "It's silly. It's irrational. It's the way I felt. No matter what, he was there behind me, supporting me, understanding me, believing in me. Loving me." She blinked rapidly and swiped at her eyes.

"Tomorrow I'm supposed to meet with the lawyer to find out what inheritance my grandfather has left me," she went on. "But I already know what he's left me. A legacy of love."

Jess put his hand over his eyes and in his mind rode the wiliest bronc he'd ever ridden, then braved the toughest bull he'd ever faced. He had to, or he'd make a fool of himself bawling in front of God and everybody.

He didn't watch, only heard Alison come back to the pew and take her seat next to her father.

Then the minister introduced the last musical piece, a baroque trumpet solo that Dan Grissom, the high school band director, sent soaring to the heavens.

As a send-off it was pure Nathan all the way. Jess knew he would have been pleased.

THERE MUST HAVE BEEN three hundred people who came back to the ranch afterward.

But not Jess.

Alison knew because all the time she was sharing recollections with Nathan's friends and neighbors, all the time she was pouring coffee and smiling her best, she kept an eye out for Jess.

He'd sat in the same row she did at the church. He'd driven back home in the car behind hers. He'd stood shoulder to shoulder with her while Nathan's body was lowered into the ground at a small family plot on the hill behind the house.

Then he disappeared.

The most she saw of him came in the middle of the afternoon when she caught a glimpse through the window. There were still ten or twelve people milling about in the living room when she spied him outside just beyond the front gate.

He was still wearing the suit he'd worn to church, and the light breeze mussed his hair. This morning Alison had thought the suit had made him look serious and remote. Now, incongruous against the backdrop of the rugged mountainside, it simply made him look lonely.

Was he?

In her dreams, of course, he had been—lonely for the love of a good woman, satisfied only with her.

In reality she'd never believed it was true. She didn't think she'd ever encountered a more self-sufficient man in her life than Jess Cooper.

But now, watching the man who stood so still looking up at the house, she wasn't sure.

IT WAS EARLY EVENING by the time Alison took a breath that she felt she could call her own. The last of the funeral dinner guests had departed shortly after four. After they did the washing up, she and Doug and Peter went through Nathan's scrapbooks sorting out the few that her brothers would take with them. Most they seemed quite willing to leave for her.

"You're the one who used to love the place," Doug reminded her. "You're the one who got us dragged back every summer."

Alison looked at him, shocked. "You didn't want to come?"

He shrugged. "Well, when I was a kid, yeah. But later on, not really. The wide world beckoned, you know—" he gave her a grin "—like it did to Dad."

Alison understood, but was surprised nonetheless. She smiled at him. "Then thank you for being so forbearing."

He reached over and tousled her hair. "No problem. It's what big brothers are for."

"And twin brothers," Peter chipped in. He was tossing the last of his gear into his duffel bag, preparatory to driving to the airport.

Alison turned to him, astonished. "You didn't want to come, either?"

"Till we got to be about fourteen, yes. Then things changed. You started making calf's eyes at Cooper."

"I never!"

Peter laughed. "You used to tag after him everywhere he went."

"He was . . . nice to me," Alison said lamely.

"I didn't think he ever even talked to you," Peter said frankly, zipping the bag shut.

"Sometimes he did."

Peter flicked her a glance over his shoulder. "Oh, yes? So passion wasn't completely unrequited?"

Alison rolled her eyes. "I was a kid." She wasn't about to admit how little her feelings seemed to have changed.

"And now you're not. Has he this time?"

"Has he what? Talked to me? Of course."

"He didn't show up today."

"He was at the funeral."

"But not here after."

She shrugged. "I'm sure he has lots of work to do."

Peter was still looking at her. "Maybe." He grinned at Doug. "Or maybe it was like old times. Maybe he's still dodging Ali."

Mortified, Alison felt her cheeks flame. "He didn't! Did he?" she asked worriedly after a moment. It was all too possible, seen from afar.

Peter turned his grin on her. "No. I just know how to get a rise out of you. And I noticed you were looking."

Alison shook her head. "Not for him," she lied.

Peter just looked at her, but Doug breathed a sigh of relief.

"Good," he said. "I'm glad you've grown up."

"Right," Peter said. He glanced at his watch. "Ready, Doug? It'll take an hour or better to get to the airport. We'd better leave now."

Douglas clicked his suitcase shut and slipped on his coat. "All set." He paused and looked at his sister. "Sure wish you were coming, Ali. I don't like to think of you all alone up here."

"I'll be fine. I was fine before you got here," she reminded him as they walked to the door.

"She's a big girl now. Besides, she has Cooper to protect her," Peter said with a grin.

Doug stopped quite suddenly so that Alison almost ran into him. He scowled. "Not funny," he said to his brother.

"Wha—?"

"Remember Cindy Brinkmiller?"

Peter's grin faded. "You don't think—"

"That had nothing to do with Jess," Alison said abruptly.

Doug's eyes widened. "How do you know?"

Oh, hell, Alison thought. She had done what Jess had asked, never telling anyone about the fight, about what he'd told her that afternoon. She didn't want to break her word now. "I just know," she said stubbornly.

"I don't think you knew anything. You were a kid."

"I knew," she insisted. "Anyway, I'm not a kid now."

"And you think that makes me feel better," he said grimly.

"I'll be fine, Doug, honestly. I won't let him seduce me. I promise." She gave him a cheeky grin.

Doug sighed, dropped a kiss on her forehead and got into the car. Peter stowed their gear in the trunk, then stopped beside the door of the car and turned to look at her. His expression was grave, his blue eyes concerned.

"Would he have to, Ali?" he asked.

TRUST PETER.

She could always buffalo Douglas. He never saw beyond his balance sheets or his stock quotes. She could put off her father and Chris by noncommittal nods and vague replies followed by questions about their pet projects.

She could never deceive Peter.

She stood in the silence, long after the car carrying her brothers had disappeared down the dirt road and out of sight around the bend. She thought about what he had asked her.

She didn't know how long she stood there before a tiny self-mocking smile crept onto her face. The question was moot. Jess Cooper was no more interested in her than he had ever been.

She had just turned to go back into the house, when she heard the phone ring. It was Gary.

"How are you? I've missed you."

Alison smiled at the eagerness in his voice. "I'm okay," she told him. "I've missed you, too," which would have been truer if she'd had more time.

"When are you coming home?"

"Tomorrow night. I have to see the lawyer in the afternoon."

"Want me to pick you up? Where are you coming in and when?"

"LaGuardia, around midnight. You don't need to, really. I'll take a cab."

"No trouble," Gary insisted. "I'll be there. Seems like you've been gone an age."

It seemed to Alison as if she'd been out of real time altogether, as if she'd somehow slipped from the present into the past.

"Gotta run now," Gary was saying. "I'm off to lift weights. See you tomorrow. Count on me."

"Yes," Alison said, but he had already gone. She set down the receiver, then went to the door, intending to latch it for the night. But behind her the radio Doug had left on was still playing, and the stillness in the yard seemed to beckon her.

She opened the door again and went out.

She stood still, letting the tranquillity settle over her.

It wasn't really all that quiet. It was simply an absence of human and mechanical noises that she experienced. No laughter, no music, no taxi horns or car alarms. Nothing save the gentle sighing of the western wind through the spruce and, off in the meadow, the lowing of the cattle as they settled in for the night.

There was no light, either, other than the narrow sliver of moon and the canopy of stars she never set eyes on in the city. She tipped her head back now, marveling at this universe that might as well not exist back in New York.

She turned slowly, relishing it, then lowered her gaze to the even blacker bulk of the mountain peaks surrounding her. She remembered doing the same thing years ago, opening her arms and turning in slow circles, embracing the natural world that most of the year, when she was in Beirut and Paris, had seemed so remote.

It was equally remote most of the time now. Even when she stood out on her terrace and stared up at the sky, picking out the few visible stars, she never lost the sense that the city was pulsating beneath her feet.

She remembered the night she'd got the news about Nathan. She'd stood there on the terrace, listening to the hoot of horns, the wail of sirens, the scritch-scratch of her downstairs neighbor Ginger, who was repotting a bonsai on her patio. Ginger's bonsai was twenty-seven years old. Older than Ginger.

Ginger loved it. Nathan hadn't. "Nature in a pot," he'd groused when Alison had taken him down to meet Ginger.

And so it was, but what was wrong with that?

The whole world couldn't live in the wilds of western Colorado, as lovely as it was. She remembered Nathan urging her to come out and visit him again, get in touch with all the things she had loved as a young girl.

And she had declined.

What was the point? All those wild desperate longings of her teenaged self had no place in her life now.

She looked back at the house, then turned and walked slowly up the hill toward the family burial plot. There she stopped and looked down at the newly turned sod.

"Thank you, Pops," she said now. "Thank you for bringing me back one more time. But I can't stay. Really I can't. There's nothing for me here."

She lifted her gaze and looked down the hill toward the bunkhouse. It was dark. Silent.

Jess was no doubt sound asleep. He was, she was sure, every bit as busy as she'd told Peter and Doug he was, and would no doubt be up at dawn tomorrow to work again.

Jess.

Her cowboy. Her hero. Her fantasy.

But reality was Gary, her job, her life in New York. There was no future for Ali Richards and Jess Cooper. Never had been—except in her heart.

HE COULD SEE her standing there in the moonlight. With the lights off in the bunkhouse, there was just enough illumination outside to make him aware of her as she stood in the yard, turning circles, her arms wide.

He swallowed, dropped the curtain and turned away.

He wasn't getting any sleep standing there watching Alison Richards. And damn it all, he needed his sleep. He had work to do and plenty of it, as soon as the sun came up tomorrow.

He sat down on the edge of the bed, started to lie down, then, as if drawn, he lifted the hem of the curtain again.

She was still there, moving up the hill slowly. He could just glimpse her slim figure moving through the darkness. Sweet, tender, caring Alison.

He shouldn't be watching her now. He hadn't seen her since the burial. He's stayed well away from the house afterward. There'd been plenty to do. More cattle to bring down, a bit of doctoring, some fence work.

Life was for the living. That was what Nathan had always said. Nathan would have understood why he'd stayed away today.

Jess's mouth quirked at one corner.

Sure he would, he mocked himself. Nathan would have looked right square at him and called him a coward. Nathan would have said he was running from his dreams, from his fantasies. From Alison.

Nathan would have been right.

Jess let the curtain fall from his fingers, lay back on the bed and folded his arms beneath his head.

So what? he said to himself. Dreams weren't all they were cracked up to be.

He only had to get through twenty-four more hours. Then he could worry about the things that really mattered in life. In twenty-four hours Alison Richards would be on her way back to New York.

FRANK KIRBY couldn't see Alison until four in the afternoon.

"He's tied up in the morning," his secretary apologized, "and then, well, you know, once you get going, you don't want to stop until you have to."

Alison could only vaguely decipher the meaning of that theory. She supposed it meant that Mr. Kirby, once committed to some pursuit became single-minded and wouldn't likely be free until then.

"You couldn't just maybe tell me what's mine over the phone," she suggested hopefully. "I'm right out here at the ranch, you know. I could simply pack it and catch the earlier flight."

"Oh, no. Mr. Kirby wants to see you," the secretary said.

So Alison spent the morning packing her bags and collecting the few things from the bedroom she'd been using that had been hers all those years ago. Then she walked out to the corral and leaned against the fence, letting the early-autumn sun warm her back as she rested her arms on the top rung and stared out across the corral and the valley, soaking up last impressions.

They would have to last her a lifetime, for she wouldn't be back. The ranch would be sold. Her father hadn't said so, of course. David Richards was the consummate diplomat, even in family matters. He would never have broached the subject of selling the Rocking R with Nathan barely in his grave. It would have been too hard on them all.

But Alison didn't delude herself.

There was no way her foreign service officer father was going to abandon his career to come back to a remote corner of southwestern Colorado and raise cattle.

No, the ranch would go. The cattle, the horses, the barns. Everything would go.

Even Jess.

And all she would have would be her memories.

She stored up as many as she could that morning. She never saw Jess, which wasn't surprising. He'd been gone since daybreak. She'd awakened to hear him riding away, but she'd deliberately lain in bed instead of going to the window to watch. There were some memories she didn't need.

Now she drew a deep breath and opened the door of Kirby and Ransom Law Offices, prepared to hear Mr. Kirby's reading of her grandfather's will. Then she would go back to the ranch once more, take whatever he left her and be on her way.

She didn't expect to see Jess.

He was sitting in the office.

Alison stared, then turned to the secretary. "Did I mistake the time? I thought my appointment was at four."

The secretary smiled. "That's right. Mr. Kirby is just finishing up his previous appointment now. Please have a seat. He'll be with you in a moment." She motioned Alison toward the seat next to Jess's. He was no longer slouched. His booted feet were planted firmly on the floor. He had begun to strangle his hat in his hands. He didn't look at her.

Alison moved to sit by him, remembering Peter's comments, knowing her cheeks were reddening as she did so. How he'd laugh if he could see her now. The secretary went back to her typing. Alison sat silently, noting out of the corner of her eye the muted plaid of Jess's shirt, the soft denim covering his thigh, the way his fingers creased the brim of his hat.

She cleared her throat. "I thought you had work to do today." She knew she sounded almost accusing, and that made her cheeks burn even more.

Jess rolled the hat's brim between his palms. "Kirby said he needed to see me."

"That's right. Dad said Pops left you something, too."

"Nothing valuable, I don't reckon," he said quickly, as if she might be thinking he'd been trying to steal her inheritance.

Before Allison could say that she had no such fears, the door to the inner office opened and Mr. Kirby ushered out his previous client and shook hands with him. Then he turned his attention to Alison and Jess.

"Sorry I'm running late. Come on in."

Alison, confused at which of them he'd been speaking to, looked at Jess. He looked back at her.

"Which of us did you want?" Alison asked finally.

Kirby looked over his shoulder. "Which? Why, both of you, of course." He sat down in his big leather chair and began shuffling through the papers in front of him. At his nod, she took the chair across the desk from him. Jess hovered in the background.

"Shut the door and sit down," Mr. Kirby said. "Pull over that chair and we'll get down to business."

"Don't you want to talk to her first, then me?" Jess suggested, which would have been Alison's suggestion, too.

Mr. Kirby aligned papers on his desk, folded his hands on top of them, then lifted his gaze and met Jess's scowling one with a wide smile. "Nope."

He cocked his head and waited expectantly. Reluctantly Jess dragged over the other chair and sat.

Mr. Kirby picked up the sheaf of papers. "Pity you couldn't have come in earlier," he said. "It's going to take a while to spell out all the conditions and ramifications."

"I could have been here anytime today," Alison said sharply. "I told your secretary that."

"Yes, but Jess had work to do, and there's no sense in going over it twice, is there?" He gave them another happy smile.

Alison frowned.

"Go over what?" Jess asked cautiously.

"Nathan's bequest to you."

They looked at each other again.

"Me?" Jess asked. "Or her?"

"Both of you."

Alison didn't look at Jess this time. She looked at Mr. Kirby, her eyes wide. "What did Nathan leave us?" she asked him quietly.

"You mean the old devil really didn't warn you? Ah, Nathan." Kirby chuckled and raised his eyes to heaven where his dear departed client was no doubt at this very moment sharing the joke. "He's left each of you half interest in the Rocking R Ranch."

Chapter Four

Half the ranch?

Jess stared. He heard the words. Minutes later they were still echoing around his head like pebbles in a saucepan, making sound but not sense. Not yet.

"—stipulations, of course," Frank Kirby went on. "Not too difficult, though, as I'm sure you'll agree."

"What sort of stipulations?" Jess heard Alison ask. He couldn't have formed the words himself. He felt cold and shivery, as if he'd just been tossed into an icy creek. It was a shock.

Half the ranch.

He said the words over slowly in his mind, testing them, probing them for meaning. Intellectually he had no trouble. Emotionally he was lost.

He shook his head numbly, then bowed it and held it in his hands, staring down between his booted toes at Kirby's worn carpet. Solid wool reality. Slightly fraying. Standard office tweed, not even rose-colored as circumstances might have warranted.

A man can't live without dreams. Jess could hear Nathan now. He could see the old man, see him sitting there at the coffee bar, fixing Jess with those deceptively mild blue eyes and asking, *What's your dream?*

His wildest dream?

The Rocking R.

And Nathan had given it to him.

Correction. Nathan had given *half of it* to him.

Slowly Jess lifted his head and focused on the woman sitting next to him, the woman leaning forward earnestly with her attention wholly fixed on whatever Frank Kirby was saying, the woman who owned the other half of his dream: Alison Richards.

"Then what you're saying is, we can sell it?" he heard Alison say, and this time the words were registering.

"I'm saying that Nathan was prepared for that eventuality, yes," Frank Kirby replied. He tapped his pen on the desk. "But he doesn't want it broken up."

Jess found his voice at last. "Which means what?" He thought he sounded rusty, as if he hadn't spoken in years, but no one else seemed to notice. *Sell it?* Hell, he'd just got it! But Alison . . .

He shot her a quick glance.

Of course she'd want to sell it. What would a New York City librarian want with half a Colorado cattle ranch, for Pete's sake?

"It means," Frank said, "that you have three choices. You can keep it." He smiled at them both. "You can, either of you, sell your half to the other. Or you can decide to sell together. But individually you can't sell your half to anyone else."

He folded his hands again and looked at them. "Very simple, really. Very clear."

"Very," Alison said hollowly after a moment.

And Jess, letting the ramifications sink in, thought it was no wonder that Nathan had always beaten him at checkers. The old coot had always had something up his sleeve. The question was, what was he trying to pull now?

Was it a simple bequest or was there more to it than that? With Nathan a guy never knew.

"Well, I'm sure you'll want to discuss it just between the two of you," Frank said, standing up and rubbing his hands together briskly. He looked hopefully at them.

Jess got to his feet, then reached out instinctively to catch Alison when she stumbled getting to hers. His hand brushed against the soft cotton covering her breast. He pulled back as if he'd been stung.

"If you need any advice, you can call on me," Frank went on, oblivious, ushering them to the door.

"Thank you," Jess heard Alison say in a voice barely above a whisper.

"Much obliged," he said, following her out.

He was almost out the door when he felt something touch his arm. "This is for you."

He turned. In Frank's hand there was a one-hundred-dollar bill.

Jess scowled. "What's that for?"

"From Nathan." Frank smiled. "He gave it to me when we made out the will. Said I should give it to you when I told you about the ranch. He figured the two of you could go out, have dinner on him and . . . talk about your future."

THEIR FUTURE?

Her future with Jess Cooper?

Alison wanted to laugh. She would have if she hadn't thought she would end up crying instead.

Oh, you foolish, crazy old man, what have you done to me now? she wailed silently as she followed Jess's truck down Main Street and around the corner on Aspen toward the Hitching Post. It was scarcely a fifty-dollar-a-plate restaurant, but they'd have had to drive clear to Denver for that.

She hadn't really wanted to go at all, and she had known from his expression that Jess hadn't, either. But he hadn't said so. He'd simply walked behind her in silence all the way out to the street. Once there he'd said, ''So where do you want to go?''

''Home?'' she'd said with a tight little smile.

And Jess had grimaced before holding out the money between two fingers. ''Yeah, right, but then what are we supposed to do with this?''

Alison sighed. ''I guess we'd better use it. He wouldn't like it if we didn't. But we'd better use it fast. I have a plane to catch.''

Jess murmured something that sounded distinctly like, ''Thank God,'' under his breath, then told her to follow him to the Hitching Post.

He was waiting for her now, leaning against the door of his truck as she turned into the parking lot and pulled in alongside him. He didn't even wait until she got out of the car before turning and heading toward the restaurant. Hurrying, muttering imprecations against her meddling grandfather, she followed him.

The Hitching Post was the nearest thing Bluff Springs had to a fancy restaurant. Catering to hunters in fall, skiers in winter and locals the rest of the year, the notched-log lodge specialized in game dishes half the year and in pasta the rest. Since it wasn't hunting season yet, linguine seemed the order of the day.

''Our specials are clam linguine or linguine with marinara,'' the hostess told them as she sat them at a table by the huge stone fireplace and handed them menus. ''The waitress will be here to take your order shortly.''

Alison glanced around the spacious room with its round tables and deep armchairs. The Hitching Post hadn't existed when she'd last been in Bluff Springs.

Except in her dreams. She remembered a fantasy in which a doting Jess had taken her to just such a place for their first date.

She flushed now, remembering the idiocies of youth. Yet she couldn't help a small ironic smile as she did so. Here they were, after all. And by stretching her imagination, she could even call it a first date!

And last, she reminded herself. One glance at Jess told her he'd never be the doting swain she'd dreamed of. He sat across from her stiffly studying the menu with intense scrutiny. He hadn't looked at her once, nor had he directed a word to her since they'd left Kirby's office.

The waitress came, smiled at Jess, mostly ignored her. Taking their orders, she disappeared again, leaving them alone. Alison sat back in her chair, studying the man across from her, memorizing him, recalling all her adolescent fantasies.

The notion that Pops had actually given her a "future" with Jess amused her. And yet somehow it made her ache as well.

Had he had any idea of what he was about, throwing the two of them together like this?

Had Nathan suspected her childhood crush?

Even to Alison's fanciful mind, it didn't seem likely. And yet...

"—have to get an appraisal," Jess was saying.

Allison looked at him blankly. "Why?"

"So I can pay you what it's worth, of course." He grimaced and eased his collar away from the nape of his neck. "By rights I should be paying you for the whole ranch," he said after a moment. "I never expected him to—" He looked away out the window, and Alison could see that he was embarrassed by Nathan's bequest.

"I didn't imagine that you did," she said quietly.

"He never said."

"No. He wouldn't." She gave a wry smile. "Pops liked his surprises."

"I'll say."

The waitress brought their salads, poured Jess a beer and gave Alison the glass of red wine she'd ordered. "Enjoy," she said brightly, giving Jess another winning smile.

He didn't smile back. His gaze never left Alison's. His fingers drummed on the tabletop. Finally he reached for his glass and raised it. "To Nathan." There was an ironic twist to his mouth.

Alison smiled. She wanted to reach out and lay her hand over his, tell him not to worry, that everything would be all right. She wondered if she was losing her mind.

She lifted her own glass and clinked it lightly against his. "To Nathan," she echoed softly and lifted the glass to her lips. The wine made her head feel light and fuzzy.

"Simmons at the bank can do it," Jess went on between bites of his salad.

Alison, watching him chew, had to drag her mind back to what he was saying. "Do what?"

Jess gave her an impatient look. "Give us an appraisal."

"Oh, right. I suppose he can."

"I don't know how I'll be able to come up with the money. Maybe we can do a land contract. If you're willing..."

"Mmm."

The waitress reappeared with their meals. Jess dug right in. Alison didn't. She watched Jess.

His head was bent, and Alison noted, not for the first time, that his hair needed cutting. She had to sit on her hands once more, this time to keep from reaching across the table and brushing back the dark locks.

It was odd, this temptation she'd always had, to touch him. She didn't ever remember feeling it with any other man. Even Gary. She and Gary held hands, of course. They even kissed. But she never needed to reach out to him. At least she hadn't yet.

Jess rubbed a hand around the back of his neck, then took another bite of his steak. "It's going to have to be a long-term loan," he said slowly. "I...I talked to Nathan once about maybe buyin' the place off him sometime. I had...hopes...but...I sure as hell didn't think it'd be this soon."

Alison listened and yet she didn't. She heard his words, understood that he expected her to sell to him, knew that indeed that was what she would do.

And yet...

And yet she found herself wondering just what Nathan had had in mind when he left half the Rocking R to her.

Her thoughts went back to the bonsai tree, to Nathan's disparaging comment about it. She knew Nathan hadn't been enchanted with her New York life-style. She knew he'd sensed her own unspoken restlessness. But had he really thought coming back to the Rocking R was the answer to her questions?

Or was it just his way of giving her options?

New York, the Rocking R or the money from its sale to pursue her dreams.

Or...Jess?

No. Surely not.

"Reckon I can get Simmons out sometime next week," Jess was saying. "When he's taken a look around, checked the books, totaled everything up, I can get in touch with you. All right?"

"Fine."

"Or we can wait until after sale day."

"Whatever." She needed to leave, to stop these crazy speculations, to get back to Gary, to her job, to her life. She pushed back her plate. "I have to get going. You can stay if you like."

"No problem. I have to get up before five." He beckoned to the waitress. "Can we have the bill?"

They had enough change left over from Nathan's hundred dollar bill to go out again. And again.

Jess offered her half of what he got back when he'd paid.

Alison shook her head. "Don't be ridiculous."

"I owe you, then."

"No."

He stuffed the bills into his wallet and tucked it into the back pocket of his jeans. He held the door for her and she slipped out past him, careful not to brush against his shirt.

The sun was below the mountains in the west, already casting a soft golden glow that heightened the color of the aspens. Alison, looking at it, couldn't help thinking how beautiful it was and how much she'd like to be around to see it.

You don't have to go. The words seemed to come out of nowhere, teasing, tempting.

She shook her head. She did have to go.

It was wishful thinking to imagine that she could just walk away from the life she'd made for herself. It was foolishness to think that she'd have anything to stay here for.

There wasn't a chance in the world that Jess Cooper was going to stop by the side of her car and beg her to stay, declaring his undying love.

The very thought of it made her smile.

"What's funny?"

She shook her head. Then she lifted her gaze and smiled at him, grateful for the chance to look at him this one last time, to smile at this man who had been her fantasy in person for so long, to wish him well, to—

"Will you kiss me goodbye?" The words were out of her mouth before she realized it.

The moment she said them, she was horrified. Her hand flew up to cover the exclamation of dismay that followed.

"I didn't mean—" she began, then shook her head helplessly because, in fact, despite her better judgment, she did. She wanted his kiss.

Why not? If she was growing up, turning her back, kissing her fantasies goodbye metaphorically, why shouldn't she do it literally as well? If this was as close as she was going to get to her dreams, surely she ought to take it. Take it and be finished.

Jess just stared at her, then blinked. He was looking at her as if she'd grown another head. His stupefaction fortified her bravery.

"Don't tell me you're afraid to?" she said recklessly, lifting her chin.

"Afraid?" Now the stupefaction was in his words.

She nodded, managing a cheeky, challenging grin. After all, what difference did it make?

In five minutes she'd be gone, never to see him again. They'd talk, of course, about the sale of the ranch. Or maybe Mr. Kirby and Mr. Simmons could do it for them. She didn't know. She didn't care.

She only knew she wanted this, even more than she'd wanted his kiss twelve years ago.

"It's a yearning for closure," Ginger the amateur psychologist would have told her.

Alison supposed it might be. It might also be no more than a desire to slake her ancient lust.

"Why not?" she said, shrugging carelessly, and smiled at him, wondering even as she did so if that one glass of wine hadn't been one too many.

Jess hesitated. His fists clenched and unclenched as he struggled with her request.

In another moment Alison knew she'd feel the veriest fool. How could she have said it?

But then he reached for her, pulled her close, wrapping those strong hard arms around her. And with a mutter that sounded very much like, "What the hell, why not?" his lips came down on hers.

It was a stunner of a kiss. In her life Alison had never had another one like it, had never even imagined there could be kisses like it!

Lips were lips, after all. One mouth was pretty much like any other.

Except Jess Cooper's.

She remembered his first kiss, the quick hard touch of his lips against hers. She'd hoped for at least that, but had expected a half-hearted indifferent brush of his lips across her cheek.

What she got was warm and eager, demanding, not a perfunctory peck at all.

It was everything Alison had ever allowed herself to dream of.

No, it wasn't. It was more.

Alison had kissed her share of men. She'd read her share of love stories, told her share of fairy tales. She knew about passion, about promise, about need.

This went beyond those things. This was something so deep, so elemental that she felt touched not just on the lips but to the depths of her very soul.

Her arms came up to clutch his back and she clung to him, dizzy and mindless.

If this was goodbye, she wondered shakily, what would happen if they ever kissed hello?

She supposed she should feel relieved that when at last Jess pulled away, he looked as shaken as she felt. His chest was heaving, his fingers dug lightly into her arms.

"That's what's known as playing with fire," he said hoarsely.

Was he warning her? Or himself?

"Yes." Trembling, Alison reached down, fumbling open the car door, and got in. Only when she was safely inside did she look at him again. His eyes met hers, dark and stormy.

"Nathan should have known better." He scowled, stuffing his hands into his pockets. "And so should I."

He turned on his heel and stalked to his truck.

HE SHOULD NEVER have kissed her.

He worked from dawn until dusk the rest of the week and all the week after. It took a hell of a lot of work to shape up a herd for shipping: three hundred odd cattle to check over and sort; yearlings and dry cows to cut out and stick in one pasture for the sale; the rest to drive down the valley to the winter pasture where they'd remain. Nathan usually hired an extra man to help out. Jess did it all himself.

Because he should never have kissed her.

He branded five summer calves besides. Treated some pink eye. Did some worming. Mended fence. Cleaned out cattle guards. Chopped wood.

And it didn't do anything to help him sleep at night because he should never have kissed her.

He'd see a flash of glossy chestnut foreleg, and he wouldn't think what a good piece of horseflesh it was. He'd think of how much the color reminded him of Alison's hair.

He'd pass Nathan's grave on his way up the hill in the morning, and he'd remember the night he'd seen the silvery outline of her curves as she'd stood there.

He'd burn his lip on scalding coffee early in the morning, and all he would recall was the heat of Alison's mouth on his.

Dear Lord, why had he kissed her?

He was thirty-four. Old enough to know better; far past the age when he'd needed to take a dare.

And it had been a dare; he could see that in her eyes. They were more wicked then he'd ever believed possible. The same sparkling blue of a deep mountain lake, just begging him to drown himself. They'd taunted and teased him unmercifully, making his whole body react.

She'd wanted it. And yet underneath he'd sensed she was just as afraid of it as he was.

And heaven knew they'd had reason to be!

It had been a humdinger of a kiss. Whoever would've thought it?

Not Jess.

Sure, he'd always found Alison attractive, even back in the days when she'd been curvy as a fence post and leggy as a colt. But he really wasn't given to dreaming, despite Nathan's best efforts.

He spent far more of his time in the here and now or thinking about the past than he did dreaming about what never had been nor likely would be. Consequently he hadn't really considered what it would be like to kiss Alison Richards.

He should've left it that way.

Knowing was hell.

At night he lay awake in bed, tossing and turning, remembering. It might have helped, he told himself, if he'd had the good sense to stay in the bunkhouse where he belonged.

But oh no, he'd had to act like the lord of the manor and move back into the house. Back into the room he'd used before Nathan had died. Back into the bed where Alison had slept.

Jess sleep?

Not on your life.

He'd spent almost three years in that bedroom, in that bed, and he couldn't have dreamed about Alison Richards more than once. Or twice. Now he couldn't stop dreaming about her—even awake.

Damn it, why had he kissed her?

"—hear what I said, Jess?" Alvin Simmons's impatience broke into his reverie.

Jess blinked, looking around, saw Alvin tapping his foot on the porch. The older man's asperity meant he'd said whatever he'd been saying more than once. "Sorry. I...got a lot on my mind."

"Reckon so," Alvin agreed with a bit more equanimity. "Not the best time to be doing this, day before the sale. But if you want all the figures on hand before the sale, we've got no choice."

"I want 'em." Even if it meant showing Alvin around the house when he wanted a shower and something to eat. Even if it meant he would be up half the night attending to last-minute details. The sooner he had Alvin's appraisal, the sooner he could contact Alison, make her an offer, get her once and for all out of his life.

"Well, fifteen, twenty minutes at most and we'll be done," Alvin promised. "You gonna sell out?"

Jess shook his head. "Buy her half," he said, crossing his fingers that the bank would agree.

"Funny business, the way old Nathan set it up, you and that granddaughter together. Coulda knocked me over with a feather when I heard."

Me, too, Jess thought. He followed as Alvin paced around the kitchen, making a note on his pad.

"Nathan always was a sneaky old buzzard." Alvin shot Jess a speculative look. "Sure you wouldn't rather make a go of it with the girl?"

Jess snorted. "Me and some big-city girl? Don't even think it."

"Reckon Nathan did," Alvin said cheerfully, heading into the living room.

Jess shook his head. "No way."

"Why'd he do it, then?"

Jess had wondered that, too. He'd been thinking long and hard about it since the day they'd been to Kirby's office. He remembered Nathan returning from New York that last time preoccupied and muttering. "Probably thought she needed to get in touch with nature again. Or maybe he wanted to put her in touch with her dreams," he said wryly. "Nathan was big on dreams."

Alvin grinned. "Then maybe she won't sell."

"She will. She took off the day after the funeral. Reckon she couldn't wait to get back to the bright lights."

"Some women are like that."

"Yes," Jess agreed. And he would do well to remember that fact instead of her scorching kiss.

It took Alvin longer than fifteen or twenty minutes to finish, mostly because he stopped every few minutes and talked. Jess followed him, dutifully answering the questions as well as he could.

He was tired and hungry. He needed a shower. He'd been late coming in, and Alvin's truck was already outside the house when he'd got back. He felt dirty, grimy and sweaty. His bad leg ached. His ribs were sore.

He leaned against the doorjamb to the attic, swaying slightly, his eyes closed, listening to Alvin poke around, tapping on rafters, knocking on the chimney pipe. Every once in a while Alvin would send a question floating down and Jess would try to come up with coherent answers.

"All done," Alvin said at last, thumping back down the steps. "I'll give you a call later tonight when I've got it all figured out." He trotted down the stairs and out to his truck, leaving Jess standing on the landing. Just as well, Jess thought wearily. Then he wouldn't have to trudge back up to take a bath.

His stomach growled, but he ignored it. Most days he wanted a shower, quick, brisk and invigorating. Tonight he wanted to soak, to lie back and let the hot water soothe his aches.

When the tub was half-full he lowered his aching body into the steamy water, sighing as the heat eased tired muscles, settling back and closing his eyes. Bliss.

He drizzled a washcloth full of hot water over his head, then sank lower, letting the water lap against his neck. By tomorrow night he would be in Denver and almost home free.

The cattle would be in the stockyards awaiting Monday's sale, he would know how much he needed to make in order to give Alison an offer, and Sam and Mal, the truck drivers, would be ready to party.

When he'd gone to Denver with Nathan, partying had been the last thing on Jess's mind. He'd been too interested in plaguing Nathan with questions about the business side of ranching to bother.

"Ain't natural for a young fella like you to be hanging around a motel on a Saturday night. Leastwise, not with me," Nathan had complained. "G'wan, get outa here."

To humor him, Jess had gone. There was always plenty of action in Denver's various bars, and plenty of willing women if a guy wanted them.

This year Jess thought he might.

One woman was as good as another, his father'd always said. And while there wasn't much Les Cooper said that Jess believed, if he was going to forget about Nathan Richards's granddaughter, he needed to prove his father right.

Yeah, he was looking forward to Denver tomorrow night. He needed to do some serious partying.

He pulled the plug and stood up. Water ran down his torso as he stepped out of the tub and reached for a towel. His stomach growled again and he sighed, anticipating dinner. He rubbed his hair, blotted his chest, then cocked his head as he heard a creaking sound on the stairs.

"You already ate, Scout," he said, slinging the towel around his neck and jerking open the door. "Don't pester."

It wasn't Scout.

"I'm back," said Alison Richards.

Chapter Five

The door shut smack in her face. Fast.

But not fast enough. Not nearly fast enough to prevent her unimpeded observation of a lean male torso, lightly matted with damp, dark hair. Not at all quick enough to shield from her sight the most essential part of Jess Cooper's masculinity. And certainly not soon enough to eliminate her clear view of his shocked face.

"What the hell are you doing here?"

Alison heard more rage than embarrassment in his voice, and that, thankfully, gave her the gumption to reply determinedly, "Moving in."

The door jerked open again. This time he was standing behind it, only his outraged face appearing around the edge of it. "Moving in?" he yelped. "Here? The hell you are!"

"The hell I am," Alison said firmly.

It had taken her three soul-searching days to come to that conclusion, another eight to get her affairs in order, take her accumulated vacation time in lieu of notice, quit her job, find someone to sublease her apartment, gather her most important worldly possessions, say goodbye to Gary and come west.

She wasn't going back now.

The door banged shut again. "Hang on. Don't do anything." She could hear him scrabbling around for his clothes. "Don't move. Just wait there. We've got to talk."

"I'll put my things in my room. It's only—"

"No!" There was a crash and he was back, poking his head out again. "No," he said in more moderate tones. "I mean, you can't. Use Nathan's room," he commanded. It was the least welcoming offer of accommodation Alison had ever heard.

"But my room is—" Fine, she was going to say.

"Mine," said Jess.

Their eyes caught and held. A dark flush lined his cheekbones. He glared at her defiantly.

His room? Her room was *his* room?

Alison smiled faintly, hugging her cat against her chest. "Fine," she said mildly. "I'll use Nathan's room."

Her grandfather's room was across from hers—Jess's, she corrected—and once she got inside, she dumped the cat on the bed, then slumped down beside him and pressed cool palms to suddenly overheated cheeks.

"Oh, my," she murmured. "Oh, my. Oh, my. Oh, Jess."

Jess. She smiled. Ah, Jess.

Jess naked. Promising.

Jess enraged. Not so promising.

But she hadn't been expecting him to welcome her with open arms. Not right away. Even she wasn't that big a fool.

Still, she'd had to come back. She'd been thinking about him since she'd left.

How could she not, given that kiss?

She'd envisioned a hundred scenarios for her return. But never Jess naked with only a towel around his neck. She grinned, then giggled, then took a deep, shuddering breath.

Get a grip on yourself, Ali, old girl, she counseled herself.

She tried. Really, she did. But the memory of his lean naked body wasn't the stuff of which indifference was made.

Still, she told herself, she'd better not dissolve into a puddle of either desire or laughter the next time she faced him. Not if she wanted her dreams to come true.

And that was, she admitted, what she wanted.

She'd lived on the memory of Jess Cooper's kiss since he'd stalked away from her at the restaurant eleven days ago.

At first she'd tried to get him out of her mind.

No such luck. As far as kissing Jess Cooper went, reality beat fantasy hands down every time. But if she'd thought the kiss was devastating when it happened, it was nothing compared to the way it made her feel later that night when she dashed off the plane and into Gary's arms.

She had run to him, thrown her arms around him, touched her lips to his and felt . . . nothing. Not a thing.

There was no hunger. No passion. No need.

Just lips, warm and pleasant. Not unlike Nathan's grandfatherly pecks. Alison felt a shaft of cold slip down her spine. She took a trembling breath. Gary seemed to notice nothing at all.

He took her bag in one hand and her hand in the other and led her out to his waiting car, all the while telling her about his newest software program, inquiring casually about her trip, not even particularly interested in her news about Nathan's amazing bequest.

"Wouldn't you even like to see it?" she'd asked him.

And he'd shaken his head. "To misquote one of our former national leaders, 'If you've seen one aspen, you've seen them all.' And, honestly, Ali, I doubt if cattle are much different."

She'd fallen into silence then, wondering, looking at Gary through new eyes. She liked him. She'd always felt comfortable with him. She'd never really expected the sort of desperate passionate yearnings with him that she'd felt about Jess all those years ago.

After all, she'd reasoned, they were the product of her age.

Now, unfortunately, she knew she was wrong. They were the product of the man.

And could she even think about marrying Gary when she knew for a fact that another man could wreak such havoc in her soul?

Gary had chatted on amiably all the way back to her apartment. He'd expected to come in. She'd stopped him at the door. "I'm really exhausted. Why don't I call you tomorrow?"

"It is tomorrow," Gary had said with a perplexed grin.

Alison nodded. "Later then, all right?" She had looked at him pleadingly and he had taken pity on her, dropping another of his dispassionate kisses on her forehead.

"All right, love. You get some sleep."

She hadn't slept. She had lain awake thinking, remembering. She had known for a certainty that she wasn't his love, nor was he hers.

And Jess?

What about Jess? a niggling little voice inside had plagued her.

Jess had been her dream. Ah, yes. But Jess was also real.

And so was his kiss.

"Pops always told me to follow my own rainbows," her father had once told her when he was explaining how he had chosen to leave the sheltered valley in southwestern Colorado where he'd been raised.

It seemed to Alison as if Nathan had handed her this one.

Was she going to hand it back to him? Turn her back on it?

Was she really going to share a kiss like the one she had shared with Jess Cooper and then simply walk away?

Could she settle for Jess's cold hard cash when she could possibly have so much more?

She began making plans to come back.

Gary thought she was crazy.

"You're moving to Colorado and becoming a cowgirl?" He had stared at her, aghast.

"Rancher," she'd corrected. "I'm becoming a rancher."

He'd taken her hands in his. "What about us, Ali?" he'd asked.

And Ali had had to admit that there really wasn't an "us." She'd considered marrying Gary not because she couldn't live without Gary, but because she'd come to see him as a means to achieving her dream of home and family. It wouldn't be enough.

She still wanted a home, she still wanted a family. But she also wanted desire, hunger, love. She'd tasted those things on Jess's lips, or hoped she had.

She aimed to find out.

She didn't say any of that to Gary. She hemmed and hawed, mumbled about needing space and trying to find herself. Gary, no fool, got the point.

"Don't expect me to sit and wait," he'd muttered. "There are other fish in the sea, Alison."

Alison nodded. "No doubt."

Ginger had squealed and clapped her hands over her mouth when Alison had broken the news to her. Then she had looked deeply into Alison's eyes and, no fool either, had asked bluntly, "What's his name?"

But Alison wasn't saying. She wasn't sharing her hopes with anyone. It could all come to nothing.

Still, she began to think perhaps Nathan had had a reason for leaving her the ranch. He must have, or he would have left her money like he'd left her brothers.

Was that reason Jess?

It seemed fanciful to think so. But she couldn't help it. Maybe it was sheer rationalization. But the dream had not died, and try as she might, she could not seem to shut it out.

So she made her excuses to Gary, ignored Ginger's questions, smiled enigmatically at her co-workers, all the while working feverishly to tie up all the loose ends in her life and return to Colorado.

Her goal had been to come and help get things ready for the sale. She hadn't really made it in time for much of the work, though she hoped that she might be of some use tomorrow morning. But from here on out, she planned to do her share.

She and Jess would learn to work together.

But if she kept seeing him in a towel and nothing but, she thought with a smile, it was going to be a little hard to keep her mind focused only on cattle.

She heard footsteps now, and Jess appeared in the doorway, barefoot and clad in jeans and a long-sleeved plaid shirt, which he was still in the process of buttoning.

His eyes went from her to the cat. He scowled. "What's that?"

"My cat. He's called Kitten. Kitten," she said, "this is Jess."

Jesse didn't look pleased at the introduction. Man and cat stared at each other, sizing each other up. Jess looked away first. Kitten sat down and began to clean his tail.

"What's this nonsense about moving in?"

Alison mustered her most optimistic look. "Just what I said. I quit my job, sublet my apartment, and here I am." She spread her palms and gave him a sunny smile.

It was a good thing, she thought, that she hadn't expected him to throw his arms around her and declare his everlasting love.

He looked horrified. "Quit your job? What the hell'd you go an' do a stupid thing like that for?"

"Because I wanted to. Because I don't have to work there anymore. Because—"

"You own half a ranch and you think you're a woman of leisure now?"

"Of course not, Jess. Don't be an idiot."

"*I'm* an idiot? What do you think you're going to do around here?"

She gave him an impatient look. "I'm going to help you with the ranch."

He had nothing to say to that. His snort of disbelief said it all.

Alison slapped her hands on her hips. "What's wrong with that?"

He pressed his lips together and looked away. "You got an hour or two, I'll tell you."

"Don't be obnoxious, Jess."

"Me? Obnoxious?" He paced an irritated circle in Nathan's small room. "You come bargin' in here right before sale day and you call *me* obnoxious?"

"I came to help," Alison said with all the patience she could muster. "Now, what needs to be done?"

He raked his fingers through his hair. "I don't believe this." He stalked another circle, kicked the bedstead, sending Kitten scurrying for cover.

"Believe it," Alison said.

HE DID.

He didn't want to, damn it all, but he did.

She had that same earnest, determined look about her that he remembered so well from when she'd been barely more than a kid. That I'm-gonna-do-this-if-I-bust-my-head-tryin' look. It was one of the things that had attracted his attention clear back then.

When all the other girls had been content simply to bat their eyelashes and simper at him, she'd wanted to learn how to rope. She'd followed him around, not saying anything, just watching, emulating, messing it up, hauling the rope back in and trying it again. And again.

Dogged. Determined.

In the end he'd taught her. Showed her how to make the loop, how to hold the rope so that the coils would slip out freely as she threw. And he'd watched her practice—her teeth biting into her lower lip as she concentrated, her nose wrinkling in disgust when she missed, her shoulders squaring determinedly as she tried it over and over.

She was looking at him with just that same determination now. He gritted his teeth.

"Hell," he muttered under his breath. He slapped his hand against the doorjamb. His stomach growled again, and he remembered he still hadn't eaten any supper. Not that he felt much like it now.

"Come on," he said gruffly over his shoulder. "You can tell me about this hare-brained scheme while I eat. If you think you're going to be the next Dale Evans, we've got some talking to do."

"Does this mean you're going to be Roy Rogers?" Alison asked him as she gathered Kitten into her arms and followed him down the stairs.

He banged a pot on the stove and reached down to yank a can of stew out of the cabinet. "Like hell."

"I'll make it," Alison volunteered.

"You won't." He jerked the opener out of a drawer and ground open the can. He didn't want her doing things for him, playing Mrs. Rancher. "It's insane, you know," he went on. "You movin' back here." The stuff of his worst nightmares.

"I don't know."

"You sure as hell don't. You don't know the first thing about ranching. You're a librarian, for cripe's sake." He slapped the bottom of the can and the congealed stew thudded into the pot.

"I can learn."

He snorted. "Yeah, how?" He paused, a possibility occurring to him. His head snapped up and he glowered at her. "You're not followin' me around all day."

"Fine," Allison said shortly. "Then I'll find out other ways."

"What other ways?" He jabbed at the stew with a fork, stirring it, making the pot bang against the burner.

"Asking questions—"

"Not me."

"—of willing people, observing *willing* people, reading books."

"Reading books?" He looked at her, incredulous.

Alison lifted her chin. "You'd be amazed what a person can learn from reading books."

"I would," he agreed. He slanted her a nasty grin. "I sure as hell would like to see you learn to rope a steer by reading a book."

"I don't have to read a book to learn how to rope," Alison reminded him. "A formerly nice person once taught me."

"The more fool he," Jess growled and slapped a huge spoonful of stew onto his plate. He kicked out a chair, sat down and, ignoring her, began to eat.

He could feel Alison's eyes on him. Doggedly he stabbed a piece of beef and stuck it in his mouth and began to chew. It tasted like his saddle.

Abruptly Jess stood and dumped the stew back into the pot.

"What's wrong?" Alison asked nervously.

"It's cold."

Which was true, of course, but which was the least of his problems.

His biggest was sitting at the table, watching him with those wide blue eyes and smiling at him with that warm, kissable mouth.

It wasn't just another bad dream. It was Alison, in the flesh, sitting mere feet away, talking about moving in, talking about taking part in the day-to-day operation of the ranch, not selling, but in fact invading his very life!

Hell's bells, Nathan, he wondered desperately, what were you thinking of?

Did the old man have a clue as to the mischief he'd wrought with his stupid will?

Of course not.

He couldn't possibly have known how Jess felt about his granddaughter. Not once had Jess betrayed more than a fleeting interest in her whenever Alison's name had come up. Not once had he admitted his attraction.

So why did he feel as if Nathan was sitting up in heaven chuckling right now?

Jess adjusted the flame and poked irritably at the lumpy mass in the pot, trying to think of something sensible to say, something that would make her realize what she was proposing was a mistake. "Nathan wouldn't expect you to go haring off doing something idiotic like this," he began.

"On the contrary, I think it's exactly what Nathan wanted me to do."

He stared at her. "You do?"

She nodded complacently.

"Why?"

She hesitated. She sat back in the chair and pulled her knees up against her breasts, wrapping her arms around them. It made Jess conscious of the length of her, of the subtlety of her curves, of how much of a woman she'd become. He sucked in his breath.

"I think," Alison was saying, "that he thought I'd be . . . happier here. When he came to New York to visit, we spent most of the time talking about the ranch."

"Hardly a reason to move here," Jess said gruffly.

Alison brushed a lock of hair away from her cheek. "No. At least I certainly didn't think so at first. But—" she looked up and gave him a smile that started his insides to melting "—I do feel freer here, happier."

He scraped the bits of burning stew off the bottom of the pan and dumped the whole mass onto his plate again. "You haven't had to do any work yet."

She smiled again. "That's true. But I'm quite willing."

He wasn't. He scowled. "And that's why you came back?" It seemed pretty vague and stupid to him. He doubted her resolve would last. He hoped it wouldn't.

"Not . . . entirely."

"So why else?" He wanted all the cards on the table, wanted to know what had prompted her, so he could do his best to undermine her.

"The kiss."

"The *kiss?*" He felt as if she'd just punched him in the gut. "Holy Mary, Mother of—" He raked his fingers through his hair. "You quit your job on the basis of a kiss?"

He shut his eyes. This couldn't be happening.

Even in his best—or worst—dreams, sane and sensible, intelligent city-bred women like Alison Richards didn't do things like this!

"It's not as idiotic as you're making it sound," she said irritably. Her blue eyes were stormy as they glared at him.

He sat down and took a bite of stew. "It isn't?" he said around the chunk of beef.

"No. Not unless you kiss every woman like that."

His head jerked up. She was looking straight at him. "Do you?"

He choked. Coughed. Alison leapt up and smacked him on the back. Finally he swallowed. She handed him a glass of water. He drank it. His eyes were watering. Damn, even eating with her was dangerous!

"Better?" Alison asked him when he'd settled back in his chair and was breathing normally. She sat down again.

He nodded, still not trusting his voice.

"Then answer my question." Blue eyes met his implacably.

"What question?" he tried.

She just looked at him.

Oh, hell. He rubbed a hand against the back of his neck, scowled, shrugged, wanted desperately to lie to her. Couldn't. Quite.

"It was only a kiss," he muttered hoarsely, knowing she could easily hear what he wasn't willing to say.

She beamed. "Not 'only.' It was quite a kiss."

He made an inarticulate sound deep in his throat.

"So," she went on guilelessly, "I thought, for Pops's sake, we ought to see where it might lead."

It was his turn to stare.

"You wanted to see where it might lead?" he rasped finally. He shoved back his chair so hard it fell over. Scout and Kitten looked up, startled, then vanished around the corner. Jess came around the side of the table to stand over her.

Alison looked up at him. "Well, I—" She gave him a helpless little shrug.

But Jess was beyond being stopped by helplessness. He reached out and took hold of her hand, pulling her to her feet, hauling her against him, touching his lips to hers.

"Here," he muttered, his mouth on hers. "Here's where it will lead."

The kiss was long and hard and left him aching. He wanted to grab her and haul her upstairs to bed and thanked God he wasn't fool enough to do it.

He stepped back, breathing hard, staring down into her astonished, wide eyes.

"Any more questions?" he said raggedly. Then he turned around and stalked out the door without looking back.

"NOT AN AUSPICIOUS beginning, was it, Kitten?" Alison said to the cat. She sat huddled in Nathan's high feather bed and stared dismally into the darkness.

It was now nearly midnight and Jess still had not come back. She had followed him to the door, but he was walking fast in the direction of the truck. So she stopped where she was.

She'd heard the truck start up and had watched him through the window as he whipped it around in the yard and gunned the engine, scattering gravel behind him as he roared off down the hill.

And that was the last she'd seen of him.

She'd washed the dishes, scoured the pan he'd burned the stew in, then carried the few things she'd brought with her up to Nathan's room.

She stayed there, hoping that if she kept a low profile for a time, things might improve. But there was no chance of them improving if Jess didn't even return.

She sighed and lay down on the bed, curling around Kitten, hugging his unresisting body against her, trying to will herself to sleep. Seconds later she sat up again.

She couldn't sleep not knowing where he'd gone. What if he'd been in an accident? What if he was lying somewhere hurt?

The memory of what the Brinkmillers had done to him was vivid in her mind.

There wouldn't be any Brinkmillers tonight, she told herself firmly.

Still she couldn't sleep. She got out of bed and padded into the hall, flipping on the light. Kitten blinked at her.

She continued along the hall to Jess's room, then stood in the doorway, looking in.

It made sense now, why the room had felt lived-in when she'd been back for Nathan's funeral. It had been Jess's room even then. He must have moved out right before they came.

Why hadn't he said? Why had he pretended otherwise? Had he felt that uncomfortable around them?

She wished she understood him better. He was such an enigma. So intense and yet so private. She had dreamed of him forever, and yet she had very little notion of what had made him the way he was.

Why did he kiss her so hungrily, then thrust her away?

She started to go into his room, wanting simply to look around, to learn more about this man who'd haunted her for so many years.

Then, far off she heard the sound of an engine. She flicked off the light, then padded quickly into his room, not looking around, but simply crossing the floor to look out the window.

She pulled back the shade and saw, down the valley, a pair of headlights moving this way.

"Thank heaven," she breathed, relieved that all her worst fantasies had come to naught.

She stood watching until he drove into the yard, cut the engine and quietly shut the door of the truck. Then she turned and ran quickly to Nathan's room, jumping into bed and pulling the covers up to her chin, pretending to be asleep.

He didn't come in.

Finally, when a quarter of an hour passed and he still didn't come in, she eased herself out of bed again and crept across the hall to his room.

The yard was empty except for the silent truck. She frowned, peering into the darkness, trying to discern movement.

There was none.

But something was different. A light in the bunkhouse.

And the very moment she noticed it, it shut off.

So he was hiding out, was he?

He'd deny it, she was sure. But that was what he was doing, as sure as she was Nathan's grandchild.

Alison sighed. It wasn't the homecoming she'd wished for, although it had had its moments, she thought with a smile, remembering him coming out of the bathroom in his birthday suit.

Still, things had gone right downhill from there.

She walked slowly back to her bed and slid beneath the covers, asking herself exactly what Jess Cooper was afraid of.

THE TRUCKS CAME up the hill at dawn. It felt as if they were rumbling right through his head. Great honking semis grinding their gears in the grooves of his brain, peeling out against the backs of his eyeballs, letting go with roaring blasts of their air horns, loud enough to explode the inside of his head.

Jess ground the pillow against his face and groaned.

What in the hell had he done to feel this way?

He wasn't so far gone that he didn't remember. He'd panicked and run. He'd taken one look at Alison Richards's smiling, hopeful face, remembered the kiss they'd shared, heard her wonder aloud where it might lead, and he'd bolted like a bronc with a burr under his saddle.

He'd started at the Silver Dollar, moved on the Moriarty's, and finished at the Blue Heeler.

"Whatcha doin' here? Ain'tcha shippin' tomorrow?" Denny the bartender at the Silver Dollar has asked, curiosity wreathing his bulldog face.

Jess had scowled into his beer. "What of it?"

Denny took a step backward, picked up a towel and began to dry another glass. "Just wonderin'," he said mildly, and when a customer called for a gin and tonic, he'd moved gratefully away.

Nearly the same had happened at Moriarty's, where old Gus had shaken his head and said, "Let it go to hell that fast, didja? Poor ol' Nate."

"Nothing's gone to hell," Jess had snapped. Except maybe him. "The ranch is fine. The cattle are fine."

"Uh-huh," Gus said. And the skeptical look on Moriarty's face had sent Jess to the Blue Heeler within minutes.

The Blue Heeler was primarily a tourist joint. Hunters with an eye for an elk or a ten-point deer hung out there. There were no hunters yet, it was too early in the year. But a busload of German tourists on their way from Phoenix to

Denver were stopping for a night at the springs and a little local color.

They watched with silent respect as Jess drowned his miseries.

"You are a real cowboy," one of them said with wary admiration, looking him up and down as if he were a tiger on the loose.

"*Ein* true American hero," nodded another. He smiled at Jess hopefully. "Can I take your picture, *Herr* Cowboy?"

Jess wished he had a six-shooter.

If he had one now, he'd think about putting himself out of his misery. He sat up on the edge of the bunk and held his head in his hands. God, how could he have been so stupid as to drink that much the night before shipping day?

How could he not, he asked himself, given the prospect of Alison's smiling, wide-eyed face?

Where would it lead? He knew damned well where it would lead. That was why he'd had to get out of there!

He staggered to his feet and pulled on his boots, then stumbled to the sink and stuck his head under the faucet. The stream of icy water on his skull nearly accomplished what a six-shooter would. He yelped, pulling back. Then, cautiously, he ducked his head again, letting the water beat against his skull so that now the outside felt as if it were being as soundly hammered as the inside.

The first truck rumbled into the yard as he was toweling off his hair. He grabbed a jacket and headed for the door.

Alison was there before him, all bright-eyed and cheerful as she talked to Sam Wiley, the driver.

Sam grinned at him. "Mornin', Jess. See you got some new help." His gaze flickered to Alison approvingly.

Jess strode past without stopping. "Hell of a lot of help she'll be. Come on. Time's wastin'."

Sam's brows lifted and he gave Alison a wink. "Got up on the wrong side of bed, did he?"

"If he even went to bed at all," Jess heard her reply behind him. He gritted his teeth and headed toward the corral.

The cattle were restless, aware that today was different, that things were about to change, and it took all Jess's concentration to get them moving toward the chute. He turned to shout at Sam or Mal to open the gate.

Alison was already there, anticipating him.

He sighed. His head hurt.

"Give her some credit, Jess," Sam said. "She's not half bad."

Jess grunted and went back to his work.

But Sam was right. She did have a pretty fair sense of what needed to be done, and she was right there, opening this gate, closing that one, trying her best to do it. He had to give her credit for that.

Still it didn't mean she ought to give up librarianing for ranching. Especially not here.

So what if she owned half of the ranch? Hadn't she ever heard of absentee landlording?

Presumably she had. And she'd been going to do it until he'd kissed her.

And what had he done last night except kiss her again?

Damnation! What was the matter with him?

Jess scowled, wiping a hand across his grimy forehead. He turned, watching the quick, efficient way she moved, appreciating the way she filled out her jeans. He wished some cow would do its worst all over her shiny new boots. He wished she'd catch a dirty wet tail across the cheek.

It wasn't going to work, him and Alison Richards being partners, working together; no matter what fuzzy little idea she had in her pretty head. She was too damned tempting, too desirable.

He wanted her.

He'd used Nathan's memory and a good dose of solid common sense to mind his manners when she'd been around for the funeral. He'd done fine for three days, thank you very much.

But he wasn't a big enough fool to believe he could keep it up indefinitely.

The hell of it was she didn't seem to want him to. "I figured we owed it to Pops to see where it would lead," she'd said.

Did that argue for a platonic relationship?

Not on your life!

And after they became lovers, then what?

"You got a problem, you gotta step back and look at it from all angles," Nathan had always said. "Get yourself a little distance, some perspective."

Jess had the mother of all problems.

"Come on, Denver," he muttered, urging the cattle toward the chute, hoping against hope that three days and three hundred miles would give him the perspective he sought.

THE CATTLE WERE LOADED by eight. Jess left Sam and Mal locking up the last of them and went into the house to get his gear.

He tossed his bag onto the bed and threw shirts and jeans into it indiscriminately. Then, grabbing his shaving kit out of the bathroom, he headed back downstairs.

Alison was just coming up.

He moved aside giving her wide berth. Only when she was safely past did he say, "When I get back from Denver, we're going to have a talk."

"Why don't we talk en route?"

"What?" He stopped dead, his hand on the newel post. "What do you mean, 'talk en route'? You're not coming with me!"

"Of course I am."

"Like hell!"

"Then I'll go with Sam."

What he said then was even ruder. "Who's going to take care of things here?" he demanded.

She shrugged. "Who was going to take care of them if I hadn't come back?"

"Brian Gonzales."

"Well, then," she said lightly, "I guess Brian Gonzales will." And she turned to head back up the steps again.

Jess, furious, strode after her, taking the stairs two at a time.

"Listen to me, Miss Dale Evans Richards, if you're gonna be responsible for half of the things that happen on this ranch, you need to do your share! You need—"

"As a co-owner I need to find out as much as I can about the livestock we're selling and about getting the best deal possible," Alison said with quiet authority. "The bottom line is what we make on the cattle, isn't it? Well, then I need to come, too." She paused. "I don't have a steady income anymore, remember?"

"That's not my fault," Jess bit out.

She just looked at him, then smiled that damnably maddening, tempting smile. "Isn't it?"

"Oh, hell." He turned on his heel and stomped down again.

He was sitting in the truck fuming when she came out a few moments later.

Sam had already headed down the hill. Mal was starting after him. Jess would bring up the rear.

Ordinarily he would've ridden with either Sam or Mal. But he wasn't letting Alison in a truck cab with them for a whole day.

Once, he'd have figured she'd keep her mouth shut and smile politely. But since she'd asked for that goodbye kiss, he realized there was no telling what she'd do.

He sat with his hands clenched on the steering wheel, knuckles whitening as he watched her come out the door. She turned back for a moment, bending down, patting something.

The cat, he thought irritably.

What on earth were they going to do with a cat?

He muttered an expletive under his breath. Then, reaching over, he jerked open the passenger door. "Come on if you're coming," he yelled. "We haven't got all day."

She came at a run, tossing her bag into the back before she scrambled in and settled down beside him, grinning. "All set."

Jess gunned the engine and they shot off down the road. She bounced forward, and he reached over and thrust her seat belt at her. "Use it."

She put it on, then leaned back against the seat and smiled at him. She'd been herding cattle since sun up and damned if she didn't smell like flowers.

He thought he'd lose his mind.

A WHOLE DAY in a truck, just her and Jess Cooper. It was the stuff of which Alison's adolescent dreams had been made.

Reality was a far, far different thing.

In her dreams Jess had taken advantage of the opportunity to declare his undying love, to hold her hand, to steal kisses whenever the switchback curves permitted.

In reality he turned on the radio, kept both hands on the wheel and never said a word.

No, that wasn't quite the truth. He would speak if spoken to. But he didn't seem to be jumping into this talk that he'd said they were going to have, though Alison allowed him plenty of time.

That being the case, she decided to bring up the subject herself. "You wanted to talk to me?"

He grunted.

"Well, I thought you said—"

"I'm trying to figure out how to say it. How to be tactful."

"Why start now?"

He ground his teeth and turned up the radio.

THE TRIP TO DENVER took fourteen hours. It seemed to Jess like four hundred years.

He should've been concentrating on the cattle, on how he needed to shape them up when he got them there, on what he needed to tell the commission man before Monday morning.

He thought about Alison and about how to get her out of his life.

He wasn't used to talking to women, especially not about personal feelings, and most especially not about sex, but he didn't see any way around it.

She wasn't leaving him any choice.

"All right," he said finally when they'd reached the Interstate without him being able to find the words. "Let's put it this way. Pure and simple, it wouldn't work."

Alison, who had been looking out the window for the last hour in complete and unnerving silence, looked at him and blinked. "What wouldn't work?"

"Going to bed with you." His face burned even as he said the words.

Alison blinked. Her face reddened a bit, too. Then she gave him a saucy grin. "How do you know unless you try?"

Jess sputtered. "Geez! What in hell would your grandfather say?"

"I don't know. But I rather think he'd have more to say to you than to me," Alison told him.

Jess snorted. His thumbs tightened on the wheel.

Alison turned sideways in the seat so she could look at him. He felt like a bug, pinned to a board.

"Let me get this straight," Alison said conversationally. "You have been sitting here contemplating the prospect of sleeping with me for almost three hundred miles?" She sounded almost amused.

His hands strangled the steering wheel. "Well, what d'you expect. You suggested it!"

"I!"

"Who said, 'Let's see where it might lead'?" He turned a glare on her. "That was you, wasn't it?"

"Yes, but—"

"Well, damn it all, that kiss I gave you yesterday, that's only where it would start, and you know it. I'm sure you're terrific in bed and all that, but—"

"Thank you. I think," Alison cut in.

"But I think if you really give it some consideration," Jess went on, determined to get it out once and for all, "you'll decide it isn't what you want, either."

"It isn't."

"But you said—"

"I said what I said because I felt like something was happening between us. That did not mean I was simply angling to go to bed with you!"

"It didn't?" He looked at her narrowly. "Then what the hell did you mean?"

Alison stared for a long moment at her hands in her lap. Then she lifted her gaze and met his. "Think about it," she suggested quietly.

Jess did.

That was more terrifying yet.

Chapter Six

"Ho, no. No way."

She couldn't mean what he thought she meant. Could she?

It took one swift glance to tell him that, yes, indeed she did.

"M-marriage." Even to him his voice sounded rusty. "You're thinking about *marriage?*"

"It's a possibility."

"Huh-uh." Jess shook his head. "Talk about things that wouldn't work."

"How do you know?"

He stared at her, incredulous. "You're serious? You think that just because Nathan has stuck us together on a ranch in the middle of nowhere we ought to get married?"

"Nathan has nothing to do with this."

"You mean if you hadn't inherited half of the Rocking R you'd have shown up to propose to me, anyway?"

"Don't be an idiot."

"I'm not the idiot here," Jess muttered. Marry? *Marry Alison Richards?* He couldn't fathom it.

"I'm not proposing to you."

"Sounded like it to me," he muttered, still shaken.

"Still, you have to admit, after a kiss like that—"

"Kisses aren't proposals, either!"

"No, but you're a man, I'm a woman. We're within a reasonable age of each other."

"And you think that's enough?"

"Of course not. Love is necessary, too."

"Love." He snorted. If there was ever an emotion he doubted, it was love. "What's that?"

"You don't know?"

"I'm asking, aren't I?"

"It's wanting to share, to care. It's when someone else's good, someone else's happiness matters to you more than your own."

"And you read all that into a kiss?"

"It wasn't indifferent."

"You've never heard of plain, simple lust?"

Her fingers clenched. "Of course, but—"

"That was lust."

"Oh, Jess." She sighed and shook her head.

"I'm not getting married."

"You said that once before."

"When?"

"The day the . . . the Brinkmillers were . . ."

She didn't have to finish. He remembered now. Too well. God, why had she been there that day?

He gritted his teeth. "And I meant what I said."

"Why?"

He shot her an exasperated glance. Damn it. Couldn't she leave well enough alone? "Some people aren't cut out for marriage. Me, for instance."

"How do you know?"

"What the hell is this, twenty questions?"

"I'm . . . curious. What made you decide? Is it for religious reasons? Did you take a vow?"

"You think it's funny?"

"No," she said quickly. "I don't know what to think, Jess. Really. I'm trying to understand."

He rubbed his hand against the back of his neck.

"Family history." He stared straight ahead waiting for her to ask what he meant by it. But she just looked at him, and he found himself explaining without the question.

"My family doesn't do marriage. Or when they do, they don't do it well."

"Your parents divorced?" she asked quietly.

"No. But stayin' together until my mother died doesn't mean what they had was good."

His hands tightened briefly on the steering wheel as he remembered the arguments, the tears, the upheavals during which his mother had moved them from relative to relative, dragging him and his sister along while his father took off rodeoing again.

"My ma died when I was ten. Dad married again. And again. Those marriages didn't work, either. One lasted six months, the other barely two years. Hardly world records. And after that, he stopped marryin' 'em and just lived with 'em. Not exactly a role model for fidelity, would you say?"

"No, it isn't." She looked at him earnestly. "But that's just one man, Jess. And he wasn't you."

"Maybe not, but he handed it down. Did you know my sister, Lizzie? She used to work at Cutter's ranch as a hired girl."

"Long wavy dark hair, beautiful big brown eyes. She used to sing. Didn't she have a . . . a child?"

Jess's mouth twisted. "Yeah. Patsy. She's got two more of 'em, by last count. All with different men, and she never married any of 'em." He lifted one brow almost mockingly. "See what I mean, Ms. Richards? It's in the blood. So don't talk to me about marriage." He stomped down on the accelerator, moving out to pass a truck.

Alison didn't answer. She sat quietly, looking down at her hands, and he felt faintly guilty about the intensity of his outburst.

"Sorry," he muttered.

"I'm sorry, too," Alison said softly.

"I don't need you feeling sorry for me."

She just looked at him. He roared past three more cars before cutting back in sharply.

"No," she said. "I won't."

They drove on without speaking, the road was wide and straight as it headed up the eastern edge of the Rocky Mountains toward Denver. As Jess drove, he glanced over at her from time to time, trying to guess what she was thinking. He hoped she wasn't thinking too badly of him, but it wouldn't have surprised him. He didn't exactly have a background to put on a résumé. She might as well know it before she got any more damn fool ideas.

Just north of Colorado Springs, he cleared his throat. "If you want to fly back from Denver, I can send your gear on to you."

"Fly back?" She looked at him, puzzled. "To Bluff Springs? Why would I want to do that?"

"Not Bluff Springs. New York."

"I'm not going back to New York. I told you that."

"But you can't stay on."

"Why not?"

"By all that's holy, woman, we just discussed that! It won't work!"

"Like marriage won't work?" Alison smiled at him. "A detached observer might say you're protesting a bit too much. Don't worry, Jess. I won't pressure you, I promise. I just said I wanted to see where it would lead. If it doesn't lead to marriage, fine." She gave a negligent little shrug and went back to looking out the window.

It made Jess want to shake her.

"You're as bullheaded as your pesky grandfather," he muttered.

Alison nodded. "Thank you very much."

SHE DOUBTED he meant it as a compliment, even though she took it as such.

He probably thought she was crazy. Maybe she was. But why not spell it out, or at least admit she'd considered marriage as a possibility.

What could he do? Throw her out?

Hardly. She owned half the ranch.

Of course knowing what she was thinking could make him uncomfortable. But he was uncomfortable now. For better or worse, her presence seemed to have accomplished that.

In any case, coming out here again was taking a risk. She knew it. And she wasn't about to increase the risk by fostering misunderstandings.

She was no longer a starry-eyed adolescent content to live on a raft of fantasies for the future.

The future was now.

And if it was foolish to lay all her cards on the table with Jess, it would have been more foolish to pretend that all she wanted was a roll in the hay.

She had no doubt that a roll in the hay with Jess Cooper would be well worth remembering. Her cheeks warmed at the very thought. But that wasn't all she wanted.

She didn't honestly know yet if she wanted marriage, either. But she was at least willing to consider the idea.

Why couldn't men accept marriage as a possibility to be explored rather than a gun to run from?

Well, she consoled herself, it had got her one thing, this honesty of hers—it had encouraged Jess to open up to her for the first time.

All she'd ever known about his family before had been what she'd heard from his grandmother all those years ago. Ella hadn't told her much, mostly that her grandchildren worried her. Lizzie was wild, with crazy dreams of being a singing star that Ella was sure would bring her to ruin. And Jess was the opposite.

"He's so quiet. I never know what he's thinking. He's not like Lizzie. He's gentle, my Jess," Alison remembered Ella saying. "He won't hurt no one. People take advantage of him and he lets them. It will get him into trouble someday. I know it will." The old lady had shaken her head.

Alison had believed in Jess's gentleness then. She told herself it must still be in there now. Only she had the feeling that perhaps Ella had been right. Somewhere along the line, Jess had lost that gentleness—or had hidden it.

He was very well defended now.

He wasn't about to let anyone in—certainly not Alison.

She turned to him now. "What do we do when we get to Denver?"

"*I* get the cattle settled in, then find me a hotel room, go out to dinner with Sam and Mal, have a few drinks, then come back and get a good night's sleep. *You* can do whatever you damned well please."

She blinked at his vehemence, but didn't argue. "Fine. I will."

She heard a soft curse and looked over at him. "What?"

"Never mind. Come with me if you want." He was scowling at her.

Alison smiled slightly, then thought of his grandmother's words. "I don't want to take advantage. I don't want to ruin your trip."

"You already ruined my trip."

Alison looked at him. He gave her a ghost of a grin.

"I meant everything I said about us. And about marriage. Just forget that. But—" he sighed irritably "—oh hell, we are partners." He seemed to hesitate over the word for a split second, but then he went on doggedly, "Half of these cows are yours. You have a right to be there, too."

Alison placed her hand over her heart and gave him her best Girl Scout salute. "I promise I'll be good."

His expression was glum. "You'd better be."

IT WAS DARK by the time they got to Denver. Alison was glad that unloading the cattle didn't take as long as loading them had, and she was delighted when Jess drove her and Sam and Mal to a downtown hotel where they all got rooms.

"Dinner in an hour," he told her briskly in the lobby, handing her a room key. He turned to Sam and Mal. "You don't mind if she tags along?"

Mal looked astonished. "Mind? Why would we mind? She's a damned sight prettier than you are."

"Better conversationalist, too, I'll bet," Sam added, grinning.

Jess scowled. "So long as all you want to do is talk."

Mal and Sam looked at Alison, then gave him identical innocent smiles. "What else?"

Jess opened his mouth, then apparently thought better of whatever he might have been going to say. "See you in an hour," he muttered and stalked off toward the elevators.

Sam looked at Mal. "He look a little green around the edges to you?"

Mal grinned. "Just a tad." He gave Alison a wink. "Your fault?"

"You mean he isn't always this cheerful?"

Mal laughed. "See you at supper."

They ate in the hotel restaurant, a dimly lit, dark-paneled room with thick burgundy carpet and hunt club prints on the walls. The chairs were leather and the tablecloths linen. It was a far cry from the pine ladder-backs and faded checkered oilcloth in Nathan's kitchen.

"We like to live right once a year," Sam told her with a grin as they sat down.

"You come to Denver every week," Jess objected.

"Yeah, but we pretend we don't. Wouldn't want to make you feel bad." Sam grinned at Alison.

If she'd worried about feeling out of place having dinner with the three of them, she learned quickly that Mal and Sam were more than willing to welcome her. And if Jess ignored her, Mal and Sam were easy to talk to. They were eager, when she asked, to regale her with stories of Nathan and the Rocking R's earlier sale days.

"Topped the Denver market twice," Sam told her over a thick slab of prime rib. "Nathan was damned proud."

"Should've been," Jess put in abruptly. "Means he did things right. I'd like to do it again." His dark eyes met Alison's, challenging her. They were the first words he'd spoken since they'd sat down, and she heard the faint stress on the singular pronoun.

Mal, oblivious to the tensions between them, grinned. "Reckon you got your work cut out for you then. Ain't gonna be easy."

"I'll do it," Jess said quietly.

"Yes," Alison agreed. "We will."

After supper all Alison wanted to do was go back upstairs and fall into bed. Sam and Mal had other ideas.

"Thought we'd take in a little of the bright lights," Sam said as they were heading back toward the lobby. He gave Alison a hopeful, encouraging look.

She shook her head. "Go right ahead. Don't let me stop you," she replied. "I'm tired. I plan on going straight up to sleep. I'll see you in the morning."

He looked disappointed, then shrugged. "Another time, then. You comin', Jess?"

Alison looked over at Jess. He'd complained in the truck about how tired he was. She knew he hadn't slept much the night before. He was looking at her, his expression brooding. But when Mal asked, he didn't even hesitate.

"Sure. Why not?"

HE MEANT to have a high old time. Certainly Sam and Mal, released from the constraint of being gentlemen for Alison's benefit, were set on having one.

It didn't take them more than fifteen minutes to find a bar with a live band, a mechanical bull and a bevy of willing women. Perfect, Jess thought.

So why the hell was he sitting at the bar drinking orange juice by himself?

Because this morning's hangover was all too recent and well recalled. Because he needed to be sane and sensible when he went to the stockyards in the morning. Because he didn't have Nathan here to make the final decisions this year. And he sure as hell couldn't count on Alison, not for advice on shaping up the cattle. She probably thought she could, though. She seemed intent on infiltrating his life.

Damn Alison.

A woman with the looks, personality and education of Alison Richards could have her pick of men. So why was she fooling around with him?

Marry Alison?

Didn't he wish!

But he hadn't been lying when he'd said marriage wasn't for him. There was no way he wanted to end up like his father with a wife he couldn't satisfy and children he didn't give a damn about.

Jess Cooper knew there was only one way for a guy like him to relate to women, and it didn't take a preacher to do it.

"Kinda glum tonight, aren't you, honey?"

He looked up as one of the willing women slid onto the bar stool next to him and gave him a smile.

He shrugged, looking her over as he did so, wishing the sight of her would light some fire deep inside him. She was pretty enough. Big dark eyes, a puffy cloud of equally dark hair.

But there was knowledge in those eyes, a kind of unspoken calculation that instead of warming him actually made him feel cold.

"Not real talkative, are you?"

He hunched over his glass. "Got a lot on my mind."

"Bet I could distract you." Her voice was soft, almost a purr.

He wished it were true.

"Probably you could," he told her gently, "if I wanted you to." Inclining his head slightly, giving her a faint smile, he set his glass down and backed away, then turned and headed for the door.

Maybe he was a fool. She would have provided some solace. It had been a long time since he'd held a warm and willing woman in his arms. But there was only one woman who interested him that way right now.

The irony was, he could have her if he married her. And the even bigger irony was that in a more perfect world he would do it in a minute.

But Jess knew better than to believe in dreams like that one.

A ranch, well, yeah, maybe he could get that with hard work, determination and Nathan's blessing. But Nathan and all the hard work and determination in the world couldn't correct his past, couldn't change the family he'd grown up in, couldn't give him the courage to try the impossible.

That said, for the moment at least, he was going to have to learn how to accomplish the extremely difficult—living day by day with Alison, at least until she'd satisfied her curiosity and once more gone away.

In the past whenever things had got too tight, whenever he'd felt commitments closing in, he'd been able to take the time-honored cowboy's retreat and ride off into the sunset without looking back.

A rancher couldn't do that.

You couldn't roll up a ranch like you could a bedroll, toss it in your truck and be on your way. You stayed where the ranch was.

Or you sold out.

Could he sell out? Walk away and leave the one dream that finally seemed to be within his grasp?

Walking away had never been a problem in the past. He'd never tried to hang on to anything, and he'd left without looking back.

You never had anything worth hanging on to, he reminded himself.

But now he did.

One time, in the first year he'd worked for Nathan after he'd come back, he and Nathan had had a disagreement. Jess, angry and feeling misunderstood, had packed up his gear and headed out the door.

"Chicken?" Nathan had called after him.

Jess had spun around, fists clenched. "Who're you callin' chicken?"

Nathan had been sitting calmly at the kitchen table, the Sunday papers spread out in front of him, looking as calm and unruffled as a sleepy hen as Jess had glared at him. He'd looked up with those mild blue eyes and challenged him. "Well, if you're afraid to stay and fight for what you want..."

"It's your ranch," Jess retorted, stung.

"And it's your life." A corner of Nathan's mouth had lifted slightly. "What're you gonna do with it, son?"

Jess had stayed.

He'd slung his bag down, stalked over to the table, glowered down at Nathan and once more argued his point. Nathan had listened, then insisted that Jess listen to him. Jess couldn't even remember which of them had prevailed. He only knew that he'd taken a deeper interest in the ranch after that.

It had really begun to matter to him.

It still mattered.

Sure, he could sell out. But he never would. Not now.

So that meant he had to stay and fight. Fight his attraction to Alison. Learn to get along with her until she left. Pray every night that his desire would fade or that the siren call of the big city would lure her away before the temptation became too much.

HE'D AGREED to call for her when he was going to the stockyards Sunday morning. He hadn't wanted to, she could tell, but she'd been adamant. "Like you said, we're partners, Jess. I need to be there, too."

So now Alison hurried to get ready, not wanting to keep him waiting. In fact she wondered if he'd show up on time.

If he'd had a hard night out on the town, perhaps he'd sleep right through his alarm. Or maybe he had stayed out so long, he wouldn't have been to bed at all. That thought made her wince.

Whichever the case, just as she finished braiding her hair, she heard a knock on the door.

He was wearing his customary jeans and long-sleeved shirt, with his sheepskin jacket hanging open, his hat in his hands. He looked surprisingly well rested for a man who had been so eager to party last night.

Or maybe, Alison thought, he wasn't so much well rested as well satisfied. The notion made her teeth clench. She drew a fortifying breath.

On the way to the stockyards Jess was all business, telling her how he intended to shape up the cattle he was selling, what size lots he figured to let them go in, what sort of prices they would be hoping for.

He was as talkative as she'd ever heard him, but at the same time he seemed distant and professional and formal. Perfectly proper. Very aloof.

Alison listened carefully, trying to digest everything he was telling her as they parked and she trailed after him, knowing as she did so that she'd forget a lot of it and have to ask again.

"Jess!"

Alison looked up to see a dark-haired man hurrying toward them. He was tall and broad-shouldered, like a football player, and, somewhat incongruously, wearing a suit. His white shirt cuffs peeked out below his spotless navy-blue sleeves, and a small blue sapphire sparkled in the center of a burgundy and navy tie. He looked like a Wall Street broker except for the boots.

Jess turned to Alison. "This is Steve Sudmeier, our commission man. This is my new partner—" once more Alison heard the fleeting hesitation "—Alison Richards. Nathan's granddaughter. From New York."

"Formerly from New York," Alison qualified with a smile. "Now I'm from Bluff Springs." She offered Steve her hand.

"I was sorry to hear about your grandfather. He was a good friend. A fine man."

"Thank you. He was. And a bit of devil, too, leaving Jess and me half the ranch."

Steve grinned. "I don't think you'll have any trouble selling it. Will she, Jess?"

"But I'm not going to. I've decided to come west instead."

Steve looked surprised. "To live at the ranch?"

Jess was shifting his feet, making impatient tapping noises with the toes of his boots.

Alison smiled. "I didn't realize how much I missed it until I came back for the funeral. And—" she shot a mischievous glance at Jess "—there were other enticements, too."

Steve's brows lifted.

"You can waste time chatting if you want," Jess said abruptly. "I got work to do." He turned to Steve. "You come over when you're finished socializing, and I'll show you how I want the cattle sorted and shaped up."

Without giving Steve a chance to answer, he turned on his heel and stalked off.

"Been working hard, has he?" Steve asked her as he watched Jess leave.

Alison sighed. "Oh, yes."

Steve slanted a glance in her direction. "I guess I ought to be, too," He hesitated. "Are you . . . spoken for?"

"I beg your pardon."

"You're not married? I didn't think you were, but enough women keep their maiden names these days that a guy can't be sure." He gave her a disarming grin.

"I'm not married."

"But that doesn't mean you don't have somebody interested. Jess, for example?" The brows lifted again.

"He says not," Alison admitted, which was putting it mildly.

"He ought to have his head examined," Steve said. "But—" he grinned "—all the better for me, I guess. Would you join me for the afternoon, then? Once we get work taken care of, I'll show you some of the bright spots of Denver."

"Thank you. I'd like that."

Why not? Steve Sudmeier seemed a nice man. And there was no point in sitting in her hotel room and pining away while Jess was out having a good time.

She might have her fantasies, but she wasn't a total fool.

IT WAS WORKING. He could handle it.

If he mentally stuck Nathan's bushy white eyebrows and thinning hair on her, padded her with thirty-five pounds and imagined she was eighty-two, it was a piece of cake.

If he talked business, speculated on prices, discussed bulls' bloodlines and the cost of feed, it was no problem at all.

Jess was feeling positively cocky by the time they got back to the hotel.

"We don't have to meet Mal and Sam for dinner this noon," he told Alison as they boarded the elevator together. "There's a good French place about half a mile from here. I'll take you to Henri's," he offered, pleased at his own ability to cope.

"Oh," she said, a tiny frown creasing her forehead. "I'm really sorry. I can't. I have a date with Steve."

"The commission man?" He should've moderated his tone a little bit. The other people in the elevator were looking at him.

"He said we'd have the afternoon free. Don't we?"

"Sure. Of course we do," he said, his tone clipped. He shoved his fingers through his hair. "Do what you want."

The doors opened on their floor. They walked down the hall together in silence, halting when they got to her room.

"I'm sorry."

"No problem. Have a good time," he managed.

Alison gave him a bright smile as she went into her room. "I'm sure I will. You have a nice day, too."

Yeah, right, Jess thought.

And how in hell was he supposed to have a nice day thinking about her going out with Steve Studly?

Chapter Seven

He had time on his hands.

He should've told Sam and Mal he'd take them up on that extra ticket to the Broncos' game. It would have been a far better way to spend the afternoon than sitting around his hotel room wondering what Alison was doing with Sudmeier.

What was so great about Sudmeier, anyway?

Sure he was good-looking and he had that toothpaste-commercial smile. But he wore a suit with his cowboy boots, for crying out loud. And his hatband looked like he never sweated at all.

Probably didn't, Jess thought glumly. And that was probably the attraction.

He ought to be glad. Alison was hankering after big-city men already. If that was true, she wasn't really all that serious about digging in at the Rocking R.

He ought to have hope.

Telling himself that, he decided to go look up the only person he knew who lived in Denver. His sister Lizzie.

He and Lizzie weren't what you'd call close. There was nothing "Leave It To Beaver"-ish about the family he'd grown up in. He'd thought "Father Knows Best" was a joke.

Les Cooper had always been on the move, trekking from one rodeo to another, one dead-end job to another, one unemployment line to another, while Jess's mother tried to keep the home fires burning. She hadn't had much success.

After his mother died and his grandmother had taken them in, Jess and Lizzie had spent even less time together. Lizzie, at thirteen, had better things to do than hang around her kid brother. She'd had dreams clear back then, and Jess had already seen the harm such dreams could do.

If they'd had little in common growing up, they'd had even less the last time he'd seen her.

That had been two years ago when he and Nathan had come to Denver for the sale.

He'd been out on the town with Sam and a couple of other guys, making the rounds of a variety of country-western bars, and to his amazement, Lizzie had been singing in one of them.

She'd cut her hair and lost weight. Her eyes were enormous. She looked like one of those paintings on velvet that Jess sometimes saw in pawn shop windows.

He'd waited for her afterward to drive her home, but she'd refused. "Tom comes to get me."

"Who's Tom?" It had been Hank, last he knew.

"My one true love. He writes gorgeous songs. They make me want to cry." She'd looked at Jess with her brown eyes sparkling. He remembered Hank as her one true love. Or had it been Danny?

"He living with you?" Jess had asked her.

"Of course."

"You marry him?" He hadn't known whether to hope she had or not.

"Marriage isn't important, Jess," she'd said, tossing her head defiantly. "Love is what matters. And Tom loves me.

He says he can get me an audition in Nashville. Wouldn't that be super, Jess?''

''Super,'' he'd echoed, but Lizzie wouldn't hear the skepticism in his voice.

''Tell you what, sweetie,'' Lizzie'd patted his cheek. ''You come around tomorrow and we'll have a good ol' sister-brother chat.'' She scribbled an address on a piece of paper.

So Jess had come around. He'd found her tiny duplex, had climbed rickety steps to ring the bell, then had shifted impatiently from one foot to the other. He was about to leave, pretty sure she'd forgotten or was avoiding him, when he saw a curtain twitch.

Moments later the door opened. A little girl looked out. ''Who're you?'' the child asked.

''My name's Jess. Is your mother here?''

''She's sleepin'. Are you her brother? She said you might come. You can come in. I'm Sue. I'm four.'' The girl stuck out her hand. Solemnly Jess shook it and followed her into the sparsely furnished living room.

A few moments later a sleepy, disheveled Lizzie had appeared. ''Oh, it's you.''

Lizzie had wanted to know what he was doing, and when he told her, she'd told him he ought to go back to rodeoing.

''I like what I'm doin'.''

She'd looked at him long and hard. Then, at last she'd shrugged. ''Livin' in one place, chasin' little critters all day? You're a strange one, Jess,'' she told him, but she was smiling. ''You always have been.''

''No stranger than you,'' he'd countered with a grin.

''I'm gonna get there,'' Lizzie had told him stubbornly. ''I believe, Jess. I'll make it. You just see if I don't.''

Jess had smiled faintly and stood up, moving toward the door. ''Good luck to you.''

His eyes had flicked from his sister, with her bloodshot eyes and smoke-roughened voice to the school photo of Lizzie's older girls stuck on the refrigerator, then to Sue who still hadn't taken her eyes off him. "Good luck to all of you."

It was probably a mistake to go back to see her again this afternoon.

Still, what else did he have to do? And if he ever got tempted to actually think marrying Alison was a good idea, seeing Lizzie ought to go a long way toward curing him of that.

There was a fresh coat of paint on the duplex when he got there. Someone had repaired the front steps. He felt a faint flickering of hope as he rang the bell.

The door opened and tall thin man looked out. Tom? Jess wondered. Or his replacement.

"I'm looking for Lizzie Cooper," Jess said.

"Don't know no Lizzie Cooper."

"She doesn't live here?"

"Nope. We been here a year. Don't know who was before that. Guess you could ask the landlady." He jerked his head toward the other side of the building.

But the landlady didn't know anything, either.

"Lizzie Cooper? She moved well over a year and a half ago. She an' the kiddies. Went east, I think. Nashville, maybe?"

"Probably." Jess gave her a ghost of a smile. "Yeah, I reckon it was. Did she leave a forwarding address?"

The woman shook her head. "Nothin' to be forwarded." She looked him up and down. "You the father of one of them kiddies?"

"No. I'm her brother. I just came up from Bluff Springs for a cattle sale, thought I'd look her up."

"Wish I could help you, but she's long gone now."

"Thanks." Jess settled his hat back on his head and made his way back down the steps.

He shouldn't have been surprised. Moving on had always been a habit with Lizzie. And every move, she hoped, would bring her one step closer to her dream.

For her sake—and that of her kids—Jess hoped it had, too.

He got into the truck and drove back to the hotel. He tried not to wonder where Alison was. At least there was football on television.

IT WAS THE DAY of Alison's dreams—lunch at one of the restaurants in the Larimer Square area, a leisurely wander through the historic district and around the botanic gardens, followed by an elegant dinner at the Brown Palace with a handsome, charming, witty man.

The wrong man.

It wasn't fair, Alison thought as Steve brought her back to the hotel that evening. He was better educated, more loquacious, tons more charming and at least as good-looking as Jess Cooper. It shouldn't have been a contest.

And it wasn't—because he wasn't Jess.

"You're very quiet," Steve said as he escorted her to her room.

"I'm tired. It's been a long day. But a very pleasant one."

"I hope we can do it again."

"I'm not likely to be in Denver again. Until next year."

"Maybe I can persuade you. Or—" he shrugged "—maybe I can come out your way."

Steve followed her to the door of her room, his hand still holding hers.

Alison smiled. "Thank you very much for a lovely day." She raised her hand and touched the front of his jacket, just as his lips began to come down.

"I don't think—" she began softly.

"Ah, good, you're back." Jess's voice sounded louder than she'd ever heard it. Steve's nose collided with hers as Jess slapped him on the back.

"Have a good time?" he asked cheerfully.

Steve rubbed his nose, stepping back. "Just fine, thanks."

"Too bad you can't hang around any longer. Alison and I have business to discuss."

"Business?" Alison and Steve said in unison.

"We are partners, aren't we?" Jess looked right at her.

Alison smiled slightly. "Yes."

"Then we have business to discuss." He put a hand on her arm.

"I can go down to the bar and have a drink until you're through," Steve suggested.

Alison felt Jess's hand clench against her arm.

She turned a smile on Steve. "Thanks very much, but I really am tired. I'll see you tomorrow."

Steve grinned. "Count on it."

Jess hauled her down the hall and into his room before she could say another word.

The door banged shut behind them. "Don't you know better than to encourage guys like him?"

"Encourage? Guys like him?" Alison stared at him, then started to laugh. "You're . . . are you jealous, Jess?"

He was pacing back and forth, but her question stopped him dead. "Of course not!"

"Well, then . . ." She spread her hands, still smiling.

"It's damned near eleven o'clock!"

She looked at him wide-eyed. "I have a curfew?"

"You were gone hours!"

"If you're not jealous, what do you care?"

"We're partners, as you're forever reminding me. What if something had happened to . . . to the cattle?"

"The *cattle?*" Alison did laugh then. "Like they all ran away or something?"

He glared. "You know what I mean."

"Ah, Jess." She crossed the room and put her arms around him, felt him tense as her hands locked against the small of his back. She touched her lips to his. "Yes. I know what you mean," she said softly.

"Damn it, Alison."

Her tongue ran lightly along his upper lip, then teasingly dipped into his mouth. Her lips rubbed gently, tantalizingly against his. "Hmm?"

He started to say something, then stopped, unable to speak and kiss at the same time. And he was kissing her. It was no longer a one-way street. Alison could feel the need in him, the hard press of desire.

And then he was pushing her away, taking deep lungfuls of air, shoving his fingers through his hair. "Cripes! That's exactly what I mean."

She looked at him perplexed. "What's what you mean?"

"Why we can't work together! Blast Nathan anyway!" Jess slammed his hand against the door. "I don't know why he ever— What the devil could he have been thinking of, saddling me with you?"

"I don't know, Jess," Alison said quietly. "What do you think he was thinking?"

The words fell into the silence and stopped him dead.

Their gazes met. Jess seemed to halt, mid-glare. And as she watched, Alison saw his expression undergo a subtle change, from anger to awareness to confusion. He sighed and jammed his hands into his pockets. He scuffed his toe on the rug.

"That manipulating son-of-a-gun." He looked at Alison, his gaze stubborn. "It won't work," he said.

But Alison wasn't so sure about that.

IF FOR MOST PEOPLE a good defense was a good offense, mending fence seemed to Jess the best defense of all.

He set out the morning after they got home.

"I'll be gone all day," he told Alison. "But I'll be in tonight to move out my gear."

"That is ridiculous." She was standing at the sink, cutting a grapefruit, still wearing her bathrobe, her hair tousled and tempting.

Jess knew it wasn't ridiculous at all. And if he didn't, seeing her in her robe, knowing how little must be under it, would have proved it to him. "Think what you like."

"I feel as if I'm driving you out," she complained.

"You are."

"Thanks very much."

"You're welcome." He started back out the door.

"Don't you want some breakfast?"

"I'll be fine."

"You'll die from hunger before noon if you don't eat something. You ate with Pops, didn't you?"

"Sometimes."

"How many times?"

He scowled. "Most of the time."

She smiled and held out half a grapefruit. "Then you can eat with me. We're partners, remember?"

Jess didn't see how he was supposed to forget.

He did his best. He stayed away at noon. He kept busy all day. There was always something to do.

And while he was gone, he pretended that nothing had changed. He imagined Nathan back at the house, puttering around, reading the livestock journals, making his soup.

He didn't let himself think about Alison.

Much.

When he did, he tried convincing himself that she'd get bored, find ranch life confining, hanker after big-city lights and yearn for all the things she'd left behind in New York.

Maybe when he got back this evening, she'd have seen how ridiculous her ranching notion was. There'd be nobody to talk to, no books to check out, no magazines to catalog. Maybe she'd have gone stir crazy in one afternoon.

Maybe she'd have her bags packed and her cat under her arm and be waiting for him to come back, so she could offer to sell out.

THE MOVERS BROUGHT all Alison's worldly goods later that morning. She had, in the course of following her father's career all over the world, become used to traveling light. But she had learned long ago that, while most things didn't matter, it was helpful to have a few favorite things to carry along, to provide continuity, to make a house seem like a home.

Consequently she was delighted when the big white van trundled up the road and left fifteen large packing containers and her few beloved pieces of furniture on the porch.

"You sure you don't want us to move 'em in, lady?" the mover asked her. "It's part of the deal."

But Alison shook her head, signing the receipt and handing it back. "I don't know where I want them yet. I have to make room."

There was considerable cleaning and weeding out to do. While Jess had kept the rooms painted and fresh, the furniture had seen better days, the oilcloth and the curtains all had been washed more often than they'd had any right to expect, and Nathan's tendency to save everything gave the house a more-than-lived-in look.

Alison had her work cut out for her.

The mover tucked the receipt in his pocket and gave her a smile. "Good luck, then."

Alison, standing on the porch with Kitten weaving between her legs, watched him drive away and knew she would need it.

As the dust from the van finally settled and the sound of the heavy-duty engine no longer reverberated in her ears, she knew that there was no going back.

"Come on," she said to Kitten, "we've got work to do."

She didn't know whether to expect Jess for noon dinner or not.

He'd eaten the grapefruit and the oatmeal she'd forced on him. He'd grabbed a couple of apples and some carrots from the refrigerator without comment. He'd said, "See you," as he'd stuffed them in a saddlebag, and he'd gone out the door without looking back.

Probably she should have asked. She hadn't dared.

She'd pushed Jess just about as far as she could. Any more and he would bolt, she was certain.

So for the time being she would handle him the way she'd seen Pops handle a skittish horse—taking things easy, moving slowly, letting him get used to her.

"You don't 'break' horses," Pops told her. "You gentle 'em."

Alison figured the same would be true of Jess.

So she hadn't asked and now didn't know if she should fix anything or not.

Better to err on the side of preparation, she decided. So she made a stew and baking powder biscuits, fixed a fresh lettuce salad, then took some corn on the cob out of the freezer and put water to boil it in on the stove.

Then while the water heated, she carried a couple of her boxes of books into the living room and set about finding them shelf space.

At two o'clock she ate the stew and salad alone. Then she went out to the barn and fed the biscuits to the Belgians that would pull the hay wagon when the tractor couldn't handle the snow. The boiling water sat cooling on the stove awaiting supper. The corn she put in the refrigerator.

After she ate, she unpacked her stereo. It was nothing compared to the high-tech quality of Peter's, but it was far superior to the tinny radio she found in Pops's kitchen. Then she uncovered the box in which she'd shipped her tapes and CDs, and before long she was wrapped in music to suit her mood.

She spent the afternoon weeding through Nathan's bookshelves, getting rid of old stock guides and yellowing issues of long-defunct magazines, accompanied first by soft rock, then by a reggae beat. She scrubbed and dusted, waxed and polished, then, humming and tapping her feet, she shelved her books alongside Nathan's own.

She stopped in the middle to stretch her back and run up and down the stairs. She used to do it in her brownstone every evening after work, for exercise. She had no doubt that she'd get lots more real exercise out here, but it didn't look as if she'd get it this afternoon. So she started on the first floor, ran up to the second floor and the attic, then went down again clear to the cellar.

That was where she discovered the shelves of home-canned fruits and vegetables. She recalled Ella having kept similar shelves, but she hadn't imagined Nathan and Jess canning anything. A little further snooping revealed that they hadn't.

The jars all had neat little labels with kitty cats or rainbows on them, and they all said, "Made Especially for You by Cathy Lee Parsons" or "From the Kitchen of Mabel Kirby" or "Yummies by Diana Lee."

Obviously Nathan and Jess hadn't starved.

On her last trip down, Alison plucked off a jar of Mabel Kirby's peaches for a pie.

The pie was sitting on the counter cooling, the leftover stew was simmering once again and fresh water was boiling for the corn, and Alison was wondering whether she'd be eating supper alone, too, when at last she heard the screen door to the porch bang shut.

In the midst of returning the last pile of books to the shelves, she stayed right where she was. She would take her cue from Jess.

He appeared in the doorway between the kitchen and the living room a few minutes later, his face freshly scrubbed, his hair still damp. His gaze found her where she sat cross-legged in front of the bookcase, a book on equine diseases in her hand.

She smiled up at him. "I'm just putting away some books. My stuff arrived today."

"So I see." He didn't sound thrilled.

"I thought I'd move in slowly, sorting things out as I go."

"Suit yourself. It's your house."

"It's also half yours."

"In name maybe. I won't be here." He shoved his hands into his pockets.

"I still think you're crazy."

He just looked at her, long enough and hard enough to make her squirm. "Crazier to stay in here," he said gruffly and turned to go back into the kitchen. She scrambled to her feet and followed him.

"I won't jump your bones if that's what you're worried about, Jess."

He shot her a dark look over his shoulder. "It's not."

"Then what is?"

"That I might jump yours."

She felt heat surge into her face. "Such a compliment."

"Not a compliment. A statement of fact."

"But you're interested—" she began hopefully.

He cut her off. "In sex. I'm interested in sex. Not marriage." He gave her a sardonic smile. "So unless you want sex with no strings attached, you won't mind me moving, will you?"

She hated his sarcasm. It wasn't like him, not the way she remembered him, not the way she'd dreamed him.

Her fists clenched, but she moderated her tone. "Well, if you can't control yourself..." she said lightly, giving him a playful smile, trying to make him smile, too.

He didn't. "Want to find out?"

She swallowed. "Not if it's only sex, Jess. No."

"Well, it is. So if you want this 'partnership'—" his voice gave the word a bitterly ironic twist "—to work, you'd better be glad I'm going." That said, he turned away and lifted the lid on the stew pot. "Smells good."

Alison, staring at him, realized that the discussion, as far as he was concerned, was finished.

Her heart was still pounding, her fists still clenching and unclenching. Deliberately she made an effort to steady herself, to tell herself that he was still running scared, that she had to wait him out, let him relax around her before she did anything else.

She smoothed her hands down the sides of her jeans. "Are you hungry?"

"Starved," he said and began ladling the stew onto his plate.

He didn't seem to be exaggerating by much, either, Alison thought as she watched him eat.

She had only a small helping of the stew. He finished it off. She ate an ear of corn. He ate three and looked hopefully around for more. He made short work of the salad and finished up with several slices of bread and butter. Through it all he never said a word. She wondered if he was still angry, but he didn't seem to be.

After he'd finished with third helpings and she got up to bring the pie to the table, she ventured, "You weren't kidding, were you?"

He was as lean as he had been twelve years ago. There wasn't a spare ounce of fat on him anywhere. Gary had to work out constantly and eat sparingly or in weeks he'd sport a spare tire.

Jess looked faintly embarrassed. "You're a good cook. And... apples don't go too far."

"You could have come home for dinner."

"I was clear up in the top meadow," he said gruffly. "A waste of time comin' all the way down." He frowned. "Did you fix dinner?"

"I had the stew ready then. And the salad. Also biscuits."

He looked around hopefully. "Biscuits?"

"I fed them to the horses."

"A whole pan of biscuits?" Jess stared at her, horrified.

"I don't think it will hurt them," Alison said quickly.

"Not them. Me. How could you get rid of them like that? A whole pan," he muttered, dismayed.

"Biscuits aren't good cold." She cut a large wedge of pie and set it in front of him.

"I'll take 'em any way I can get 'em."

"You sound as if you've been starved for weeks." She gave him an arch look.

He looked up, still chewing. "Nathan brag about his cooking, did he?"

"No. I didn't mean Pops. I found all those jars in the cellar from Mabel Kirby and... and Diana somebody—"

"Lee," he offered helpfully.

"—and Cathy Parsons and, for all I know, Betty Boop!"

He grinned. "Nathan had quite a fan club."

"I don't suppose it was Nathan they were trying to impress," she said irritably. Then, because she couldn't help herself, she asked, "Are they part of the 'no strings attached' brigade?"

Jess grinned. "Not Mabel Kirby. She's attached to Frank."

Which didn't answer Alison's question about the other two. She got up, turned her back and began scrubbing the plates fast and furiously.

She didn't want to feel this shaft of pure jealous rage, but she couldn't help it. She had no doubt that whatever interest Jess had in them, it went no further than his interest in her. But even that knowledge didn't help.

"Aren't you gonna have a piece of this pie?" he asked her. "It's good."

"I'm not hungry. I'll get fat eating this much every day."

"A body's got to eat. This isn't library work, you know. D'you miss it?"

"No. But I've only been away from it a week. Why?"

He shrugged. "A man can hope."

"You're not getting rid of me. I'm here to stay." Alison sat down opposite him again. "Speaking of which, we need to talk about a fair division of labor."

"I suppose you're gonna herd cattle now?"

"I don't know. You tell me." She looked at him hopefully.

He scowled. "I told you to go back to New York. Look how much good that did."

Alison dismissed that. "You should be getting a salary for what you're doing. I know Nathan paid you for your work around here, and now you're doing it for nothing."

"I own half the ranch," he reminded her. "Anyway, I didn't get paid much in money. I took most of it in cattle. A fair bit of that herd is mine."

"So I don't really own half."

"You own half of the property and half of about two thirds of the herd. I should be paying you rent for pasture."

"Don't be silly."

He lifted one brow. "Weren't you?"

"I just don't want to take advantage, Jess. I know Nathan cooked, and I can do that. But what else do you want me to do?"

He hesitated, a faint flush crept into his face. He looked away.

"He kept the books and made notes," Jess said after a moment, a rough edge to his voice. He nodded toward a file cabinet in the corner of the kitchen. "It's all in there. Not that he needed to refer to it. He had it all up here." He tapped his head, then sighed. "Helps when you're deciding which to keep and which to sell. How many calves they've had, how those calves have done. He was a master at that. You can go through the files. See if you can make heads or tails of 'em."

"I'll put them on computer."

"Computer? Why?"

"It's a wonderful analytical tool. It can make all kinds of comparisons."

Jess grunted doubtfully.

"Come help me unpack it," Alison suggested, "and I'll show you how to use it." And maybe that way he would see that she could be of some use. Maybe that way he'd begin to get used to her.

"Can't. I got work to do."

"It's dark."

"Not field work. Movin'."

LATER THAT NIGHT, after he'd moved, she had unpacked the computer by herself. She set it up in the living room and entered the first file. Then she shut off the light and climbed the stairs to go to bed.

But instead of going into Nathan's room, she turned the other way, going into her old bedroom. The room that Jess had just moved out of.

From the window she looked out over the yard, across to the barn, the shed, the bunkhouse.

There was no light now. He was asleep, just as he had been asleep twelve years ago when she'd stood here, a young and dreamy teenager, staring down at the place where she knew Jess lay.

Then she had wanted to lie with him, to sleep with him, to love him and to wake up in his arms.

She wanted that still.

He wanted it, too. Tonight he'd said so in no uncertain terms.

The problem was, for him that would be the answer to everything; for her it would never be enough.

Chapter Eight

She was getting under his skin. It was harder every day to pretend that nothing had changed.

Oh, the thick dark greens of pine and spruce stayed the same. The aspens turned ivory and gray as they did every year. Barbed wire was barbed wire, any way you looked at it. The cattle still took up most of Jess's time.

But at night when he came in for supper, Alison was there.

Changes were being made. She interspersed the beef and potatoes that he was used to with chicken stir-fries and hearty French stews. When he came in at night the house was redolent with a variety of exotic and enticing smells.

The wide pine plank floors were waxed until they shone. She uncovered a pair of Navajo rugs in the attic, aired them and spread them on the living room floor.

Pictures appeared one by one, in the living room and up the stairs into the hall. Some were photos of her parents and grandparents, her brothers and herself. But one day he was startled to see the photo of himself and Nathan framed and hanging alongside her parents' anniversary photo.

Another day he came home to find she'd been digging through Nathan's clippings and had found several about Jess's rodeo career. Jess winced, watching her pore over them. The next day he hoped to find them in the trash. Instead they were framed and on the wall in his former bedroom. Alison took him by the hand and dragged him up to see.

"It's a memorial," Alison told him cheekily and dug her fingers into her ribs. "All I have of you until you come to your senses and move home."

"I am home," Jess told her gruffly.

She laughed and ruffled his hair.

He could still feel the touch of her fingers that night when he went to bed.

She hung art prints, as well. Alison's taste was more eclectic than Nathan's Kentucky Derby winners. It ran to R.C. Gorman prints and others of sailboats and tropical-looking stuff that Jess thought she said were done by someone called Homer Winslow.

Jess thought it was an improvement, but he didn't tell her.

He didn't comment at all. Not when the prints went up, not when the floors got shiny, not when new yellow gingham curtains and place mats appeared in the kitchen and the oilcloth disappeared.

But he noticed, and at night he lay in the bunkhouse and touched his hair, remembering her fingers there, touched his mouth and remembered her lips.

It was like being tortured.

All he could do was hope that when she finished the house, she'd get bored and restless, and decide she'd had enough.

She got a job.

"A job? Where?" he demanded. She'd sprung it on him in the middle of the meal. He had his mouth full, and he almost choked demanding an explanation.

"Not full-time," she said patiently. "Just three afternoons a week. I'm helping set up a library in town. We're taking book donations to start it. I'm donating a lot of Nathan's, a lot of the fiction, a little of the husbandry and some of the stud books and magazines, too. If you don't mind," she added quickly.

"Me? Why should I?" She could donate any damned thing she pleased, including her time, if she'd just leave.

"They're half yours," she reminded him. "We're partners."

He shut his eyes.

He didn't see how he was going to make it. He was so damnably aware of her. And day after day, week after week, the awareness didn't go away.

It grew.

He sat in the kitchen eating supper as quickly as he could, knowing he needed to get out of there, if he was going to keep from touching her, kissing her. It didn't keep her from touching him.

Nothing blatant. Nothing he could take and hold up and say, "You're coming on to me!" making it an accusation. And maybe, he conceded, she wasn't. Not intentionally.

But it was happening nonetheless.

The casual touch on his arm when she wanted to show him something. The way they seemed to always end up passing each other in narrow doorways, so that her hair brushed his shoulder or her breasts brushed his chest. It was enough to drive a man to drink.

So was the way she could provoke him with a mere comment. She said the damnedest things.

Tonight, for instance. It was Wednesday. Alison had gone into town to spend the afternoon helping with the fledgling library and then picking up some new curtain rods. Jess had agreed to mount them after supper.

He was standing on the counter, with his back to her, screwing the rod into the wall, grateful that there could be no accidental physical encounters here, when she said, "We got an unusual donation for the library today."

"Mmm." He didn't turn around.

"All about men's buns."

The screwdriver slipped and gouged into the wood.

"It was quite interesting," Alison went on conversationally. "There was the usual, the swimsuit sort of thing, and underwear, of course. Slacks don't do much for a man, you know. But jeans—" there was a pleasurable sigh coming from the other side of the room, moving closer "—some of them were pretty impressive."

"Al-i-son," through gritted teeth.

"Not as good as yours, though."

He heard the teasing lilt in her voice. He tried not to react. It was like trying not to breathe. His whole body tightened—notably, among others, the part he was sure she was studying. He fitted the screwdriver back into the screw and gave it a savage turn.

"You're especially nice in chaps," she went on. She was so close he would swear he could feel the heat of her breath against the back of his leg.

"We're thinking of having a money-raising benefit to get the library off the ground. Cathy Parsons suggested we take our own set of local photos like the ones in the book, then auction them off. What do you think? Want to be my model?"

He glared down at her. She was standing right below him, her hands on the counter, looking up and grinning her head off.

He stepped on her hand.

"Jess!" she howled. She tried to yank her hand away, catching his pants hem, twisting and pulling.

"Damn!" He turned, slipped, then skidded, and landed hard on the floor facing her, breathing hard. Their noses were scant inches apart. He clamped his jaw shut. His fists clenched.

"I suppose you're going to say no," Alison said after a moment.

It was the last straw.

He grabbed her forearms and held her so they were almost nose to nose. They didn't touch.

"What do you want from me, Alison?" he demanded. "Just what the hell do you want?"

He hoped his fury would scare her. He hoped she would back off, say, "Nothing," shrink away.

She didn't move, didn't even seem to be breathing hard, though her pupils were dilated and her eyes had never seemed so blue. She was so close he could even smell the lemony scent of her shampoo. She just looked at him, her gaze steady. That was bad enough.

It was worse when she smiled. It was a sweet smile, a wistful smile, a gentle smile that he was sure would undo the best intentions of any man who didn't run from it.

"You don't have to ask, Jess," she said in a voice as gentle as her smile. "You know."

SHE'D JUMPED the gun.

She'd pushed too hard and sent him running in a panic. Jess had bolted the house after their encounter last night, and had taken off in the truck, spraying gravel every which way. And, though she'd stayed awake until two, she never heard him come back.

She'd spent the evening cursing her tendency to overplay her hand.

"Slow and easy," Pops used to say. "Slow and easy."

She should have known better. She must've been behind the door when patience was passed out.

But, damn it, she'd had enough.

For days she'd felt him watching her every move, and not with antipathy, but with awareness. She'd seen brief flickerings of desire in his eyes when they'd passed too closely in the hall, had heard the quickening of his breath the evening she'd shown him the clippings she'd framed and hung in the bedroom.

She knew he wanted her. She knew he liked her. She suspected sometimes that what he felt even went beyond liking.

But he never gave in.

He hedged, he stonewalled, he ran.

She was at the end of her rope.

He didn't come in for breakfast. She went out to the barn and found him saddling Dodger. He looked hollow-eyed and miserable, with bloodshot eyes and unshaven cheeks.

"I suppose you're not hungry," she said.

He glanced at her. "I'd barf."

"Found too much solace in the bottle, did you?"

He looked at her, his expression haunted. "Too much bottle and not enough solace." His voice was rough. He finished saddling Dodger and brushed past her, leading the horse out of the barn.

She followed him. "We're two human beings, Jess. We have needs, feelings."

His mouth twisted. "You do. Not me."

"No feelings? No needs?"

He swung into the saddle and sat looking down at her. His jaw was tight. "None I can't handle if you let me be."

"Oh, Jess."

"Oh, Jess," he mocked. "Don't push me, Ali. We're partners. No more, no less."

DINNER WAS an awkward meal. Jess was quiet. Alison was hurt. She didn't believe his protestations, was certain he felt more than he said; but his words were painful nonetheless.

And though she knew she would challenge him in time, she didn't feel tough enough to tackle him over them yet. They ate in silence, Jess hurrying, though whether it was to get into town to get the welding done, as he said, or whether it was simply to get away from her, Alison didn't know.

He was putting on his jacket when she said, "I hesitate to ask you, but there are a few things I forgot yesterday at the grocery store."

"Of course I'll get them."

"I wasn't sure you'd want to be bothered."

Jess's jaw tightened. "Don't be stupid, Ali. We're—"

"Partners," Alison finished for him dryly. "Yes, I know." Their eyes met and held.

There was no telling how long they might have simply stayed looking at each other, no telling where the discussion might have gone from there, for at that moment they heard a car coming up the road.

Jess looked at her quizzically. Alison shrugged. He pushed back his chair, going to the door to see who it was.

"A friend coming for tea?" he said archly. "Or perhaps more 'interesting' donations for the library."

Alison, dishing up blueberry cobbler, joined him at the door. "No one I know."

"A tourist, then," Jess said, opening the door. "Little late in the year for fall color now." It was the first week in November, and they'd already had several light dustings of snow.

The car door opened and a woman got out.

Alison thought she was about her own age, with an ash-blonde pageboy haircut, a neat business suit and high heels. Not common attire among visitors to the Rocking R.

Jess went out on the step to meet her. "You lost? Can I help you?"

"Mr. Cooper? Jess Cooper?"

He looked surprised. "Yes, ma'am."

She smiled. "Then I'm not lost. I'm Felicia Darrow from the Department of Social Services. You're Elizabeth Cooper's brother?"

Jess nodded warily. "Lizzie? Yeah. What's she done?"

The woman gave him a sad, sympathetic smile. "She hasn't done anything, Mr. Cooper. But I'm afraid I have to tell you—" she hesitated, then plunged in baldly "—she's dead."

The color drained from Jess's face. He took a step back, and Alison found herself holding on to his arm.

"Dead?" The word came out as a croak. "What happened? When?"

"In March."

"Where? How? She wasn't sick?"

"No. She was in Nashville. It was an accident. She must have been preoccupied or something. She was crossing a street against a light..."

She didn't have to say anything more.

Jess didn't speak, simply stood there as if he'd been turned to stone. Yet Alison could feel the rapidly beating pulse in his arm, felt him tense, then quiver as a shudder passed through him.

"What the hell'd she think she was doing?" Jess muttered. "Was she drinking?"

"Not a drop. I gather she was simply euphoric and not paying attention. I understand she'd just been offered a recording contract."

Jess stared. Then, "Jesus Christ," he murmured. It was more prayer than blasphemy, and Alison felt him almost sag against her.

"Lizzie," he muttered. "Damn it, Lizzie..." He turned hard eyes on the social worker. "That was months ago," he protested after a moment. "How come nobody told me before now?"

"We didn't actually find out your whereabouts until last Friday. We'd been looking for several months. One of our regular case workers was doing a follow-up and managed to contact a Mrs. Blodgett, Ms. Cooper's former landlady. She said you'd dropped by looking for Lizzie. She remembered where you were living. And—" Felicia Darrow shrugged and smiled "—here I am."

"Yeah." Jess shook his head, clearly still having trouble comprehending. "Well, thanks. I'm obliged, your comin' all this way just to tell me about her."

"You're welcome." Felicia Darrow smiled again. "But that isn't precisely why I came. It was because of the children, really."

"The children? Oh. Yeah." He straightened up, running a hand through his hair. "Lizzie's kids. Who's takin' care of Lizzie's kids?"

"It seems," said Felicia Darrow, "that you are."

THERE WAS NOTHING, Jess found, like inheriting three children to take one's mind off one's loins. Suddenly his preoccupation with Alison seemed the least of his problems.

He walked around in a daze the rest of the day, not going to town, not doing the shopping or getting the welding done, just thinking—or trying to.

But he couldn't make sense of it. Felicia Darrow was like a bad dream who had got back in her car and driven away. By nightfall he had himself almost convinced that he'd hallucinated the whole thing.

He was even seeking out Alison in the hope that she would confirm it. He'd left the house once, right after supper. But sitting down in the bunkhouse by himself, mending tack, had been torture. All he could see in his mind's eye were miniature versions of Lizzie, staring up hopefully at him. All he could imagine is how ill equipped he was to fulfill that hope.

Facing Alison, enduring the temptation of being around her, seemed, for once, preferable.

"She isn't seriously going to show up here tomorrow with the girls, is she?" he asked, coming back into the kitchen.

Alison was sitting at the computer. She'd been typing when he came in, but she stopped now and looked up. "Miss Darrow?" She gave Jess a sympathetic smile. "I think she is."

He raked a hand through his hair. "I can't believe it. What in the hell am I going to do with three girls?"

"Raise them?"

"Me?" He'd said the same thing to Felicia Darrow. "You've got to be kidding," he'd said to her.

But she hadn't been. And when he'd continued to protest, she'd shown him a copy of Lizzie's will. It had been right there in black and white, staring him in the face. Three pages of legalese. But what it boiled down to, in Jess's eyes, was one line: "I leave the custody, care and supervision of my minor children, Patricia, Dorothy and Susan, to my brother, Jess Cooper."

"It doesn't make sense." He'd said it to Felicia Darrow then. He said it again to Alison now.

"She must have thought you were the best person," Alison said.

Jess snorted. "The only one, more likely."

"What about their fathers?" Alison rested her fingers on the keyboard. "She could have named them, couldn't she? But she didn't."

"Those jerks?" Jess felt angry at the very thought. "They never even hung around to see their kids, not one of them! I could do a better job than they could!"

Alison gave him a gentle smile. "Lizzie must've thought so, too."

Jess just stared at her. She was looking at him with such confidence, such faith.

"God!" He dragged his palms across his face. "This is insane. I don't know anything about girls!" He shoved himself up on the counter and banged his heels against the cabinet below.

Alison smiled. "That's not the impression you like to give."

He looked at her sharply, then groaned. "Oh, hell, and I suppose I have to worry about men like me now, too!"

"I suppose you will."

"I think I'm going to throw up."

"A tough guy like you?" she chided gently. "Come on, Jess."

"Three girls? I can't!"

"Sure you can." She hesitated. "I'll help you."

He looked at her suspiciously. "Why?"

"We're partners?" She said the words softly, almost warily. There was a faintly teasing lilt to her voice as if she were throwing his words back in his face, but she seemed serious, too.

He hunched forward, resting his elbows on his forearms, linking his fingers. "Hell."

She got up and he heard her moving toward him. "What do you want to do?"

He gave a short half laugh. "Take off and never look back?"

"Realistically."

"Cripes, I don't know." He shook his head. "All I know right now is that there are only three people in the world I feel more sorry for than for myself—Patsy and Dottie and Sue. I can't imagine getting raised by me."

"You don't think you can do it?"

For just a moment Jess stiffened at the challenge in her tone, then he sagged again.

"I don't know," he said, his voice low. "I just don't know."

"You can do it, Jess," she told him. "Together we can."

Together?

Like a couple, did she mean? Married? Is that what she was getting at?

He tensed. "I'm not getting married!"

Alison stepped back as if she'd been slapped. "Don't be an ass, Jess. Did I ask?"

He rubbed a hand against the back of his neck. "No, of course not. I'm sorry. It's just... I don't know. I'm not thinking straight."

"No, you're not." Alison's tone was clipped, and he knew he'd really offended her.

"I'm...sorry," he said again. He bowed his head. She was standing scant inches from him. And though, minutes ago, he'd been anxious for her presence, now he wished she'd step back, move away, give him some space. It was too tempting, having her standing there.

He wanted to reach out to her, hold her, have her arms around him, holding him.

He wanted to hang on. Tight.

He didn't dare.

"They're not your problem," he said gruffly at last.

"They're girls, not problems, Jess." Her voice had lost some of its edginess. She sounded gentler. "You've got to believe that, if it's going to work."

"Fine for you to say. You can take the next bus out of here."

She reached out and grabbed his hands, holding them tight, her action and her touch so astonishing him that he looked straight at her. "For the last time, Jess Cooper," she said with steel in her voice, "I am not leaving."

A corner of his mouth twisted. "You must be a glutton for punishment, then."

She shrugged. "Maybe. But I've made up my mind. I have no intention of leaving. Especially now. From what I gather, your nieces have had a pretty rough year. They're going to need some stability and security. I can help you try to give them that."

"Yeah? And when you get fed up? When you decide it's time to—"

"Don't say it, Jess."

He sighed, said a rude word, chewed his lip. "Okay." He lifted his eyes and met hers. "But how?"

"By getting involved with them, by caring about them and showing them that you do. That *we* do. By making them feel like they belong."

"And that's gonna be enough?"

"It's a start."

Jess bent his head, looked at her hands holding his, thought about his past, about the way he'd envisioned his future. He thought about Alison, all that was sweet and warm and womanly, thought about those three little girls he didn't even know. He thought of a million potential disasters that lay ahead. He understood better than he ever had the old adage about being damned if he did and damned if he didn't.

"What if we blow it?" he said. "What if *I* blow it?"

"I thought cowboys believed in 'try,' Jess. Is it better not to try?"

"This isn't bronc ridin', for cripe's sake!"

Alison shook her head. "No." Her hands were still clasping his, her thumbs rubbing gently along his wrist bones. Her touch was undermining him, lessening very reasonable fears.

"I've never—"

"They need you, Jess."

He shut his eyes. His fingers tightened around hers. But what about what *he* needed? Had anyone ever thought about that?

He lifted his gaze and met Alison's. Her eyes were warm and blue and very bright.

He sighed. "Maybe you're right."

SHORTLY BEFORE NOON he saw Felicia Darrow's car barreling up the road. Jess held his breath for a split second, hoping against hope that she'd be alone.

She wasn't. She pulled up next to the gate, shut off the engine and got out.

Slowly the other car doors opened, too.

Lizzie's daughters got out, looked around, saw him, hesitated. Then the tallest took the hand of the youngest and the three came toward him.

He remembered the littlest one, though she was taller now. The other two had been only faces in photographs the last time he'd seen them and scarcely more than toddlers the time before that. The oldest, he was startled to note, was almost a woman.

Felicia Darrow came with them.

"This," she said briskly as they reached him, "is your uncle Jess. Mr. Cooper, these are your nieces. Pasty," she nodded to the eldest, who looked at him in unsmiling assessment, "Dottie—" the middle one seemed to be eyeing him with frank curiosity and perhaps a bit of hope "—and Sue."

They all stared at him.

Jess stared back, hoping desperately to find some rush of family feeling, something that would make these girls less than total strangers to him. He felt, except for a surging sense of panic, curiously blank. His fingers clenched and unclenched, wrapped suddenly in other fingers, warm and supportive. Alison's. He hung on.

"Sue," he said, looking at the littlest one. He found his voice a bit rusty, "Remember me?"

Dark hair swung back and forth emphatically. "Nope."

"I'm sure you'll make lots of new memories," Felicia Darrow said optimistically, turning toward the car. "Go get your things out of the car, girls. They don't have a lot," Felicia Darrow confided to Jess and Alison. "They've moved around so much, poor dears. It's been so hard on them."

"I'll help you," he heard Alison say, and he felt her fingers give his own a brief squeeze before letting him go. She followed the girls toward the car.

Felicia Darrow laid her hand on his arm. Probably, he thought, because she must have sensed he was ready to bolt. "I know you haven't had much time to prepare, Mr. Cooper, but—" she smiled earnestly "—believe me, it wouldn't be easy if you had a month."

He rubbed a hand against the back of his neck. "I guess," he muttered.

"They're lovely girls. I've enjoyed knowing them. I know you will, too. You'll do just fine." She fished in her handbag and handed him a card. "If you have problems or questions, feel free to contact me. I'll do whatever I can to help."

Jess stood there, watching helplessly as she moved to say goodbye to the girls, giving them each a handshake and a brief hug. He saw her tell them something that made them look over at him. Then she shook Alison's hand, smiling, and Alison nodded and smiled in return.

When she reached the car, Felicia Darrow turned and gave him a wave. "Bye, Mr. Cooper. Bye, girls. Good luck."

Jess and his nieces looked at each other and knew they were going to need it.

PERHAPS SHE'D BEEN overconfident. Believing that strong, tough, capable Jess could do anything had been a way of life for Alison.

She'd never seen him like this.

Even battered and bloody, after the Brinkmillers had pounded him into the ground, he hadn't had the stunned, desperate expression on his face that Alison saw now.

She shepherded the girls right past him into the kitchen, saying, "You must be hungry. I'll bet you'd like some dinner."

She opened the cupboard, handing down plates. "Here, Dottie, you take these over to the stove. Patsy, you can dish things up. Sue, wash your hands after petting the dog."

The girls, all apparently willing to do something if it meant feeling less awkward, moved to do what she said.

Alison wiped her sweating palms on her jeans, saying, "Help yourself to the milk and start eating. I'll be right back."

Jess hadn't moved an inch. He still stood in the dirt by the fence, looking dazed. When she came up to him, he turned slowly to look at her, but his gaze was unfocused. He looked numb.

"Jess?"

"I can't!"

"Damn it, Jess. Grow up! These girls are depending on you. They need you!"

He shook his head. He was looking at her as if he wasn't even seeing her, as if he were somewhere else altogether.

"Come on, Jess!"

And when he still didn't move, she did the only thing she could think of. She grabbed him, pulled his head down and kissed him. Hard.

If the kiss Jess had given her that night after their dinner at the Hitching Post had awakened her, this one, she hoped, would wake him.

It wasn't a gentle kiss. It didn't seek, nor did it ask. It demanded. Her tongue thrust into his mouth, teasing his, her teeth nipped his lips, her hips pressed into his, and she didn't let up until she felt him respond.

When she stepped back, he was glowering at her, breathing hard. Alison glowered back at him.

"You're playing a dangerous game, Ali," he growled.

She lifted her chin. "This isn't a game, Jess. This is our life. And it's their life now, too. It's time for dinner. Come on."

She turned on her heel and walked back to the house, not waiting, pretending not to see the three faces in the window peering from behind the curtain, pretending not to care if Jess followed or not.

When she got back in the house she found that the girls had arranged themselves around the table where they were eating, whispering quietly among themselves.

She got her own plate and joined them, smiling, crossing her fingers of the hand that lay in her lap. At last she heard the sound of a boot heel on the steps.

When the door opened and Jess entered, the eating stopped.

The girls all looked up, watching, waiting, their eyes on Jess.

Alison tried to look unconcerned as she smiled at him. She got to her feet and moved toward the stove where she dished up his food.

He hesitated in the doorway, then sat down. She put his plate on the table in front of him. He picked up his fork, but he didn't eat.

Slowly he lifted his gaze and looked from one girl to another. "I'm sorry about your mother." His voice was low and ragged, as agonized as Alison had ever heard. She hated herself for having forced him, even though she knew she could have done nothing else.

Patsy met his gaze, then nodded solemnly. "Thanks."

Jess swallowed, then went on, "I don't have a clue about raising kids, which I suppose I probably shouldn't admit." He shrugged. "I reckon you'll find it out soon enough," he added with a ghost of a grin. "So we'll just have to do the best we can. You guys, er, girls, and me."

Sue nodded her head, hair flopping in her eyes which went from him to the woman at the other end of the table. "And Alison," she said with a little smile.

Jess's gaze lifted and met Alison's for a long moment. She still ached from their kiss. She wondered if he did. His expression gave nothing away.

"Yeah," he said quietly. "And Alison."

HE WAS A COWARD and he knew it.

Bu he couldn't hang around. He got through dinner because there was food to eat, an excuse not to talk, something to do with his hands. The moment the meal was over, he was on his feet and moving.

"I'm off for town," he said quickly, heading toward the door. "I got that welding to see to and all."

"Today?" Alison was staring at him as if he'd grown another head.

He jammed his hat on his head. "Damn right, today. There's work to be done."

The look she gave him told him he wasn't fooling her. It made him mad. "You need that shopping done, too," he reminded her.

"We won't starve if you wait a day."

"No, but the cattle will if I don't get the welding done, and we have to wire that piece again." So it wasn't precisely the truth. It was close.

"D-d'you feed a lot of cattle?" Dottie asked. It was the first question either of the older girls had ventured. Jess looked at her, startled.

"About three hundred."

Her eyes widened. She reminded him of Lizzie when she looked like that.

"Maybe Dottie would like to come along," Alison said.

Jess glared at her. He looked with dismay at the girl still sitting at the table.

"If she likes cattle. Do you, Dottie?" Alison gave the girl an encouraging smile and got Dottie a tentative one in return.

"Yeah," the girl said quietly. "But I don't know much about 'em."

"You'll learn," Alison said. Her gaze shifted and she looked at Jess expectantly.

He scowled at her, hating her for trying to back him into a corner. He hadn't asked for this, damn it. He took off his hat and rubbed his hand against the back of his neck. "I reckon it'd be kind of boring for a kid."

Alison gave him an arch, disapproving look.

Jess didn't care. He backed toward the door. "I'll be home before supper." And he let the door bang shut behind him.

He didn't turn around to see if anyone was watching as he headed for the truck. He whistled for Scout, started the engine and took off as fast as he could.

The truck jounced from one rut to another as he took the road far too rapidly. He'd have yelled at Alison if she'd driven it that fast. But he couldn't help it.

He needed some of that distance and perspective Nathan had always been talking about.

How in God's name was he going to raise three girls? Girls who reminded him of a past he wanted to forget and a future he never wanted in the first place!

He thought about Felicia Darrow and her blithe, "I know you'll do just fine. Give me a call if you have any questions or problems," and his foot stomped down on the accelerator even harder.

Hell, yes, he had questions! A heap of them. And didn't she think being saddled with his sister's three kids was a problem?

And talking of problems, what about Alison?

Damn Alison, anyway!

What a time to kiss him!

It was like kicking a guy when he was down. He didn't have any defenses left!

The truck bottomed into a pothole with a resounding crack.

Jess winced. All the more so, seconds later when, back on the road again, he could hear the tinny clanking of his muffler dragging against the gravel.

By the time he'd reached Bluff Springs, five miles away, he still didn't have perspective and he doubted if he ever would!

"I DON'T THINK Uncle Jess likes us much," Sue said as she sat at the table and watched Alison and Patsy do the washing up after supper.

"The hell with him, then," Patsy said, thumping the glass she was drying onto the counter with such force that Alison cringed. "We didn't ask to come here."

"It isn't that he doesn't like you," Alison began carefully, feeling as if she were stepping into an emotional minefield. "I'm sure he does. It's just been a shock for him. Hearing about your mother, getting used to the notion that he has new responsibilities."

"That he doesn't want," said Dottie flatly. She tipped back in her chair, making it balance on two legs.

"I wouldn't say that," Alison protested, not because it wasn't true, but because she hoped he'd change his mind.

He hadn't come back from town until almost supper time. Before Alison could even raise an eyebrow at the length of time his supposedly short trip had taken, he thumped seven bags of groceries on the kitchen table, muttered something about damned potholes and new mufflers, and took himself off to put some newly welded widget back on his tractor.

"That's a lot of groceries," Alison had said to his rapidly retreating back. A lot more than had been on her list.

"Reckon they'll get eaten," he replied over his shoulder.

"Supper's almost ready. Don't you want to eat?"

"Nope. Got work t'do."

They hadn't seen him since.

Alison and the girls had soup and sandwiches for supper. For dessert Alison had made them sundaes with the ice cream and chocolate syrup that hadn't been on her list.

It was the ice cream and syrup that gave her hope.

She knew enough about Jess now to know that he did care about his nieces, that he wanted to welcome them, even to love them, but that he didn't have any idea how to go about it.

She remembered what he'd said about his background and guessed that he didn't have a lot of experience along those lines.

She did. And there was nothing more she would like than to show Jess how it was done, to share in the doing of it with him.

Sue seemed to accept Alison's explanation about Jess's reticence with equanimity, wanting to believe. She knew that Patsy and Dottie were frankly doubtful.

"How's he gonna get used to us, if he isn't around us?" Patsy asked.

Alison smiled. "Give him a little time."

It wasn't until after the girls had gone to bed that Alison expected him to reappear. He hadn't had any supper, after all.

She waited for over an hour, sitting at the kitchen table, using her grandmother's old treadle sewing machine as she put pleats in the new living room curtains.

Every few minutes she got up and peered outside, hoping to see him coming, checking at least to make sure that the light in the barn was still on.

Just past eleven the barn was dark when she looked. And even as she watched, the window in the bunkhouse lit up.

"Ah, Jess," she murmured.

She put her sewing away, made two meat loaf sandwiches, filled one thermos with hot soup and another with cold milk, then dished up a bowl of ice cream and drizzled chocolate syrup on top.

Nudging open the door with her knee and closing it with her elbow, she carried the tray of food across the porch, down the steps and across the yard.

She kicked the door of the bunkhouse. "Jess?"

The door jerked open. "What's wrong?"

"I brought you some supper." She didn't give him a chance to object, stepping past him into the room, setting the tray down on the bare wooden table, then busying herself laying out the silverware and straightening the napkin.

He was bare-chested and barefoot, and the top button on his jeans was undone. She stared at it, then dragged her gaze away to meet his eyes.

He looked away. For a moment she thought he was going to ask her to leave. Finally he closed the door. "You didn't need to bother," he said gruffly.

"I needed the excuse."

"Why? Because I took off and left you with my problems?"

"Not exactly."

He snagged his shirt off the hook by the door and pulled it on, but he didn't button it. He looked at her warily. "What, then?"

She swallowed. Their gazes locked. And Alison knew she was looking at him with her heart in her eyes.

He groaned, then reached for her, pulling her into his arms. And she came willingly, needing his touch, starved for it. And he seemed equally starved. His hands were all over her, gliding down her back, pressing her against him, moulding the line of her hips, her bottom. Her hands slid up beneath the tails of his shirt, rubbing against the rough hair of his chest, learning the shape of his muscles, the firm strength of his shoulders.

"This is crazy," he muttered against her mouth, even as he kissed her again. Harder. Longer.

"No," Alison insisted. "It isn't."

"It is. Nothing's changed." His face was in her hair, his thumbs caressed the line of her jaw. He was trembling.

Alison shook her head. "It has." She sought his mouth, traced his lips with her tongue, felt a tremor run through him, then another, felt his hips surge against hers.

"I love you, Jess," she whispered.

He stopped cold.

She could feel his heart pounding a hundred times a minute. His chest was heaving. His muscles clenched and unclenched spasmodically as he pulled back and fought for control. He shook his head, the look he gave her dazed yet fierce.

"No!"

She touched his cheek. He winced and pulled away, crossing the room, bracing his hands against the window frame, staring out into the blackness. Alison could see through his shirt the quick rise and fall of his back.

She came to stand behind him, touched him lightly, traced a line down the length of his spine. "I do, Jess. It's true."

He shook his head. "Don't."

"I can't help it." She slipped her arms around him from behind, clasping them together just below the waistband of his jeans, touching him there. "I love you." Her lips touched the nape of his neck. She flicked out her tongue. He trembled violently and pressed himself against her hands.

Then his own hands dropped and caught hers, holding them tight against him, not moving them. She could feel the heat of his desire, could feel the urgency of his need and the quick, shallow gasps of his breathing.

"No," he said through clenched teeth. "Don't. Please, don't, Alison. I . . . don't . . . love . . . you."

Chapter Nine

He shut her out. He shut them all out.

But it wasn't because he didn't like them, Alison realized. Jess was afraid.

At first she didn't believe it. It was hard to think of a man like Jess being afraid of anyone—especially a woman who loved him and a trio of little girls. But as the days went by, there was nothing else she could think.

For the most part she deliberately kept her distance from him, talking to him as little as possible, generally leaving rooms when he came in. She couldn't pretend that his words hadn't hurt.

She didn't want him hurting the girls, though, the way he'd hurt her. So at times she overcame her own better judgment and stayed to speak to him. Then she took him to task.

"They think you don't like them," she challenged him after the girls had been there nearly a week and he'd barely said more than a dozen words to each of them. She followed him to the sink after dinner, making her point.

"Of course I like them," he snapped, ignoring her while he washed his hands.

"Then prove it."

He glared at her. "How?"

"Talk to them. Show an interest."

"You're doing that."

"*I'm* not their uncle! Ask them what they're working on, what they're interested in. You could ask Sue about the kindergarten field trip to the fire station. You could give Patsy a hand with her algebra. Heaven knows, I'm no good at it. And, as for Dottie, you could show her the tractor or take her to feed the cattle."

"The tractor?" He stared at her as if she'd lost her mind.

"She loves anything to do with the ranch. Especially what makes it work. Like tractors. And horses. And you."

Dottie watched Jess far more than her sisters did. Alison recognized in her a kindred spirit, not only in her absorption with Jess, but also in her determination to be a part of the life of the ranch.

Dottie was always up first thing in the morning, coming downstairs to feed Kitten and Scout even before Alison did. She wanted to feed the horses, Alison knew, but given no encouragement by Jess, she hadn't dared.

"Let her feed the horses and hang around a bit."

Jess glanced at his watch and headed for the door. "I'll try."

Alison watched him go and hoped he remembered, hoped, for Dottie's sake at least, that he dared.

He did better than she could have hoped.

"I thought I'd sort through Pops's *Western Horseman* magazines this afternoon," Alison said when Dottie banged in from school. "Want to help?"

"Can't," Dottie gasped, eyes shining. "Uncle Jess gave me a ride up from the bus on his horse, an' he asked me to help him put the salt licks in the pasture!"

The expedition to set out the salt licks was a success, better even than Alison had hoped. Dottie was beaming when she came back, and after supper it emboldened her enough to ask if she could help feed the horses that night.

Jess was already headed for the door. His eyes flicked for an instant to connect with Alison's, read the challenge in them, then came back to his niece.

He nodded. "Don't see why not."

Dottie was on her feet like a shot.

Alison knew it wouldn't be quite as easy with the other girls.

Patsy was the least willing to accept his interest or his help. As the oldest, she was the one who had always been responsible for maintaining the girls' sense of identity as a family, keeping them together. She wasn't ready to relinquish her role until she trusted that someone else was going to do it as well or better.

Jess's taciturnity meant to Patsy that he didn't care. When he finally did show some interest, his questions, awkward and hesitant as they were, got only monosyllabic answers.

"I can't force her to like me," he told Alison late one night when the girls had gone to bed and he'd come back to the house to get a roll of tape.

"She already does like you. She's just defensive."

Like you, Alison wanted to add. She didn't. He was doing the best he could. He and Dottie fed the horses together every evening. He even came in some nights and played checkers with her.

Alison got the tape out of the cupboard and set it on the table. She expected him to pick it up and leave.

He didn't. He picked it up, spun it on his finger, shifted from one foot to the other, then asked if she'd heard an evening weather report.

"Snow," she said. "And more snow." She went back to the file she was putting onto the computer.

Jess moved toward the door, then stopped. "What're you working on?"

Alison looked up at him, startled. It was the first time he'd expressed even the slightest interest in what she put on the computer. "The cattle. I'm putting Pops's records in."

"Yeah?" He really did seem interested.

She hesitated. She hadn't encouraged him in the least since that night at the bunkhouse. There was just so much rejection a woman could take.

She looked at him closely, saw something in his expression that made her wonder. "I'll show you what I've got, if you like," she offered after a moment.

She saw his Adam's apple work. His tongue slid over his lips. His eyes met hers, then flicked instantly away.

"Not tonight," he said, turning and hastily opening the door. "See you."

"Jess!"

He looked back.

"Don't forget the tape."

SHE WAS ANGRY with him. Probably she had a right to be. But damn it, Jess thought, wouldn't she be angrier if they made love and that was all there was to it?

Women wanted protestations of love. They wanted rings and weddings and happily ever afters. He couldn't promise anything like that.

So it was better to resist.

But now she was angry.

He could tell from the way she was avoiding him. She barely spoke to him directly—except to chew him out about the girls. She never smiled at him anymore. She acted as if she wished he was dead.

He hated it.

He wanted her smiles. He liked her laughter. He missed their conversations, their arguments, the little daily things they shared.

But he was afraid of them, too. He wanted them back. He wanted *her* back. But she said she loved him.

Jess didn't think he could handle love. But if they got back on their earlier footing, would he still be able to resist?

AFTER THE NIGHT with the tape, Alison started once more to hope.

"I'm an incurable optimist," she told her reflection in the mirror that night as she went to bed. "Or a damned fool."

She wasn't sure which.

Not until the night Jess finally connected with Sue.

If Patsy was difficult to reach, Sue presented a different set of problems. Jess had little in common with a kindergartner. Sue's interests centered on whatever current holiday or field trip her class was preparing for and the ongoing saga of her well-traveled dolls.

Sue loved her dolls. They were the part of her universe that she could control. Sue gave them adventures that would have made Indiana Jones cringe. They always had plenty of cliffs to climb, rivers to ford and problems to solve.

They also had happy endings, the sorts of endings, Alison began to realize, that Sue wanted in her own life and was determined to provide.

Within days of her arrival, the dolls had moved to a ranch, worked transcribing files onto a pretend computer, loved to read books and spent a lot of time feeding cattle.

They also argued some and kissed a lot.

"They're gonna get married," Sue told Alison, "an' have a family. Isn't that a good idea?"

Alison agreed that yes, it was.

In fact, as the days went by, Alison found herself becoming more engrossed in the lives of Sue's dolls than she ever had in any soap opera. Sometimes she wished she had a set of her own.

One night during the week before Thanksgiving, Jess came in to play checkers with Dottie. Patsy was making clothes for the dolls out of remnants Alison provided, and Alison was hemming a skirt. The two of them were sitting side by side on the couch while Jess and Dottie sat at the table and Sue spread her dolls out on the floor below.

The checkers game went quickly, Dottie taking them all.

"You were letting me win," she accused Jess.

"I was not!"

"Humph," Dottie snorted. "You beat me last night."

"Last night Alison and I had gone shopping," Patsy put in without looking up.

Alison caught a glimpse of Jess just then. He got quickly to his feet, raking his fingers through his hair. "I gotta get going."

"How come you never play with me?" Sue asked.

He hesitated. "I could play you at checkers tonight," he offered wryly.

"I can't play checkers. You want to play Alison and Jess?"

Alison froze.

"Play *what?*" Jess asked, frowning down at her.

"Alison and Jess. My dolls. That's what their names are," Sue said. "They got a ranch, too, so you'd know how. You can be Jess if you want to."

Jess's gaze jerked up to meet Alison's. A tide of red flooded his face.

Alison's own cheeks were hot, but this wasn't her fault. She looked back at him expressionlessly.

"Here." Sue handed Jess a dark-haired boy doll. She tugged on the hem of his jeans. "Come on. Sit down."

"Don't do it," Dottie warned. "She'll make you kiss her."

Jess's eyes widened. "What? Kiss who?"

"The dolls. Course they kiss," Sue said firmly. "They're gettin' married. Come on." She jerked his pants leg once more. "I'll show you."

Jess hesitated. He looked from the disapproving Dottie to Alison. There was speculation in his gaze.

She hoped her embarrassment wasn't showing. She wished he'd say no, and knew that for Sue's sake she should be wishing the opposite.

Jess sat, folded himself cross-legged on the floor, holding the doll gingerly as if it might explode in his hands.

"Now what?" he asked his niece.

"First you gotta put him on his horse. Mama bought me this horse for my birthday last year." She handed Jess a glossy plastic white stallion. "Isn't he be-yewt-i-ful? His name used to be Whitey. But now it's Dodger," she said proudly.

Jess cleared his throat. "Like . . . my horse?"

"Course," Sue said.

She waited patiently while he fitted the doll onto the horse and ventured a quick, desperate glance at Alison, who did her best not to giggle. He looked at Sue for further instructions.

"Now you gotta feed the cattle."

"Oh. Right." Jess looked around for the cattle, confused.

She pointed toward the area at the base of the sofa right by Alison and Patsy's feet. "Over there. You gotta pretend some things, Uncle Jess. The toy people don't make cows, you know."

Jess edged himself over, carrying the horse as he went.

Sue, watching, sighed. "Not like that. Jess rides better than that," Sue told him. "Do it right, so's he's real."

Jess did his best to gallop the horse until he was sitting practically on Alison's toes. He shot her a quick sideways glance. She swallowed. His eyes narrowed. He picked up her sock clad foot.

"Jess!"

He ignored her. "Is this the food?" he asked Sue, a grin quirking one corner of his mouth. His thumb tickled the ball of Alison's foot.

Alison wiggled her toes, trying to pull away and tuck her feet under her. "Jess," she protested again.

Sue giggled. "Yes, that's it."

"How do I feed it to the cattle?" Jess asked. "Shall I saw it off?" His finger drew a line across the base of Alison's toes, sending a shiver up her spine.

"No, silly, you just grab it and pull," Sue advised.

In a second Alison's sock was off and Jess's warm callused fingers closed around her bare foot. "Like this?"

Sue nodded, her eyes like saucers.

"Now the other one," Jess said and, before she could move, Alison found her other foot had been captured and that sock stripped off as well. Jess's fingers played with her foot making the horse nudge her toes.

"He's nibblin' you," Sue exclaimed, delighted. She bestowed an approving smile on her uncle. "Dodger likes the cattle's food, doesn't he?"

"You bet," Jess agreed, his hands still holding Alison's feet. "It's great stuff." He shot Alison a wicked glance. "Maybe I should try it, too."

Alison felt herself blushing even more hotly. "I don't *think* so," she said, still trying to tug her feet away.

Sue danced the girl doll up alongside the one Jess was holding. "Here's Alison to help you," she said.

Both dolls then started tickling Alison's feet. She gave a tiny shriek and managed at last to pull away.

"I think the cattle have all been fed," she said, tucking her feet up under her.

"Too bad," Jess said solemnly. "Now what do we do?" he asked Sue.

"Well," the little girl thought about it a moment, started to speak, hesitated, then went ahead. "You should kiss her."

Jess froze.

Alison did, too. There was such a thing as pushing too far, too fast.

"Sue, I don't think—" she began.

"Listen. Sue, I—" Jess said at the same time.

Sue gave a mighty sigh. "The dolls, I mean. I tol' you that. Alison helped him, and he wants to thank her. So he kisses her. See?"

She gave the real Alison an impatient glare, then turned her gaze onto her uncle. The look she gave him was only slightly less exasperated. "Come on," she said.

Jess fumbled with the doll then angled it toward the one Sue was holding, touching its face briefly to hers.

"Not like that," Sue said. "Here. I'll show you."

She took the doll from him and stood them on the ground, pressing them together, doing her best to wrap their arms around each other. Their lips met. Sue held them that way. It was a long and, if her expression was to be believed, supremely satisfying kiss.

"Oh, yuck," said Dottie, making gagging sounds.

Patsy gave a long, low wolf whistle.

Alison wished the earth would open right where she sat.

Jess swallowed, stared, swallowed again and didn't say a word.

After a a considerable interval Sue looked at Jess, pulled the dolls apart. "See?" she said to her uncle. "Like that. Get it?"

Jess cleared his throat. "Got it."

HE HAD IT, all right. Bad.

And every day it was getting worse.

He couldn't stop it.

He and Brian Gonzales, Mike's son, would take the tractor and the wagon out in the morning to feed the cattle, and instead of paying attention to what he was supposed to be doing, he'd be daydreaming about Alison.

He'd ride along the fences, checking things out in the afternoons, and he'd remember kissing Alison with the same abandon that Sue's dolls showed. He'd be trying to chivvy a cow out of a thicket, and he'd be thinking about the way her hair had smelled, the way her lips tasted, the way her hands had touched him.

He should've known his daydreaming would get him into trouble.

It was late on the Monday afternoon before Thanksgiving that it happened. He was riding Dodger through some oak scrub, trying to get some cattle out, thinking about Alison, the way he'd left her, rolling out gingerbread dough on the kitchen table.

She'd worn a dish towel apron tied around her waist. The sleeves of her navy plaid blouse were pushed up to her elbows as she bent over the pastry board. The top two buttons were undone, giving him a tantalizing glimpse of a lacy white bra and creamy flesh beneath.

The kitchen was warm, and she had a flush on her cheeks and a smudge of flour on her nose. He'd wanted to kiss it, kiss her. Wanted to undo the rest of the buttons, let his fingers slide down the softness of her curves and learn—

"Ow! Hell!"

He guessed it was a rabbit that made Dodger start, jerking to the side, then lunging forward, knocking him against the oak scrub.

Whatever it was, one moment he was in the throes of red-hot passion, and the next his left knee—his bad knee—was consumed with a white hot pain.

He swore, gritted his teeth, wanted to howl. He jerked back hard on the reins. "Stay put, you stupid fool! Oh, damn. Oh, hell."

He held himself absolutely rigid until the sharpest edges of the pain began to recede a bit, then tested his knee gingerly, running his fingers over it, feeling the almost immediate swelling. He put a little weight on it in the stirrup and winced.

Still, nothing was broken. He wouldn't have been able to put any weight on his leg at all if it had been.

He should go back to the bunkhouse right now and put ice on it. But it would only feel worse before it felt better, and he had the rest of this section to do.

He urged Dodger forward. "Keep your mind on your work," he muttered to the horse, then recalled where his own mind had been. "And I will, too," he added roughly.

It was a good thing he kept going.

There was a break in the fence near the top of the pasture. If he'd left it overnight, there was no telling how many cattle would've been gone by morning. Three were already up into the national forest land, standing in the trees looking down at him as if daring him to do something about it.

It took him longer than he would have liked to get them back. They were balky, perverse, intractable cows. The sort that always found their way through the fence and didn't take kindly to being brought home.

His knee was swollen stiff by the time he finally got them back on their own side of the fence, dismounted, repaired the fence and tried to swing back into the saddle again.

He couldn't do it. Bending his knee was a near impossibility. Putting all his weight on it while it was bent, then using it to lever himself into the saddle was an actual one. He shut his eyes momentarily, waiting for the pain to abate, then went around to the other side. Dodger shied nervously, unused to such goings on.

"Hold still, you stupid horse."

But Dodger didn't. He made nervous noises, stepping sideways, dragging Jess as he attempted to put his right foot in the right stirrup.

"Damn it, I said, hold still!"

Clenching his teeth, anchoring his right foot as well as he could, Jess heaved himself into the saddle. Dodger whinnied, pulling madly.

"For God's sake!"

It took him until well past six to make it back down to the ranch. Dottie was standing at the gate, waiting for him in the dark.

"Where were you?"

"Some cattle got loose. I had to bring 'em back, then mend the fence." He eased his foot out of the stirrup and slid carefully to the ground.

"You should've waited for me. I could've helped."

"You can do me a favor now, if you want." He handed her the horse's reins. "Take care of Dodger."

"All by myself?" She stared at him wide-eyed.

"As long as you do a good job."

She beamed. "You know I will!" She turned and started leading Dodger toward the barn, then stopped. "Will you tell Ali where I am?"

"I'm not goin' up to the house tonight. I'm not really hungry."

Dottie looked disbelieving, then shrugged. "If you say so." She tied Dodger to the gate, then took off running toward the house.

Jess hobbled his way toward the bunkhouse. He knew he couldn't get past Alison without limping. And he knew she'd fuss if she saw his knee.

He might have been able to handle her fussing other times. Not now. He was too vulnerable, and he knew it. A few sympathetic murmurs, a kiss to make it better—he grimaced—and he wouldn't stand a chance. He had to stay away completely.

He winced as he removed his boots with the bootjack, then unzipped his jeans and eased them over his knee. It was bigger than the biggest grapefruit he'd ever seen.

He probed the swollen discolored flesh gingerly, tried to bend the joint, shuddered and limped over to the sink. He should use ice, but ice meant going up to the house. He soaked a cloth in cold water, wrung it out and wrapped it around his knee. Then he hobbled back to the bed and lay down.

God willing it would be better by morning. God knew it had to be. There was work to be done.

SO HE WASN'T hungry, huh?

Alison almost snorted when Dottie gave her the news. More likely he was not up for another evening playing "Alison and Jess."

She'd seen his face that night. She'd seen the way he'd avoided the house after dinner every night since.

"Oh, Jess," she sighed. "Just when you were getting through to them."

The problem, she was fairly sure, was that they were also getting through to him.

Well, fine. But if he was just doing it to avoid the latest Jess and Alison episode, it would serve him right to go without supper.

The dolls hadn't kissed once tonight. "Alison" had taught "Jess" how to make gingerbread men.

"Should we take Uncle Jess one?" Sue asked. She was thrilled with the little cookie men and had bitten their heads off with great relish.

"Not if he hasn't eaten his supper."

"But, Ali—"

"No," Alison said firmly. "He can have one after breakfast."

But Jess didn't come in for breakfast, either.

"Was your uncle in the barn when you went out this morning?" she asked Dottie on the way to the bus.

Dottie shook her head. "I thought he'd come in early for breakfast."

Maybe he had. Jess was unpredictable. He did things in his own time on his own terms.

It didn't do to pressure him.

At least that's what she told herself until he didn't come up for dinner, either.

Alison stood staring out the kitchen window down toward the bunkhouse. The tractor was back. She could see the rear end of it just peeking out from the barn. They had finished a little later than usual, she'd noted. But Brian's truck was gone, so they must be done.

"Maybe you should take him a gingerbread man after all," she said to Sue.

"Even though he didn't eat?"

"Even though."

Sue grabbed two off the plate and took off running. Ten minutes later she was back. ''He said thanks, they were good.''

Alison frowned. ''And that's all?''

''He tol' me not to be late for school. Is it time to go?'' Sue looked at the clock. ''The big hand is on the nine.''

''It's time,'' Alison said as she shrugged into her coat and handed Sue her book bag. Normally she dropped Sue off at kindergarten on Tuesday, then worked on the library until school was over. ''What was he doing?''

''Sittin' in bed.''

''Just sitting on the bed?'' That didn't sound like Jess.

''Not on the bed. In the bed.''

''*In* it?'' Alison stomped down on the accelerator, shooting them out of the yard and down the gravel road toward the highway.

Sue nodded. ''He said he was restin'. I didn't think big people took rests.''

Alison didn't think Jess did. ''I'll look in on him.''

''You can take him another gingerbread man, if you want to.''

Alison didn't bother.

She dropped Sue off at school and came right home, stopping the truck in front of the bunkhouse.

She knocked, waited until she heard, ''What is it?'' then opened the door and went in.

Jess was, in fact, in bed, a stockman's journal in his lap. He scowled at her. ''Why aren't you at work?''

''Why aren't you?''

''I'm resting. Any law against it? Don't you think I work hard enough for you? It's half my ranch, too, remember? I can take a break if I want.''

Alison folded her arms across her chest and looked down at him, waiting until he stopped and looked at her, a faint flush on his high cheekbones.

"Are you quite finished now?" she asked.

He scowled. "I'm finished."

"Then tell me what's wrong."

"Nothing's wrong."

"Liar."

He glared at her. She stared impassively back.

"Get out of here, Alison," he said finally. "I don't come bustin' into your bedroom, tellin' you what to do."

"You can if you want." It just popped out. She hadn't meant to say it.

But, having said it, she wasn't sorry.

"Look, I don't know what your problem is, but you won't solve it sulking down here. If you're really afraid of Sue and her dolls again—"

"I'm not afraid of Sue and her dolls!"

"Then what?"

He stared out the window, trying to ignore her. She didn't go away. Finally he plucked irritably at the blanket. "I hurt my knee."

"Your knee? Let me see it. How did you hurt it? What happened?" Alison was reaching for the blanket even as she spoke.

"Damn it. That's exactly why I didn't come up to the house. I knew you'd make some big blasted deal out of it."

"It's not a big blasted deal? Then let me see it."

She didn't wait for him to comply, just pulled the blankets and sheet back.

He wasn't wearing any jeans.

Wouldn't you know, Alison thought. Every time she saw him bare-legged, she never got a chance to appreciate it. She began unwrapping the plastic-wrapped damp towel. When she finished, she winced.

"Oh, Jess."

"Oh, Jess," he mimicked in a mocking tone. "I knew you'd fuss."

"Call it what you want. You need to see a doctor."

"A doctor can't do anything. It's not broken. It's the same knee I hurt bronc ridin' three years ago. It's sore that's all."

That wasn't the word Alison would have used.

"You shouldn't be walking on it."

"I'm not."

"You went out and fed the cattle."

"Brian did most of it."

"Dottie and I could have done it."

Jess snorted.

"Dottie and I *will* do it," Alison said, "until you're well again."

"You're not strong enough."

"You'd be surprised. Come on." She reached for his arm, trying to help him up.

He stayed right where he was. "I'm not going anywhere."

"You're going to the doctor, Jess. And then you're moving into the house. Unless you end up in the hospital."

"I'm not going to any damned hospital."

"Fine. The house, then."

"There's no room."

"Sue can move in with Dottie, and Patsy can have the attic. She'd love it."

"But—"

She gave him a saccharine smile. "Chicken?"

He glared. "Dumbest thing I've ever heard."

"Dumbest thing I ever heard is you saying that you're staying down here." She tossed him his jeans. "Put your pants on. I'll carry your clothes while you're getting dressed."

"I don't need—"

"I don't need an argument. Put your damned pants on, Jess, or I'll do it for you."

He gritted his teeth. "Get the hell out of here, Alison."

She picked up his clothes and left.

When she got back, he was dressed and coming out the door. She moved to slip an arm around his back for support, but he brushed her away.

"I'm fine."

"Of course you are. That's why you're limping, you stubborn cuss."

"I never denied it." Grimacing at every step, he moved slowly across the bunkhouse porch.

"Stop at the truck," Alison said. "I'll take you to see the doctor first."

"I told you, I don't need a doctor."

"You will if you don't stop at the truck."

He turned to glare at her. Her gaze moved pointedly from her foot to his knee.

He went white. "You wouldn't."

"Want to bet?"

JESS WAS RIGHT about one thing—the doctor couldn't do much.

"Banged it up good, didn't you?" Charley Moran said, shaking his head as he looked at it. "With a knee like yours you oughta be paying closer attention to where you're going."

Jess muttered something under his breath.

Charley grinned. "But then, I reckon I can see where you might have your mind on other things these days. Hell of a lot of swelling. Didn't you put ice on it?"

"Didn't have any."

"Refrigerator not working?"

"I'm staying in the bunkhouse."

Charley gave him a long assessing stare. "And nobody'd bring you any?"

"I didn't ask."

Charley rolled his eyes.

He took X rays, then shrugged. "Nothing visible, which doesn't mean you're imagining it," he said with a grin.

"It's just the same old thing," Jess said gruffly.

"Probably ligament damage, yes. When the swelling goes down we'll take a closer look."

"Here." He handed Jess two fat pills and a cup of water, waiting while Jess swallowed. "That's for pain," Charley said. He scribbled out a prescription. "They'll help with the swelling, too. And take them, you damn fool. Don't be some macho tough guy. Get out of that damned bunkhouse, too. Somebody needs to keep an eye on you."

"I can take care of myself."

"Right," Charley said. He didn't mean it.

He opened a closet in his office and fished out a pair of crutches. "Use these for a week or so." He fitted them under Jess's arms and walked with him back out to the waiting room where Alison sat.

"Keep him off it completely until the swelling is down."

"I've got work to do," Jess argued.

"And a family to do it," Charley said unsympathetically. "Lucky you. Bed, fella. Rest. Lots of it. In the house. Got it?" he asked Alison.

She nodded. Jess glared.

Charley turned to his nurse. "Give Jess an appointment in three weeks." He handed the prescription to Alison. "Make him take them."

"I will," she promised, holding the door for Jess, who swung himself out on the crutches like a man who knew well how to use them.

"He didn't have to give it to you," Jess grumbled as they headed for the truck. "I'm not a child."

Alison looked at him doubtfully. "You must've done a good imitation of one, then."

But she let him prove it by allowing him to maneuver the crutches and negotiate the step and the door by himself.

It was difficult as hell. His knee was killing him. He wouldn't admit it.

Still, he waited in the car while she filled the prescription. Then he looked at her with surprise when she drove to Bluff Springs's only fast-food place. "I'll be right back."

Moments later she came out with a hamburger, a soft drink and French fries. She handed him the bag. "I thought you might be able to use this."

He took it, letting it sit in his lap, untouched. He felt ill-humored and sulky and he wished he could get mad at her, but it was hard when she wasn't bullying him.

His stomach growled. But he lasted until the edge of town before he opened the sack.

"Thanks." It wasn't very gracious.

"You're welcome," she said.

Alison drove up as close to the house as she could get. She took the groceries and opened the gate. She didn't help him. He wouldn't ask her to, even though the pain killers were beginning to make him woozy and he almost fell up the steps.

She left the groceries in the kitchen, then went ahead of him up the stairs, stripped the sheets off Sue's bed and was beginning to put on clean ones when he finally hobbled, exhausted, into the room.

She glanced up. "It's a pity all the bedrooms are upstairs. I'll have the bed ready in just a minute."

He leaned on the crutches, his knee throbbing. "What's Sue going to say when she finds out I've stolen her room?"

"Yippee, I imagine," Alison said dryly. "You have no idea how many times she's asked why you stay in the bunkhouse."

She straightened the quilt, then folded it back and patted it. "All set."

He didn't move.

"Jess?"

"All right," he said irritably. "I'm coming." But he almost stumbled when he did.

In an instant Alison was at his side, helping him maneuver so that he could ease himself down onto the bed. He leaned the crutches against the wall and lay back, his eyes closing.

"Come on, Jess." Before he could react, she was helping him move sideways, lifting his legs onto the bed.

He let her. He felt too fuzzy to protest. Even when her fingers deftly unbuttoned his shirt and slipped it from his shoulders, he just looked at her.

Not until she pressed him back against the pillows and set to work unfastening his jeans did he finally rouse himself.

"I knew you'd be having your wicked way with me if I came up to the house," he muttered, looking up at her as she bent over him.

Alison licked her lips. She made him raise his hips so she could slide the jeans down his legs. "Is that what I'm doing?'' she asked. He thought her voice sounded a little breathless.

''Isn't it?'' he asked hoarsely.

''What do you think?''

Chapter Ten

It was the effect of the pills, of course, that was causing this euphoric haze through which he was experiencing the world. At first he tried to fight it, blinking his eyes, muttering imprecations at Charley for having prescribed them.

But then it was too much trouble. It didn't seem worth the effort. Besides, his knee didn't hurt so much anymore. If she wanted to fuss, let her. Maybe if he slept . . .

When he woke, the haze was still there, making him feel warm and well cared for. Voices sounded soft and slurred, and colors blurred a bit around the edges.

Alison came in and offered him a glass of water, and he could hardly seem to lift his head. When she put her arm around him and helped him up, he couldn't find the words to protest. His head lolled in the curve between her arm and her breast.

He felt lighter, happier. He even smiled sleepily at the girls when they came to check on him after dinner.

"Don't worry, Uncle Jess," Dottie assured him. "Alison and Patsy and I can take care of everything."

You can't, he wanted to tell her. But she looked so earnest, so sweet, that all he could do was mumble. Then he shut his eyes and slept again.

He didn't remember anything else until Sue, clad in fuzzy cat pajamas, came padding in to say good-night. She kissed him solemnly and said, "I'm glad you came in to stay, Uncle Jess. I wanted you to."

He saw Alison standing behind her, watching them, smiling. He smiled back muzzily, even when she said quietly, "I told you so."

SHE WATCHED him sleeping. Crept in after the girls were in bed and stood just inside the doorway looking down on him, afraid to go closer for fear of waking him.

He had drifted off with the light still on, a book on cattle diseases open beside him on the bed.

She was surprised he'd even made an effort at it. The pills Charley Moran had prescribed had done a stunning job of making Jess woozy and amenable.

So amenable, in fact, that she felt faintly guilty every time she touched him, as if she were taking advantage. Imagine being able to undress Jess Cooper with no more protest from him than one faint wisecrack and a smile.

When the girls got home, they had further undercut any moves he might have made to reassert his independence. Horrified to find out that he'd been hurt, they went rushing upstairs to hover over him, wanting to know how they could help, what they could do.

If Uncle Jess needed a glass of water, he had it before he could move his toe. If Uncle Jess wanted to listen to the radio, it was beside his bed before he'd finished saying the words.

After an initial protest or two, Jess had given in, seeming to relax, allowing them to wait on him. In fact, Alison realized, he seemed almost amazed and a little awed by their concern.

She had to admit that she was concerned, too. She hoped he would rest now, doing what Charley told him he needed to do to get well.

She leaned closer, trying to see if he really was asleep at last.

He was lying on his back, the comforter bunched down near his waist. His navy T-shirt outlined in dark relief his muscular chest.

Two day's worth of stubble shadowed his cheeks, highlighting his high cheekbones and the lean lines of his face. Jess's face was still tough, even in sleep. Only the dark rumpled hair that ruffled across his tanned forehead and the equally dark, thick half moons of lashes against his cheeks lent softness to his features.

Alison slipped closer. Reaching down, she picked up the book, marked his place, then set it on the bedside table. All the while she never took her eyes off Jess.

It seemed strange to think about how many times she'd dreamed of him here in her room.

How many times had she lain awake at night and imagined what he would look like unguarded, asleep?

And now it was happening.

Did dreams come true? Did the lives of librarians and cowboys really meet?

Deliberately she pinched herself on the arm. It hurt. Smiling at her own foolishness, she reached out and brushed the hair back off his forehead.

His brows drew together slightly. His lips parted. He sighed.

And Alison couldn't resist the temptation.

''Playing with fire,'' Jess had called it.

But Alison wasn't playing. She hadn't been playing since she'd moved back from New York.

She leaned down and touched her lips to his. Gently this time. She didn't want to wake him. She only wanted to tell him that she understood.

She wasn't hurt any longer. She knew that it wasn't that he didn't love her. It was that he was afraid to.

It was going to be up to her to teach him not to fear love, up to her to wrap him and his nieces in the warmth and love with which she'd been raised.

"I'll do it, Jess," she promised him. She touched his cheek, rested her palm against his stubbled jaw, saw his mouth curve slightly.

Her own curved, too. "I love you, Jess. And whether you believe it or not, you love me. I'll show you."

HE SLEPT LATE. Later than he ever remembered sleeping in his life. The sun was halfway up in the damned sky and he was just coming around.

He flung back the comforter and swung his legs around, wincing as he did so. But his knee felt better, not as stiff, nor as swollen. He reached for his jeans.

"What do you think you're doing?"

His head jerked up. Alison was standing in the doorway, hands on her hips, smiling at him. He yanked the comforter back over him.

"Getting up, obviously. What the hell were you thinking of, letting me sleep this late? Those cattle need to be fed!"

"They have been."

"They aren't just gonna stand there politely waitin'—What did you say?"

"I said they'd been fed. Brian and I fed them."

He stared at her, shook his head slowly, disbelievingly.

"I told you we would."

"Yeah, but—" He stopped and frowned at her.

"Brian knew what to do."

"Who drove the tractor?"

"Me."

"*You?* Since when do you drive tractors?"

"Since this morning at six-thirty."

"You just went out there, flipped the ignition on and took off."

"Well—" she grinned "—it was a bit more complicated than that. More gears than I'm used to."

"Brian taught you?"

"I'm a librarian, damn it. I read the manual!"

He stared at her, dumbfounded. "You learned to drive the tractor reading a book?"

"Amazing, isn't it?"

"Mind-boggling."

"In any case you don't have to worry about the cattle. Get back in bed and I'll bring you some breakfast."

He hesitated, mind still reeling at the thought of Alison, manual in hand, figuring out the tractor, then helping Brian load up the bales and taking them out to the stock.

"You were . . . all right? I mean, you got back all right? You didn't wreck anything?"

She sighed. "No, I did not 'wreck anything,' thank you very much. Honestly, Jess." She gave him a long-suffering look.

"You could've. You could've got yourself killed," he grumbled. "Tractor accidents happen all the time."

"I read that in the manual, too. Rest assured, I was very careful. But I'm glad to know you care," she added with a smile.

He muttered something under his breath.

She grinned. "Stay in bed, Jess. I'll bring you some dinner."

"I'll come down."

"That's not what Dr. Moran said."

"Charley's an old woman."

"Not to my way of thinking."

Jess's brows drew together. "What's that supposed to mean?"

"Charley Moran is a good-looking man."

His eyes narrowed, his scowl deepened.

"Not as good-looking as you are, though," Alison winked. "I like dark, grumpy men best."

"Hussy," he muttered.

She grinned.

She brought him dinner and more of Charley's miserable pills, hovering over him until he'd swallowed them. Later she brought him the mail, then a computer analysis she'd done on the growth of their yearlings.

And all the while his good sense and his firm resolution about staying clear of Alison Richards were turning to mush.

He lay there watching her adjust the curtains, the sunbeams outlining her blue-jean-clad curves, and he wished he could slide them right off her.

He dozed intermittently as she read him a letter from her brother, Peter, detailing a date he'd gone on with his latest lady friend, and Jess dreamed that he and Alison were dating, too.

His mind fuzzed. He tried to talk logically, think coherently. He said something that made Alison laugh. He didn't know what. He only knew she had the sexiest laugh he'd ever heard.

After she'd read him the letter she made him take a nap.

"A nap?" He looked at her, horrified.

She pulled the curtains shut. "A nap. And if you take a good one, maybe you can watch Mickey Mouse Club reruns with Sue when you get up."

She blew him a kiss and went out, shutting the door, leaving him only Kitten for company.

They stared at each other doubtfully from opposite sides of the room. Then Kitten got bored and went to sleep.

Within minutes Jess did, too.

He did get to watch a Mickey Mouse rerun with Sue. Afterward he ate supper in bed, while Dottie sat at the desk, eating hers and keeping him company.

"We drew straws to see who could come up and eat with you," she told him. "I won."

Jess stared at her. "You lost, you mean," he joked, but she shook her head.

"Nope. We all wanted to, but Alison said you probably didn't need that many people all at once. Alison takes very good care of you, doesn't she?"

Yes, Jess thought. She did.

She was back after supper with another pill.

"Haven't I had enough of these today?"

"Last one," she said. "To get you through the night."

While he was in the bathroom, she straightened his sheet and plumped his pillow and folded the comforter back. When he came back, she was standing in front of the dresser, her hands knotted in front of her, watching him, smiling.

In his hazy afternoon dream she'd been waiting just like this, eager yet apprehensive, wanting him. The way he wanted her. He shook his head.

Sue poked her head around the corner of the door. "You wanta play 'Alison and Jess'?"

Alison and Jess? Oh, God, yes.

Jess looked at Alison. "How about a little Alison and Jess?"

"Not tonight." Alison smiled. "It's time for your uncle to go to bed."

"I've been in bed all day."

Alison ignored him. "He's had quite enough stimulation."

"He could always use some more," Jess said hopefully.

Alison gave him a baleful look. "Not tonight." She touched Sue's shoulder. "Uncle Jess needs to sleep."

"No, 'e doesn't," Jess tried to protest. But the damned pill was already taking effect.

He could barely keep his eyes open. He slumped sideways onto the pillow, letting Alison lift his feet and turn them under the comforter while Sue patted his hand.

"'S'your fault," he mumbled to Alison. "Knockin' me out like this."

She smiled. "It's the only way I can control you," he heard her say. "And me."

SHE HEARD A YOWL, then a crash. Her feet hit the floor before she was fully awake.

"Damn!"

It was Jess's voice, furious, pained. She ran into the hallway. Jess was on the rug, struggling to get up.

Alison knelt beside him, mind still fuzzed by a dream—a dream of Jess. "Are you all right?"

He managed a sitting position, but stayed there, clutching his knee. "Swell," he muttered.

Alison began patting him in the dark, trying to see how badly he was hurt. "Can you get up, Jess?"

"Of course I can get up."

"What happened?"

"Ask the damned cat."

"Oh, heavens. I forgot about Kitten. He usually sleeps on the hall rug," she said apologetically.

Kitten wasn't a snuggler. He liked to be where people were, but he also liked to keep his distance. "Here, give me your hand." She began hauling him to his feet.

He seemed taller in the moonlight, more imposing. Alison's hands were more than ever aware of the muscles beneath the soft cotton of his T-shirt. She'd been dreaming when she'd heard the noise. A warm dream. A wonderful dream.

Pieces of it floated through her head now as she helped him. She had been touching him then, too. Soft touches. Loving touches. Touches that she'd been dying to give him all day. All month. Ever since she'd returned.

They stood scant inches apart now. Alison felt her pulses quickening under his scrutiny. She was suddenly conscious of her thin nightgown, of his state of undress. She swallowed, brushed her hair back from her face and looked directly into his eyes.

Abruptly Jess shook his head as if trying to clear it. "I need a drink."

"I'll get you a glass of water."

"I didn't mean water," he said hoarsely.

"Well, water's all you're going to get. Go back to bed and I'll bring it to you."

He didn't go. "Bein' thirsty's not the only reason I'm up, Alison," he said at last.

"Oh." She looked away, even more flustered. "Of course. I'm sorry." She stepped out of his way, and he swung past her toward the bathroom.

She stood and watched as the door shut. She ought to go back to bed. She ought to turn on her heel and vanish into her room.

But she couldn't.

She had lived with him for weeks now. She had learned his strengths and his passions. She had become his partner, his friend.

But it wasn't enough; she wanted more.

She wanted what she had dreamed of since she was fifteen, what she saw in his eyes, but never yet had heard from his lips.

She wanted Jess Cooper's love.

Of course, he might send her away. He already had. He'd lied—to protect himself. Because, although Jess had been fighting her from the start, he was fighting himself, too, far more than he'd been fighting her.

Something existed between them, something strong and vibrant and growing. Something that all the resistance and stubbornness and determination he could muster still hadn't killed.

She waited for him.

He swung out into the hallway and stopped when he saw her standing there.

She didn't back down.

He swung past her toward the bedroom, careful not to hit anything. She followed.

He leaned the crutches against the bedstead, then sat down. Wincing, he swung his legs in. Only then did he look up at her, his eyes challenging. "I suppose you came to tuck me in?"

Alison ran her tongue lightly over her lips, drawing courage, then nodded. "By all means," she said.

With great care, she drew the comforter up around him and smoothed it across his chest, then tucked it in around him. She let her hands linger slightly as they brushed his shoulders. Then, just before she straightened up, she shoved an errant lock of hair off his forehead.

His eyes were dark, heavy-lidded, watching her every move. She felt momentarily awkward and foolish. She licked her lips, then dared to smile at him.

Then he tilted his head. His eyes narrowed. "No good-night kiss?" His tone was sardonic, almost as if he was daring her.

He should have known better.

"Damn it, Alison! Wait a—"

But Alison had waited long enough.

The dream would not be denied. Her lips came down and touched his, hard and warm.

She felt his initial resistance, felt his tension, his desperation. And then he was kissing her, too.

And it was like the other times he'd kissed her, hungry and demanding. And yet it was more.

Those had been kisses under protest, kisses that promised an end almost before they'd begun.

This wasn't a goodbye kiss. It was hello.

It was a promise, an acknowledgment, an omen of things to come.

And Alison rejoiced in it, gave herself over to the sensation of it.

This was the Jess she'd been waiting for, the man she'd been dreaming about. And, even as she knew it, she knew her dreams hadn't held a candle to the real man.

He was leather and soap and horses and something purely, indefinably Jess. And she drank of his kisses with a thirst unimaginable. She felt as if she'd been in a desert for a lifetime, as if she'd been parched for years. And Jess seemed to feel the same.

When at last she pulled back, purely to breathe and for no other reason, her heart was slamming against her ribs. She'd never felt so desperate. She wanted more, wanted...

But before she could even begin to articulate it, Jess was kissing her again, drawing her close, pulling her onto the bed beside him, kissing her the way she'd always imagined being kissed.

And Alison thought, yes, oh, yes. Like this.

Exactly like this.

She snuggled closer still. Her hands touched his dark hair, stroked through it. Her fingers shaped the curve of his ears, her thumbs brushed against his temples, wanting to memorize them all.

Jess's hands found her shoulders, flannel soft, slid down her back and drew her closer, tracing the curve of her spine, sending goose bumps in their wake. Her breasts pressed into the comforter between them, and she heard him groan. Then he reached up and dragged the comforter away.

Now only the softness of her nightgown separated them. She could feel the hard muscles of his chest beneath her nipples. Pressing closer, she sensed the pounding of his heart against her own.

He nipped gently at her lips, then, as they parted, teased them with his tongue, letting it slip inside her mouth, and she shivered at the pleasure of it. She returned the favor and smiled at the shudder that coursed through him.

It was odd how she felt so right doing this with Jess. It wasn't something she'd done with Gary or any of the few other men she'd dated in her life.

She supposed she should have felt nervous. She wasn't a bit, because she'd been here before—in her dreams.

With anyone else she would have bemoaned her lack of experience, would have hesitated, feared making a fool of herself, feared panicking at the last moment.

With Jess she was not afraid. It was right.

She framed his face with her hands. Her thumbs caressed his cheekbones, her lips touched his nose, his brows, his eyelids.

"Ah, Jess," she murmured. "My Jess."

She'd said the words in her mind for years. And in her mind he had agreed.

In reality, since Nathan's death, he'd denied her. He'd argued, resisted, walked away.

Not tonight. He didn't walk away. Nor did he argue.

He just looked at her, his eyes dark and wondering. His hand touched her cheek almost hesitantly.

She looked down and her lips curved in a tiny smile. "You're all untucked again. You'll get cold."

A corner of his mouth twisted. "Not likely."

She moved away, starting to pull the comforter back around him. His hand shot out and caught hers. "Don't go." There was a ragged edge to his voice. "Stay...awhile."

Forever, Alison thought. *I'm staying forever.*

"Yes," she said softly. And she kissed him with such hunger, touched him with such abandon, that she broke his control.

He wasn't made of stone, damn it.

He'd tried. Oh God, he'd tried.

Ever since Alison Richards had come back into his life, he'd been resisting her. She hadn't made it easy, with her smiles and her enthusiasm and that curvy little bottom of hers. But he'd done it, and he'd survived.

Until now.

Now he was finished. He couldn't fight her any longer. Didn't want to.

He wanted her. Needed her. Now. Not in his daydreams. Not in his fantasies. In his bed. Tonight.

He'd done his best to think about the long term. God knew he'd tried.

But the long term had always been hard for Jess, and never worse than now. With her body toe to toe and nose to nose with his, their hearts pounding in unison and their lips touching, the long term had ceased to exist.

He could feel her cheek, her breast, her knee. Her leg moved up his thigh, nudging him.

He made a sound deep in his throat, then reached down and took hold of her gown, drawing it up over her hips, past her waist.

The backs of his fingers brushed against the narrow band of lace at her hips. He paused, imagining the way it looked, letting his fingers find out. The lacy panel curved on around toward her belly. And as his fingers followed, he felt her take a quick breath. He waited a moment, feeling tremors in his own fingers as he deliberately slowed the pace.

Then, when he felt her move restlessly against him, he continued, stroking the soft firm flesh of her belly, letting his hand slide beneath the fabric, moving lower, touching the soft curls there.

Alison swallowed, tensed, then her own hands began to move on him. One played lightly across his chest, drawing tiny circles around his nipples, then dancing down farther, brushing against the elastic of his shorts. The other, the one lying against the bed, managed to begin a subtle exploration of the back of his thigh.

Jess shifted, lifted his knee, gave her room, gave himself over to the sensations she was evoking.

He didn't know how much more he could take, how much longer he could last.

But her soft, gentle explorations were too exquisite to resist, too heady to deny, too rare to push away.

He'd never made love like this, so slowly, so tenderly. He'd never known a woman like this.

Alison.

He was afraid to believe it, afraid he would wake up and find out he was dreaming the way he'd been dreaming all day, except that now his dreams had reached new heights, surpassing his wildest imaginings.

But it was no dream.

She was here in his arms, warm and willing. And though it might be the stupidest thing he'd ever done, he couldn't stop. He wanted her too badly, had wanted her too long.

He left off touching her just long enough to skim the nightgown over her head and the lacy underwear from her hips. He struggled to remove his own shorts, winced as he moved his knee and felt Alison's hand on his, stilling him.

"Careful," she murmured. "Let me."

Her fingers hooked inside the elastic and eased them down his hips, slipping them gingerly past his knee. When they were off completely, she knelt on the bed at his feet, looking up at him.

Slowly, carefully, he drew her up and over him, looking all the while deep into her eyes. He felt her tremble, knew he was trembling himself.

"Jess," she whispered again. "My Jess."

And he knew she was right. He did belong to her the way he'd never belonged to another woman.

Then moving just as slowly, carefully and tenderly as he had, she brought him home.

He shut his eyes. His teeth clenched. He felt a fine sheen of sweat break out on his forehead. His fingers bit into her hips, lifting her, then lowering her.

He saw her own teeth clench, her body tense, her breathing quicken. Her dark hair tossed as she caught his rhythm and began to move.

The pace quickened, sweeping both of them along together, pulling them apart, driving them on. And then, at last, when he thought he could stand it no longer, they became one.

It took an instant . . . and an eternity.

It shattered him and made him whole. It wasn't what he had imagined. It was far, far more.

Jess folded Alison against his chest and heard her wildly beating heart echoed by his own. He stroked still-trembling hands down her damp back, drew the comforter up and settled it around both of them, making them their own little cocoon against the world.

He wished it could be like this all the time, wished that he would never have to let her go, that morning would never have to come.

He had tasted wonder moments ago. He had felt magic. Alison Richards had touched a part of him that until now he'd never known.

Alison lifted her head from his chest, looked at him in the silvery light. Her eyes were wide, concerned. "Are you...all right?"

"All right?" The words came out sounding rusty, as if he hadn't spoken for a very long time.

"Your knee, I mean."

He'd never noticed. He flexed it slightly. "It's fine. Don't worry." He hesitated, smitten with sudden worries of his own. "Are you? All right? Was it . . . ?"

She smiled at him then. It was an angel's smile, pure and sweet. She touched her lips to his. "I've never been better in my life, Jess, believe me."

And Jess lay back and shut his eyes, felt them sting slightly and didn't know why.

He swallowed, drew one deep, steadying breath and then another. He folded one arm under his head and listened to the gradually slowing rampage of his heart.

He tried to tell himself that nothing had changed, that life was exactly the same as it had been half an hour ago. But he knew, even as he tried to convince himself otherwise, that this was new territory, alien and uncharted.

He didn't know what to say, what to do. He only knew one thing: how he felt. It amazed him.

Gently he stroked Alison's hair with a still-trembling hand. "Neither have I."

Chapter Eleven

Bliss. Serenity. Gratification. Wholeness.

One word alone couldn't begin to describe the feelings Alison had when she awoke the next morning at the sound of the alarm.

On two and a half hours sleep she should have been feeling miserable and exhausted.

She felt perfectly splendid, if you please.

She yawned and stretched luxuriously, wriggled her toes and flexed her shoulders. Then she simply lay quite still and let the events of the night play through her mind again. And as she did so, she reveled in the unaccustomed tenderness in her body, in the pure contentment of her mind, in the peaceful satisfaction of her emotions.

She had crept back to her own bed shortly before four, leaving Jess reluctantly. He didn't awaken as she left. He'd been holding her close, his arms wrapped around her as if he didn't want to let her go. She hadn't wanted to go, either. But she knew she had to.

It wouldn't do for Dottie to stumble in on them together if she got up before the alarm. There would be a time and a place to share with Jess's nieces the new developments in their relationship, but Alison wanted it to be one of their choosing, not an accidental morning discovery.

Now she sat up, still smiling as she did so, feeling as if she was hugging a very wonderful tiny secret to herself. She scrambled out of bed, dressing quickly in jeans, a shirt and a pullover sweater. Then she ducked into the bathroom long enough to wash her face and teeth and comb her hair.

She caught a glimpse of her face in the mirror and actually grinned. Yes, she did look as if she had a secret. Her cheeks were rosy, her eyes bright.

She drew a deep careful breath and went back out into the hall. The door to Jess's room was open a crack.

Unable to resist taking a peek, she eased it open farther. He was lying on his side, facing the door. One arm was curved around the pillow, holding it the way he had held her. She longed to slip back under the comforter with him, to love and be loved by him once more.

She lingered a moment longer, then blew him a kiss. "Tonight," she promised him—and herself. Today she would show him her love in another way, by helping him and his nieces grow together as a family.

She had the dressing made and the turkey stuffed by the time Dottie appeared, tucking in her shirt and looking at Alison through sleepy eyes. "Whatcha doin'?"

"Putting the bird in the oven. If we're going to be out in the pasture all morning, I won't have time later. Besides, I'll need to make the cranberry sauce then, and the pies."

"All that?" Dottie looked taken aback.

"Of course. It's Thanksgiving." Alison finished stowing the bird in the oven, then turned and gave Dottie a hug. "Come on. Let's get Patsy up, too. If she helps, we can get done that much faster. There's lots to do."

Brian was already loading bales of hay onto the wagon, when they got to the barn. He was, as always, quick and efficient, and today, at least, Alison had a fair idea of what she was supposed to be doing.

Dottie, of course, already knew, and Patsy learned quickly.

It was hard work, heavy work, sweaty work, even in freezing temperatures. But once they got out in the pasture, they developed a sort of rhythm with Alison driving the tractor, Dottie cutting and stripping the twine, while Patsy separated the bales into leaves and Brian lifted them and tossed them down to the waiting cattle.

It took them three trips to carry and distribute all the hay. It was almost eleven o'clock by the time they got back to the barn.

"Would you like to come in for pumpkin muffins?" Alison asked Brian as they finished.

"You can tell Uncle Jess we're doing a good job," Dottie added.

Brian grinned. "You got yourself a deal." He fell into step with Patsy. "I hear you're going to the dance with my brother."

Patsy smiled a little shyly. "He asked me," she admitted.

"What dance is that?" Alison asked.

"They call it the Snow Ball," Brian told her. "It's the high school Christmas dance."

"Sounds like fun," Alison said. "When is it?"

"Two weeks from tomorrow," Brian said. "Luke's talking about renting a tux."

Patsy started to say something, then sighed and chewed her lip. Alison took a couple of quick steps and caught up with them.

"We'll have to make sure your dress is pretty special then, won't we?" she said to Patsy.

Patsy gave a helpless little smile and shrug. "I guess so."

"Brian," Dottie broke in, "Davy says you've got a lot of horses. Can I come over some day and look at them?"

Davy was another Gonzales brother, one who was Dottie's age. Brian shrugged. "Sure. Just get off the bus with him after school."

Dottie turned to Alison. "D'you think maybe Uncle Jess'd let me get a horse? I could help him even more if I had one."

"That's something else you'll have to ask him."

Brian drank two cups of coffee and ate five pumpkin muffins while Alison rolled out pie crust and Patsy, following her directions, made the cranberry sauce.

She wanted to forget it all and run up the stairs to see Jess. Yet at the same time she felt strangely reluctant.

She wondered how he felt about it—about her—now.

What if he regretted it?

He had been so determined, had resisted so long that she couldn't help worrying. This morning, when she'd peeked in on him, she hadn't given it a thought.

Now, having had four hours to contemplate the issue, she felt unaccountably nervous.

Dottie appeared in the kitchen. "Uncle Jess needs a cup of coffee. I told him I'd bring it, but he said he was coming down."

And when Alison looked up, there he was.

He wasn't smiling. He stood leaning on his crutches, looking at her, and she saw in his expression all the worries and nervousness she'd felt herself.

Seeing that, all her own worries fled. She smiled. She loved him, and she was glad she had finally shown him how much. She hoped—prayed—that he was glad, too.

"Jess?" she said softly. She offered him her heart with her eyes.

He hesitated, swallowed, licked his lips, bit down for a moment on the lower one. Then he smiled, too.

Alison felt as if she might laugh aloud, might dance around the kitchen, might make a complete and utter fool of herself. She started grinning, wanting to go to him and hug him, to show him her joy.

But Jess wouldn't thank her for that.

He was a private man. Last night he had loved her and she wanted to tell the world. But that was risky. For the moment it was enough to tell him in silence, with only her eyes and her smiles, that she loved him too.

She nudged out a chair with her foot, waving floury hands in his direction. "Come in. Sit down."

He hobbled over to the table. Dottie poured him a cup of coffee, and he sat nursing it and eating a muffin, while Brian sang their praises, assuring Jess that his cattle were being well fed.

"Good," Jess said. He gave his nieces an approving look. "You've done great." Then his gaze lifted and his eyes met Alison's. "Thanks."

She finished crimping the crust on the pie, blew the flour off her nose and a lock of hair out of her eyes. "You're welcome."

Always welcome, she told him with her eyes, *in my bed, in my life, in my heart.*

Carefully she washed her hands and dried them, stepped over Sue who was playing with her dolls on the floor and as casually as possible reached out and took Jess's coffee cup and filled it again. He looked up at her. She took a sip from it, then set it down in front of him.

His hand lay still on the tabletop for a long moment. Then carefully he picked it up, cradling it in his palms, breathing in the fragrance. He looked up at her. Their eyes met. He touched the rim to his lips, drank where she had drunk, his gaze never leaving hers.

"Do you think these cranberries are cooked yet?" Patsy asked.

"What? Oh, let me see." Alison went to look at them.

Jess still talked to Brian, listened to Dottie, sat with one arm around Sue who'd come to lean against him. But wherever she moved, Alison felt his eyes on her, and she thanked God, because she knew it was just a matter of time until once more she felt the touch of his lips.

IT HADN'T TAKEN her long to figure out that, as far as Jess and his nieces were concerned, Thanksgiving was a holiday that had been celebrated in social studies class, not at home.

Last week when she'd asked Jess whether he wanted the meal at noon or in the evening, he'd said, "What difference does it make?"

"I want to do what you're used to." She thought it would help to preserve whatever traditions his family had observed.

"I'm used to feeding cattle and eating beef stew out of a can."

"For Thanksgiving? But surely Pops—"

Jess shrugged awkwardly. "Oh, the last couple of years we've been invited out and he insisted that we go, but it doesn't matter to me. I don't care."

"Well, I do," Alison told him.

Patsy and Dottie had shown about as much enthusiasm as Jess.

"We could get hamburgers at the take-out," Dottie had suggested. "Then you won't have to cook."

"I'm going to cook," Alison assured both of them. "We're all going to cook. It's part of the holiday. Part of the sharing. It's important."

Sue had been enthusiastic at first, when she'd thought it had something to do with the Indians eating the Pilgrims. Once her misconception was corrected, her interest waned.

Alison didn't let their indifference discourage her. It took time to develop appreciation for a holiday like Thanksgiving, she told herself philosophically... time and the experience of love that went with it.

Personally she relished the holiday.

Ever since she could remember, in whatever corner of the world they'd found themselves, the Richards family had made a point of celebrating this very American tradition, though they hadn't always done everything the traditional way.

She remembered a Thanksgiving in Mexico when they'd had turkey *mole* and another in Bangkok when they'd had a chicken, peppers, and water chestnut stir-fry.

But while the food often changed, everyone pitched in, and the Thanksgiving spirit always remained the same.

Her parents had taught them that Thanksgiving was a time to remember the past with gratitude, to look toward the future with hope and, most especially, to give thanks for the joys of the present, for the people one found oneself sharing it with.

Alison had never felt more grateful than she felt this year as she prepared to celebrate with Jess and the girls.

She had known it wouldn't be simple for the five of them to become a family.

But slowly, surely, things were coming together, figuratively and—she smiled at the memory of last night's loving—literally.

She got down her grandparents' best silver and set Dottie and Sue to polishing while they watched the football game with Jess. Then she went back into the kitchen to help Patsy wash the seldom-used, slightly dusty wine and water glasses, and all the while she marveled how far they had come.

"Five of each?" Patsy asked her dubiously, holding up the glasses.

Alison nodded. "Yes, please. And then you can help me put the tablecloth and napkins on."

"In the dining room? Seems like a lot of trouble."

"It is," Alison replied cheerfully. "But it's worth it."

"I guess." Patsy turned on the water and squirted some dishwashing liquid into the pan.

Alison dried the glasses as Patsy washed them. "I didn't know you'd been asked to the dance. What kind of a dress do you want?"

Patsy kept her eyes on the glasses. "I dunno."

Alison touched her shoulder. "Don't you want to go? Don't you like Luke?"

Patsy's head jerked up. "Of course I like him! I just... just—" her shoulders lifted "—I don't know if we were still going to be here."

Alison set one glass carefully on the counter and picked up another. "Why wouldn't you be?" she asked gently.

In the living room, as if it were in another world, she could hear Sue chattering over the football announcer, heard Dottie give a little squeal and Jess say, "Oh, yeah. Look at him go!" Alison kept her eyes on Patsy.

The girl sighed, and flicked a strand of dark hair out of her face with soapy fingers. "Oh, well, you know. This won't last, us staying here."

Alison stopped drying the glass. "Why not?"

Patsy didn't look up. "It never does," she muttered.

Alison wanted to put her arms around the girl and hold her. She wanted to give Patsy all the security and stability she'd never had. She wanted to say, *Yes, it will. We'll do it. We'll be a family.*

She couldn't.

Not yet.

They would say it together, she and Jess. But first they had to settle things between themselves. They were making progress, yes, but their love was too new. Too fragile.

"You don't put your heaviest saddle on a fresh broke horse," her grandfather had often said.

You didn't ask a man, used to going it alone, to suddenly take on the responsibilities of the world. She had no doubt that Jess would do so in time.

But so far he hadn't even asked her.

And until he did...

"You'll be here for the Christmas dance," Alison said firmly after a moment. She could promise that much at least. "And for Christmas."

Patsy looked skeptical.

"I promise," Alison said. "I'll help you find a dress in town. Or if you can't find one special enough, we can get a pattern and some material."

Patsy just looked at her, eyes wide. "I've never made anything like that before. Not a real dress. A fancy one."

"You sew for Sue's dolls all the time."

"But those are just from scraps."

"They start out as scraps," Alison corrected. "They turn out to be beautiful clothes."

"But...what if I wreck it?" Patsy asked, concern evident in her deep brown eyes.

Alison smiled. "I don't think you know your own abilities. And, anyway, if you sew something wrong, you can always rip it out and try again. Everything I've ever made has seams like that," she admitted ruefully. "What do you say?"

There was a tiny smile on Patsy's face, almost the first one Alison had seen there since the girls had arrived. "Thanks," Patsy said softly. "I say, thanks, Alison."

THE POTATOES were cooked and Patsy was mashing them. The cranberry sauce had jelled and cooled and was in place on the table. The green beans and Dottie's fruit salad were waiting, all ready to go. The table was set, gleaming with old china and highly polished silver. At last Alison pronounced the turkey ready to carve.

She called Jess.

He limped into the kitchen and leaned on his crutches. "What's up?"

"You get to carve."

He looked at her, dismayed. "I don't know. I've never..." His voice trailed off and he looked away, as if casting about for a means to escape.

But she wasn't going to give him one. If he didn't have traditions of his own yet, ones worth keeping at least, they would start some here.

"Nathan always did," she said softly and held out the knife for him.

He hesitated, then nodded. He set the crutches aside and took the knife.

"I could read to you out of my *How to Carve a Turkey* book," Alison offered with a grin.

One dark brow lifted. "You have one?"

She gestured to the new bookshelves in the kitchen which he had helped her hang.

He shrugged. There was a hint of a smile around his mouth. "Read away," he said gruffly.

Alison read. The book even had pictures. She held them up at appropriate intervals just like the well-practiced librarian she was.

The girls came out to watch.

Jess grimaced. "Just what I need, an audience."

"You're doin' good, Uncle Jess," Dottie told him.

Sue's fingers snaked out and snitched a piece of meat from the plate. She popped it into her mouth. "Very good," she said through the mouthful.

Jess tapped her fingers with the fork. "No stealing," he told her with mock seriousness. "You get caught stealing, you have to do the dishes."

Sue's eyes widened. "Really?"

He nodded. "It's a tradition."

She looked at Alison for confirmation. "Is it?"

Alison smiled. "A tradition has to start somewhere. But I think, in this case, we can all do the dishes together. Finished?" she asked Jess, looking at the platter piled with meat.

"You tell me."

"It's fine," Alison told him. "Better than I could do. And you'll improve."

"We gonna have turkey every night until I get it right?"

"Often enough," she promised. "Another one at Christmas. And then next Thanksgiving. And the next." Her eyes met his. She smiled. "Right?" she asked softly.

Jess cleared his throat, pressed his lips together, then gave her a faint answering smile. He laid his hand on Sue's shoulder. "Come on, gang. Let's eat."

JESS HAD NEVER HAD a Norman Rockwell Thanksgiving before, the type you saw on television and hanging on the walls in doctors' waiting rooms. He'd never believed in them.

Now he did.

Or maybe he believed in Alison.

Certainly it was Alison who'd made it happen.

It had begun almost before dawn, with the sound of Alison tiptoeing through the hall, with the faint creak of the bedroom door, with the sight, through his lashes, of a tousled and beautiful Alison Richards standing in the doorway looking down at him.

He'd missed her when she'd left, had wanted to hold her back and make her stay.

He hadn't dared.

What they had shared had been wonderful, more wonderful than he ever could have imagined. Too wonderful to last?

He knew that was possible.

In any case, he couldn't hold her then. What if she regretted it? What if...?

The worry made his gut twist.

Even if she'd enjoyed it every bit as much as he had, he still couldn't make her stay. There were the girls to be considered. He didn't want Alison embarrassed in front of them. If Dottie or Patsy or even Sue walked in on them, it would change everything.

Jess knew things were changing, anyway. But he didn't know which way and he didn't know how far. And he certainly didn't know, any longer, the limits of his own control.

When Nathan had left him half the ranch, he'd been pleased; who wouldn't have been? But he'd felt an unholy sense of panic all the same.

With the bequest had come responsibilities, potential, expectations. It was as if he'd been given the best wild horse in the world—a bronc that, well broke, would be the finest saddle horse imaginable.

All Jess had to do was break him.

And so he'd begun. He'd taken a deep breath, dug in his heels and hung on, doing his best.

And just when he'd felt as if he was beginning to get a sense of the horse's rhythm, fate had tossed him a beautiful crystal ornament, saying, "Here, catch. Hold on to this, too."

And "this" was Alison.

Alison. The most beautiful person ever to touch his life. The sweetest, the kindest, the strongest.

And he knew he could break her if he wasn't careful. What had happened between them last night was fragile and tentative. She'd told him that she loved him. But for Jess sex didn't necessarily mean love—except with Ali. He'd been almost afraid to hope.

Then she had peeked into the room, had stood looking down at him. And coward that he was, he hadn't admitted that he'd seen her.

But the look on her face had given him faith.

When she'd come back inside after feeding the cattle, he'd thought she might come upstairs. But Dottie had appeared instead, full of news about the cattle and more news about the holiday preparations going on in the kitchen. It hadn't taken him long to realize that Alison had plenty to do, that even if she wanted to, it would be unlikely that she would be able to come to him.

Finally he could resist no longer. He was drawn from his bedroom lair by the tempting smells and the soft sounds of shared laughter emanating from the kitchen. But mostly he was drawn by a need to see Alison again, to test her feelings. And his own.

Her eyes and her smile told him all he needed to know. And if they hadn't, the way she had touched her lips to the rim of his coffee cup and silently invited him to do the same would have.

It had been a promise. And he had spent the day basking in the sense of expectation, the warmth, the caring.

And as the day went on, she'd wrapped them in it—all of them, himself and the girls—drawing them into the spirit of sharing and thanksgiving that she had grown up knowing.

And now he sat at the table, set with white linen and damask napkins, laden with holiday fare made by Alison and each of the girls. He looked down the table, past the three bowed heads of his nieces, and met Alison's smiling eyes.

"Do you want to say grace, Jess?" she asked.

His throat felt tight, as if half the turkey were lodged there. He wanted to. He couldn't. "Will you?"

Alison bent her head. "Bless us, O Lord, and these thy gifts which we are about to receive through your bounty."

She lifted her eyes for a moment, letting them linger briefly on the girls before they connected once more with Jess's. "And thank you especially for giving us each other," she went on. "Help us keep on giving to each other. Please give us the courage to be what you would have us be. Amen."

THE GIRLS, after considerable urging, straggled upstairs to bed, first Sue, then Dottie and finally, half an hour ago, Patsy.

No one had wanted to leave the cozy living room, the warm fire, the casual sporadic conversation that they'd enjoyed all day. And Alison had been glad because it was what she wanted, after all, to make them a family.

But she also wanted something else: she wanted time with Jess. Alone.

She'd thought he wanted it, too. But as soon as Patsy went up, he'd got to his feet hastily, stretched and yawned, then said, "Think I'll turn in, too."

Alison had stared at him, nonplussed, as he moved to bank the fire. Then she'd swallowed her hurt, put the dog out one last time, shut off the lights and followed him up.

By the time she got there, he was in his room with the door shut. She stared at it, felt her throat tighten, felt a faint ache begin to grow somewhere deep inside, and turned to go into the bath.

She took her time, soaked in the tub, told herself it didn't matter, that of course he was tired, that it didn't mean he didn't care. And finally, when the water had grown cold and she was shivering, she pulled the plug and stood up, reaching for the towel.

She remembered the time she had come back and surprised him, had caught him naked and unaware. Last night she had seen him naked again, and he had been very aware indeed.

She bit down on her lower lip, blinked hard and dried off briskly, swallowing hard against the rising sound of his name in her throat. She wanted him so badly. Worse tonight than the night before.

But she wouldn't go to him again.

She tugged her nightgown over her head and ran a comb through her hair, looking at herself in the mirror. It had been eighteen hours since she'd stood here, smiling at herself in possession of a giddy wonderful secret.

What secret did she hold now?

She flicked off the light and opened the door. Everything was dark. Quiet.

Alison eased her way carefully along the hall, avoiding the even darker blob that was Kitten's sleeping bulk. She hesitated a moment outside the girls' door, then slipped in. They were sound asleep, Dottie with the current issue of *Western Horseman* sticking out from under her pillow, Sue with

"Alison" and "Jess" tucked in neatly next to her. They were kissing, the way Sue had shown Jess that they could.

Alison shut her eyes, heard a sound, turned.

Jess stood in the doorway.

He didn't have his crutches and he was leaning against the doorjamb. He looked at her, his expression unreadable. Then slowly he limped in, came to stand beside her, looked down at the girls asleep in their beds.

She heard him swallow and felt hard, callused fingers touch hers. "Thank you," he whispered. "From all of us."

Alison heard the ragged edge to his voice and smiled. She turned to look up at him. "Anytime," she told him. "All the time."

His hands slid up her arms, pulling her close, drew her with him out of the room, into the hallway. And Alison went with him, unresisting.

"Please," he murmured against her hair. "Come to me."

And Alison framed his face in her hands, touched her mouth to his lips and breathed her deepest prayer of thanksgiving as she whispered, "Oh, yes."

Chapter Twelve

Their loving was silent yet passionate, hungry yet tender. The perfect ending to a perfect day.

And afterward, when Alison lay snuggled in Jess's arms, her head on his chest, one hand trailing, stroking across his thigh, she turned her head, kissed him lightly just above the breast bone and said so.

"I've had some wonderful Thanksgivings in my life," she told him. "But this one is the best by far."

She felt his hand caress her cheek, felt his breath tease her hair. "It's my best, too," he said after a moment. His voice sounded slightly hoarse.

"I love it every year. I love the sense of family, the sense of continuity, of wholeness," Alison went on. "I remember feeling that way when I was really small. No matter where we were—Mexico, Lebanon, Spain—my parents took the time to celebrate, to share. It was different every year. And yet—" she smiled "—somehow it was always the same."

"It was always the same for me, too," Jess muttered after a moment. He sounded tense, almost angry.

Alison lifted her head and looked into his eyes. "Tell me," she said softly.

He shook his head. "It doesn't matter now."

She rested her chin on his chest, reached up her hand and threaded it through his hair. "You matter, Jess."

He pressed his lips together, looked at her from beneath hooded lids. The lines of his face seemed harsh and cold in the moonlight. She could feel the tension in him, as if an internal battle was being waged.

Finally he sat up, lifting her away, pulling up his knees, wincing a bit, then wrapping his arms around them. "You want to know what Thanksgiving was like for me? Besides beans in a can since I've grown up?" he asked harshly.

Alison nodded. "Yes." The word was barely more than a breath.

"It was my mother savin' up everything she could out of the rent money, tryin' to get a little bit ahead, hoping like hell my old man might send a bit so she could put on a little extra. And then her cookin' whatever she could get. Sometimes a turkey or a chicken or, once, a piece of venison a neighbor gave us. An' then we'd wait, hopin' that my father would come. He'd always promise he'd be there." Jess swallowed and rubbed his hand across his face.

"I could hardly wait. I'd run down the road to see if I could see him comin'. And I used to stand there, watching, waiting. Expecting him, you know? Counting on him." His voice was ragged. "And then finally I'd have to go home alone. Ma and Lizzie'd be standing on the porch, waitin' too, lookin' hopeful, and then kind of sad, and my mother'd shake her head, but she wouldn't say anything. She never said anything."

The words seemed dragged out of him, his voice ragged, his fingers clenching into fists against his knees, then unclenching, hanging limply. He rested his head on his knees.

Alison touched Jess's calf, rubbed her hand against the hair-roughened skin, kneaded the tight muscles.

Slowly he lifted his head. He didn't look at her, but stared out across the room toward the moonlit window. But Alison knew he wasn't seeing the gently falling snow.

She pressed her head against his knee, slipped her arms around him, holding him, feeling the shudder that ran through him.

In her mind's eye she could see what Jess had seen, the hopeful faces, the dawning realization, the resignation.

"I don't ever want to do that to anyone," he said, his voice shaking with emotion.

"I know." Alison soothed him, stroked him, kissed him. "You won't. I have great faith in you, Jess. I love you."

His head came up and he looked at her. She reached out and touched his cheek. He caught her hand in his and held it against his face, pressed his lips into her palm.

"I love you," she whispered again and showed him what she meant.

For a moment he held back, resisting, fighting her and himself. And then his control broke.

"I need—" he muttered.

And Alison met those needs, loving him and relishing the love she received from him, the eager hunger of his kisses, the fine tremor of his fingers as they stroked her heated flesh, the hard thrust of his body as it melted into hers.

And in the still, silent aftermath of their loving, with Jess asleep in her arms, Alison said one final grateful prayer for the day—and for the man—and went to sleep with a smile on her face.

SHE AWOKE with a start, realizing where she still lay, at the same time she realized she was alone in the bed. She sat up, looking around in the darkness, picked out movement, heard the soft sounds of clothes rustling.

"Jess?"

"Shh. Go back to sleep."

"But it's—" she glanced at the luminous dial of the clock "—past five. Brian will be coming. And Dottie—"

"I'll do it."

"Your knee—"

"—is a lot better. I can't lie in bed forever. There's work needs to be done."

"But—"

"No buts, Alison. I'm not stayin' in bed."

He finished buttoning his shirt, shoved it into his jeans and crossed the room to drop a quick kiss on her forehead. "Much as I wish I could," he said with a wry grin, then turned toward the door.

Alison scrambled out of bed. "I'm coming with you."

"But—"

She smiled and shook her head. "No buts, Jess, just like you said."

It was the only way she could keep an eye on him. And it didn't take Alison long to realize that he really should have stayed in bed.

She watched him limping as he helped Brian load bales into the wagon and bit her tongue on what she would have liked to say to him. She knew better than to chastise him in front of Brian and Dottie. But, damn the man, that leg needed more rest.

She was happy to note that even Jess seemed to recognize the problem by the time they had finished with the cattle and were heading home. It wasn't nearly as difficult as she had imagined, to extract a promise from him that for the rest of the day, while she and Patsy went into town to shop for a dress, he would stay in the house.

"Off your leg," she added for good measure when he quite readily agreed. "You can read to Sue or play checkers with Dottie."

"Or we can read the horse book," Dottie said eagerly. Dottie had recently discovered Nathan's cache of stud books, and she spent hours poring over them, deciding which horses she most wished she owned and consulting Jess whenever she couldn't make up her mind.

Alison smiled. "You do that," she said. "And we'll see you by suppertime. We'll bring a pizza from town."

Patsy scarcely said a word all the way in to town. But her reticence didn't mean she wasn't interested, Alison was beginning to realize. A quiet demeanor and a careful lack of enthusiasm were Patsy's way of defending herself.

Alison didn't know, but she suspected that Patsy, like her uncle, had seen her fair share of disappointments. Alison wanted to teach them both to hope.

Bluff Springs had three dress shops, one in the old downtown area and two in a small strip mall west of town. They tried them all without finding anything that Patsy or Alison thought suited her.

"I think you should make one," Alison said and she whisked Patsy off to look at fabric and patterns.

Here they were luckier. They found a pattern with a fitted bodice and a high waist that would complement Patsy's developing figure, and a full skirt that would swirl through the dance. They also found a deep green velvet and a sparkling, iridescent matching taffeta.

"Yes," Alison said, holding the fabric up next to Patsy's face. "Oh, yes."

Patsy looked panic stricken. "I've never sewn velvet," she whispered. "Or taffeta."

"Don't you want to?"

Patsy hesitated, then bobbed her head, her dark brown eyes sparkling. "Yes. But—"

Alison smiled. "No buts. Your uncle and I agreed. It's a house rule."

"It—it's very expensive." Patsy made one last protest.

"And worth every penny," Alison told her as they carried both bolts to the cashier. "Out of the remnants you can make Sue's doll a Christmas dress."

Alison found a pattern for a girl's Western shirt in Dottie's size. "I hope Grandma's old treadle survives all this sewing."

Patsy nodded. "Me, too."

The saleslady measured out the velvet, then turned a smile and inquisitive eyes on Patsy.

"You're Jess Cooper's niece, aren't you? I'm Betty Wells. My daughter, Carrie, is going to the dance, too. Do you sew well?" she asked Alison.

"Patsy's the seamstress. I'm going to be moral support."

Betty Wells gave Patsy a smile. "Good for you." She put the fabric and sewing notions into a bag. "I don't suppose you'd be interested in being moral support at the dance, too, would you?" She looked hopefully at Alison.

Alison turned to Patsy. "What do you think?"

"Would you want to?" Patsy asked, and Alison heard that familiar studied indifference in her tone.

"Very much," she said firmly. She gave Betty Wells a smile. "We'll be there."

"A DANCE?" Jess stopped dead in the middle of the snow-covered pasture and looked at her, horrified. "You said we'd go to a high school dance? Cripes, I never went to a high school dance when I was in high school!"

"You don't have to dance," Alison said soothingly, laying a hand on his arm as they walked. They were headed toward a small stand of spruce to cut the perfect Christmas tree.

The trees here were all the right size and close enough to the road that they wouldn't have to carry their tree miles on foot.

Thank heavens, thought Alison, since Jess, even five days after Thanksgiving, was still limping.

"We've only got to chaperon. Stand on the sidelines and drink punch and smile," Alison said.

Jess made a doubtful snorting sound and trudged on.

"I suppose you'd rather stay home and play checkers with Dottie?"

"I'd rather stay home," he said, slanting her a grin. "But I can think of a few other things than checkers I'd rather be doing."

Alison tilted her head. "Oh? Polishing the silver maybe? Reading the stud books?"

"Keep trying," Jess said. "I reckon you'll come up with it." His fingers squeezed hers gently. Alison squeezed back.

The girls far outdistanced them, bouncing on ahead, nibbling candy bars Alison had brought and, between bites, pelting each other with snowballs. Even Patsy was showing enthusiasm today, as she had been, more and more, since they'd brought home the pattern and the fabric and begun work on her dress.

"I found one!" Dottie yelled at once, pointing at a spruce twice as tall as she was.

"Me, too!" Sue hollered, hugging a little lopsided one to her chest.

"Or maybe this?" Now Dottie had found another. Then Patsy did.

Jess leaned against a fence post and pulled Alison back into his arms, his breath lifting the strands of hair by her ear, making her quiver.

"Do you think they'll ever decide?" Alison asked.

He nibbled her ear. "I don't much care if they do or not."

Neither did Alison. She watched the girls bob and skitter among the trees with amused indulgence, content to snuggle in Jess's arms. To someone who had always bought her trees off lots on corners in New York or Paris or wherever, they all looked wonderful.

"Let Uncle Jess decide," Patsy said finally, and her sisters agreed.

"Me? What do I know?"

"You know best," Sue said simply.

And Jess just looked at her, taken aback.

"Come on, Uncle Jess," Dottie urged. "Pick one."

"It doesn't matter which we choose really," Sue said with cheerful matter-of-factness. "We can use the other one next year."

Next year.

It was so casual. So confident. And so welcome that Alison wanted to rush over and hug the little girl.

She didn't, because she knew that Sue wouldn't understand why her offhand acceptance meant so much.

Next year.

Alison looked at Jess. He was looking at her. There was something infinitely vulnerable in his gaze.

Then slowly he nodded, took the saw Patsy handed him and made the cut.

They all took turns towing the tree down the hill and across the pasture. First the girls, then Alison and Jess.

Dusk was falling as they went, turning the sky a purplish red in the west, fading almost to indigo in the east. Just above the horizon Alison saw the evening star. And below it the trees stood in dark ragged silhouettes against the pink snow. The girls' parkas, lime and neon orange and turquoise, were bright splashes of color as they hurried through the twilight. They were laughing, still pelting each other with snowballs, ducking each other in drifts.

Alison smiled, then smiled more broadly as Jess's free hand came and took hold of hers.

"Want some help?" she offered. He'd been pulling the tree for quite a ways.

He smiled. "A little sustenance would be nice. Some instant energy."

"I'm all out of candy bars."

"Then I guess I'll have to settle for a kiss, won't I?"

And Alison slipped her arms around his waist and lifted her mouth to meet his. "I guess you will."

IF THE STARLIT mountainside was a natural fairy-tale setting, the Bluff Springs High School gymnasium, decked out for the Snow Ball celebration, was a man-made one. Shimmering, glossy white and foil paper snowflakes hung from invisible threads, catching and reflecting the arcing strobe lights. An old-fashioned sleigh, heaped with gaily wrapped presents, stood at one end, and a lavishly decorated Christmas tree, lit with hundreds of twinkling colored lights, graced the other.

"I'm nervous," Patsy confided.

"Don't be," Alison said as they stood waiting while Luke deposited their coats in the foyer of the gym. "You're one of the loveliest ladies here."

She lifted Patsy's hair and spread it against her shoulders so that it lay in a glossy dark cloud against the deep green velvet.

"You really think it looks all right?" Patsy was still worried. "Not...homemade?"

"Only if Christian Dior whipped it up on his sewing machine."

Patsy giggled, then turned. "What do you think, Uncle Jess?"

"That if I could dance, I'd be in line to ask you," he said, his voice gruff.

Patsy looked astonished. Impulsively she put her arms around him and hugged him hard. "I love you, but you're nuts," she said.

Jess blinked, then rubbed a hand between his starched white collar and his neck, then grimaced. "Probably. Otherwise I'd be home and playing checkers tonight."

Luke appeared then, looking almost as uncomfortable as Jess, in his rented tux and pleated white shirt. He gave Patsy a shy smile. "Ready?"

Patsy flicked a quick glance at her uncle, then at Alison. Both of them smiled at her. She nodded and held out her hand to Luke. He took her into the dance.

Alison looked at Jess. He was watching Patsy, his face taut, his expression unreadable. She touched his sleeve. "Jess?"

"Hmm?" Then he gave his head a little shake, held out his arm and slipped her fingers through it. "Oh, yeah. Right."

At a small-town high school dance, if you didn't know everyone at the start of the evening, Alison discovered that you knew most of them by the end. Betty Wells introduced her to several teachers and parents. And those she didn't meet seemed to come by as she and Jess sipped punch and watched Patsy swirl in Luke's arms.

The first was a teacher of Dottie's, who was also the parent of one of the high school boys. She cornered Jess right after the first dance, squeezing his arm and smiling. "I'm Dottie's English teacher, Arletta Sprague. You've got a bright one in that girl, Mr. Cooper."

"Thank you," Jess said politely.

"I mean it. I thought from the first she was quick. Always raising her hand, always on top of things. But we just got her test scores back and, my goodness, they were incredible."

"She does like to read," Alison agreed.

"And she's lucky to have you to encourage her," Arletta Sprague went on. "But she'll need a lot more before long. She can go places, that girl."

"She's been places," Jess muttered into his punch.

Arletta looked momentarily blank, then seemed to catch his meaning.

"Well, yes," she said, then added brightly, "and that even makes it more amazing, what she's able to do. Dottie has amazing potential. I'm counting on you to encourage her." She gave Jess's arm another squeeze and hurried off to refill her punch glass.

Jess looked at Alison over the rim of his glass. "I thought all she read was stud books. Is she that good?"

Alison smiled. "She does have a lot of potential."

"Well, look who's here!" a voice boomed behind them.

Alison looked around to see Frank Kirby. She hadn't seen him since the day he'd read them the will. He beamed at them and cuffed Jess on the arm. "Fancy meeting you here."

"Yeah, how about that?"

Frank winked. "So Nathan was right after all. I thought about calling you the other day. Fellow rang me from Denver, looking for a ranch to buy. But from what I hear, you two aren't selling." He smiled, cocked his head and studied them both for a moment, then nodded approvingly. "Nathan would be pleased."

Jess lifted his brows. Alison smiled. "Yes," she said softly. "I think he would."

A sudden swell of music almost drowned out her words.

"Not dancing?" Frank asked.

"Not me." Jess nodded at his knee.

"Ah." Kirby nodded, then looked at Jess. "But would you object if I. . ." He smiled and held out his hand to Alison.

Alison looked at Jess. He shrugged. "Go ahead."

Frank Kirby was a good dancer. He didn't have to look at his feet and count his steps as he twirled Alison around the room. He could even talk while he did it. Alison talked, too, and smiled, but always she kept her eye on Jess.

One woman after another seemed to appear at his side, talk for a few moments, brush against him, lay a hand on his arm, smile, then move on.

Alison liked the part where they moved away.

She was glad when the dance was over, when Frank Kirby took her back to Jess's side. He was talking to a tall willowy vision in a shiny purple dress and matching turban. She had her hand on Jess's arm.

"This is Alison Richards, my ranching partner," Jess introduced them offhandedly. "Diana Lee, Patsy's home ec teacher."

"How nice," Alison smiled tightly, remembering all those canned "yummies" in the cellar. "Did you make your dress?"

It was pretty clear Christian Dior hadn't, she thought uncharitably, then felt immediately ashamed of herself when Diana smiled.

"Yes. But Jess says Patsy did, too, and it can't hold a candle to hers. She has such a wonderful sense of color and design, as well. I've been encouraging her to start thinking about fashion college after graduation. It's never too early to start planning, is it?"

"Never," Alison said.

"There are some excellent ones in New York. I had a friend who went to one. She worked in Paris for a while, and now she's in Milan." Diana shook her head. "I wish I'd had an opportunity like that. I'd love to travel, see the world."

"You should," Alison said. "You'd love it. Paris, Milan, New York. Go for it." *Go far. Fast. And get your hands off Jess.*

"I will," Diana said earnestly. "I don't want to be stuck in a backwater like this forever." She turned determined blue eyes on Jess. "And you make sure Patsy isn't, either."

The music began again and one of the science teachers appeared at Diana's elbow. "May I?" he asked her.

She smiled and held out her arms to him and they floated away.

Alison looked at Jess. His eyes were hooded, his expression brooding.

The music was slow, slightly bluesy, moodily romantic. The lights began to dim, casting the room in a soft silvery glow.

Alison lifted the punch glass from Jess's hands and set it on the table. Then she slipped into his arms, putting one hand in his and the other on his shoulder, then rested her cheek against his shoulder.

"I don't—"

"You don't have to dance," she promised him. "Just sway a little."

He swayed. His grip on her hand was hard and warm, so were the fingers splayed against the back of her red wool dress. He bent his head, and his forehead rested against the top of her head. She moved her head a little, felt the slide of his smooth-shaven jaw against her hair. Then she drew a breath and held it, savoring the faint hint of leather and pine, the indefinable essence that was Jess. She snuggled closer. Jess's grip tightened.

Yes, Alison thought, her body moving to the music. *Hold me. Love me. Now and for the rest of our lives—just like this.*

The music wrapped them in their own little world until suddenly she felt Jess jerk. He lifted his head, and Alison pulled back, too, looking around.

There was a man standing just behind Jess's left shoulder, a hopeful smile on his face.

"It's a cut-in dance," he apologized. "I'm Tom Quinn, Patsy's gym teacher. May I?"

Jess hesitated, then stepped back. His hands fell away. "Be my guest."

Before Alison could say a word, Tom Quinn stepped forward and took her in his arms and danced her away.

She did her best to smile at Tom Quinn, did her best to listen to him tell her how he'd just come to Bluff Springs, too, how he'd taught in Denver for five years and was looking for a temporary change. He was going back, he said. He wanted to travel, see more of the world.

Alison thought of asking him if he'd thought of dating Diana Lee. But by then he'd gone on to talk about what a good volleyball player Patsy was, how hard she tried even though she was rather short for the game.

"Short people have to try harder," he said, with a self-deprecating grin, and Alison realized for the first time that he wasn't quite as tall as she was.

"There's nothing wrong with being short," she told him. Gary had barely looked her in the eye, either.

Tom smiled. "I'm glad to hear you say that." Then, "Are you serious about Jess Cooper?"

Alison pulled back, blinking at the sudden question.

Tom shrugged. "Why beat around the bush? I'm attracted. I admit it. I want to know what my chances are."

Alison shook her head, then smiled to take the sting out of her words as she said quite frankly, "Not good."

THEY GOT HOME a little before midnight. Luke had taken Patsy out with some of the kids to get a pizza. He promised they'd be home within the hour.

"You'd better be," Jess had told him with such authority that Alison had giggled.

She'd snuggled against him in the truck all the way home, resting her head on his shoulder and slipping her shoes off to tuck her cold feet up under her coat. In her head she could still hear the music, could still feel Jess's arms around her.

They had "swayed" together once more, right at the end. She had taken his punch cup away again and pulled him onto the floor, determined that this time no one should come between them.

But this was a "no cuts" dance, and they had it all to themselves.

Jess had held her, lightly, carefully and yet securely. He hadn't said a word.

He scarcely spoke all the way home. He seemed withdrawn, distracted.

Alison knew how to reach him, though, and she would…later. For the moment she was happy just to be with him, to touch him, to smile at him.

She went upstairs to check on the girls as soon as she got home. Jess did a last check of the barn.

He was out there a long time. Luke brought Patsy home, came in for a few minutes and left again. Still Jess didn't come.

Patsy went to bed, smiling and humming snatches of dance tunes. Alison got undressed and put on her nightgown. Then, wrapping her robe around her, she padded softly into Jess's room and looked out the window toward the barn.

The night was clear and cold, a full moon spilling bright silver light across the snow-covered yard. The light went off in the barn at last. The door opened.

Jess came out. Stopped. Stood looking up at the house.

Alison waited, watching him. For the longest time he didn't move, just stood still looking up toward the house. Then he did, walking slowly, still with the trace of a limp.

She heard him come in, heard his footsteps on the stairs. She went out into the hall to meet him. She touched the fine wool of his suit jacket, felt the tension in his hard-muscled arm.

"I love you," she said, brushing a kiss along his jaw.

She felt a muscle twitch beneath her lips. Jess shut his eyes, bowed his head. She tugged his hand.

He loved her that night with something akin to desperation, as if he needed all that she could give . . . and more.

Alison sensed it from the start. She felt it in the tremor of his hands as he stripped off her nightgown, felt it in the harshness of his breath against her cheek, in the frantic need with which he joined his body to hers.

She cherished it—cherished him—and met him with an equal need of her own.

THE NEXT MORNING he was up and gone to load the wagon before Alison was even awake. She dressed hurriedly, woke the girls, then went after him.

"You don't want to overdo it," Alison told him. "What will Charley say?"

"He'll say I'm fine," Jess told her gruffly. "Stop worrying. It's startin' to snow. Go on back to the house."

Alison went. She walked slowly, taking her time, enjoying the gently falling snow, the delicate frosting of the house and trees, the beauty that she seldom took time to appreciate in the city.

Jess would say that snow was cursed hard to work in, that it mucked up the roads and hid the cattle's feed. But she knew he relished it, too.

She'd seen him often enough, sitting astride Dodger, just staring off at the mountains or tipping his head back and, when he thought no one was looking, catching snowflakes on his tongue.

Jess.

Tough. Tender. Strong. Gentle.

"Jess," she said softly as she climbed, the steps, "whom I love."

Dottie and Patsy appeared in the doorway in front of her. "Doesn't he want help?"

Alison shook her head. "He says not."

"We could all go," Sue said. She held Kitten in her arms and was still wearing her fuzzy cat pajamas.

Alison smiled, picked her up and gave her a hug. "How about if we make him a good breakfast instead?"

The girls all nodded. The tractor started up and rumbled out from behind the barn toward the lane. Alison, still holding Sue, turned and waved.

Jess looked at them, all clustered there on the porch, hesitated a moment, then waved back.

IT WAS STILL SNOWING late that evening. The Rocking R had become a winter wonderland. Of course work would be harder, of course they might be snowed in, of course there was a price to pay for the beauty of it. Alison was willing to ante up.

She curled in the corner of the couch, the afghan wrapped around her, Kitten and Scout both sprawled on the braid rug in front of the fire.

It was quiet now, though an hour ago the living room had rung with the shouts of Sue and Dottie who got overexcited whenever they played a game of Pit. Jess could quell their noise with a look, but Jess had been out at the barn. She and Patsy and the younger girls had been on their own since supper.

Now the girls were in bed, the fire was burning down, and the room was lit only by the light of the fire.

When she'd been little, Pops had called it "sparking time," and Alison hadn't known what he meant until Doug had explained.

"Courting," he'd told her. "You know—" he'd looked faintly embarrassed as only a twelve-year-old could "—mushy stuff between guys and girls."

Alison thought it was time for a bit of that tonight. Or even a little more than a bit.

"The *M* word, you mean," she said aloud to herself. "Marriage. Or the *P* word. A proposal."

It seemed possible. They loved each other. There was no question about that. And Jess had been looking a little nervous all day, skittish almost. He'd kept his distance most of the day, but she'd caught him looking at her with that hungry, desperate look in his eyes.

Alison smiled. She heard the door open. Heard it close. Heard Jess get a drink of water. Shut off the kitchen light.

And then he was standing in the doorway, looking down at her. She smiled again, opened her arms, beckoning him.

He flexed his shoulders, cleared his throat, ran his fingers through his hair. "Alison."

She sat up, let the afghan fall away. "Come here. You must be freezing. I'll warm you up." Her grin was impish.

He didn't smile.

She did.

It was going to be a proposal. She could feel it.

But it wouldn't be easy. Not for Jess.

She patted the couch. "Come and sit, Jess."

He came in. He didn't sit. He stuffed his hands into the pockets of his jeans, rocked back and forth on the soles of his feet. "We need to talk, Alison," he said finally.

She nodded, waiting, suppressing her eagerness to say it for him, to give him her answer: "Yes, oh, yes!"

"I think we ought to sell the ranch."

Chapter Thirteen

"Sell the ranch?"

"You heard what Frank said last night. He's got a guy who's interested. He wants what we've got..."

Jess was talking quickly, staring at the fire, not even looking at her. His forearms rested on his thighs, his fingers knotting together. He shot her a swift sideways glance. "It only makes sense."

Alison gaped at him. Her mind reeled.

Sell the ranch? What kind of a proposal was that?

She tried to marshal her thoughts, create some sort of coherence out of the chaos she'd just stumbled into.

"What if...*I* want what we've got?" she asked him at last.

She was proud of herself. Her voice didn't quaver, it didn't rise shrilly at the end of the sentence. She sounded composed, not frantic, which was how she felt.

"You don't," Jess said abruptly. He got to his feet, wincing as weight came down on his knee. He began pacing the room. "I mean, you might think you do, but it won't last." He looked at her as if beseeching her to agree with him, then began pacing again.

"What do you mean it won't last?" There was perhaps a hint of shrillness now.

"You're an intelligent woman, Alison. You've got a college education. A degree!"

"Two of them," Alison said quietly. She didn't know what difference that made.

"Yeah, *two* of them. You don't need a degree to feed a bunch of cattle, to mend a blinkin' fence! It might be fun for a while, but it's gonna get old fast. And startin' up some two-bit library isn't gonna make any difference. You'll be miserable. You'll hate it. Like you said to Diana last night."

"I said to Diana?" She stared at him.

"New York, Milan, Paris. All those places you've been! You'll miss 'em. You won't want to be stuck here." He stopped in front of the fireplace and turned to face her.

Alison took a careful breath. She strangled the afghan with agitated fingers and tried to articulate what she was hearing. "Let me get this straight. You want to sell the ranch to make me happy?"

"Yeah. Besides, you'll want to get married, have a family."

"Yes." She agreed with that. She looked at him with her heart in her eyes.

"Well, then—" He spread his hands.

"Well, then, what? I'm supposed to go to Paris and marry someone? Who? I love you! You know that, Jess."

He grimaced. "You could do a lot better, a hell of a lot better, than me. That guy you were dancin' with last night, the blond guy—?"

"Tom?" She couldn't even remember his last name.

"Yeah, Tom. Frank says he's just takin' a little break, then he's gonna head back to the bright lights. You could go, too, and—"

"Jess! I danced with the man. He didn't ask me to marry him!"

"You know what I mean," he said stubbornly.

She shook her head. "I don't. I don't want him. I don't want anyone but you. I think you're losing your mind."

"Finding it, more like," Jess muttered. He shoved his hand through his hair. "We've got to sell."

"I thought the ranch was your dream, Jess," she said after a moment.

"Dreams aren't that important."

Alison felt as if he'd punched her in the stomach. She stared at him, saw the fierceness in his face, then anguish in his eyes, and knew he didn't believe what he was saying. "Don't give me that!"

"It's true."

"It isn't! You don't want to try. You want to give up."

"I don't want to, damn it! I've got to!" He was glaring at her now. Cords stood out on his neck.

"Besides trying to do the best for me," Alison said with as much irony as she could muster, "why?"

"Because—because of the girls."

"They love it here!"

"Maybe. But they need better than growin' up out on some backwoods ranch! You heard what Dottie's teacher said last night. You heard Diana talkin' about Patsy's potential, about how she ought to go to New York. You reckon either of 'em are gonna realize any of that potential here? Hell, no, they're not! They need schools where they can learn what the rest of the world is like. They need chances, opportunities! We sell the ranch, and I can send 'em to boarding school."

"Boarding school?" Alison stared at him, aghast.

His jaw thrust out. "What's the matter with that? They'd get the education they need there. They'd have opportunities!"

"They wouldn't have a family!"

"Lucky them," Jess muttered in a voice so low she almost couldn't hear. His words made her cold.

She wrapped her arms against her chest as if doing so might warm her, but it didn't. The cold wasn't outside, but within.

"And for 'educational opportunities' you'd sell the Rocking R?"

"Why not? I don't need this place." He kicked at the rug beneath his toe. "I can go back and work for somebody else. It's all I ever expected, anyway." He bent his head, staring at the floor.

"But is it what you want?" she insisted.

His eyes came up to sear her. "Damn it, Alison, it doesn't matter what I want! It's what *they* need!"

She leapt to her feet and slammed her hands on her hips. "What they need, Jess, is an uncle who will stand by them, who will be there for them, who will love them!"

His jaw clenched, his face became a mask. He looked right past her.

"I want us to sell the ranch, Alison," he repeated. The words were flat and hard and cold.

"You won't discuss it? You won't try?"

"I won't let them get settled in, expecting things, counting on things..." His voice trailed off. "It wouldn't be fair."

"And this is fair?" Alison's voice shook.

"Life isn't fair!"

"No," she said quietly. "It's not. But that's no excuse for giving up. Let's be honest, Jess. You can rant about my supposed inability to adjust and the girls' need for educational opportunities, and you can rave on and on about how I need to be protected from myself and they need to be protected from the inadequacies of a rural education. But when it comes right down to it, Jess, it isn't us you're protecting at all, is it? It's you."

THE TRUTH HURT.

And there was no doubt about it: Alison had cut right to the heart of the truth. He shouldn't have been surprised.

He knew she wasn't going to buy his altruism argument. Not that there wasn't an element of truth to it.

But, damn it, he thought, as he carried the last of his gear back down to the bunkhouse, a little bit of hurt now, a little bit of anger, was better than years of disappointments and a lifetime of frustrated hope.

And he knew, if he didn't walk away now, that was what the future would bring.

He slung all his clothes in a heap on the table. He'd put them away in the morning. Tonight domesticity was beyond him. If it hadn't been snowing so hard he could barely see his hand in front of his face, he'd take Dodger out and ride.

He needed space. Wide open space. No walls. No fences. No commitments. No demands.

He'd felt the pressure building for weeks. He'd known what was happening, sensed himself being drawn into the web of family life that Alison and the girls represented. And after an initial instinctive resistance, he hadn't fought it.

Not the way he should have.

He should have known better. But he'd been lulled by smiles and encouragement, by wide blue eyes and a gentle touch. And so he'd ignored his better judgment. He'd let down his armor and had allowed himself to simply take it a day at a time. And damn it all, because it seemed to be working, he'd dared to begin to believe.

Until today.

It was funny the way the mind worked, how it stored up images a guy thought he'd forgotten—*hoped* he'd forgotten—and then, out of the blue—they'd come back to haunt him.

He'd driven the tractor around the corner of the barn, half thinking about how much work there was to be done and half thinking about how he was going to see that Dottie got challenged and Patsy eventually made it to New York, wondering whether Alison was as happy as she said she was, and he'd looked up to see them all standing there on the porch.

Only as he looked he hadn't seen Alison and his nieces smiling and waving anymore. Instead he saw his mother and Lizzie, standing and waiting, twin looks of hope and expectancy on their faces.

And then, when they saw him—and him alone—their expressions had changed.

Jess had never hated his father more than he had in those moments. He'd never felt so helpless.

Until now.

Now he could see a time when Alison and the girls would look at him with those same identical expressions. He could see the hope and eagerness in their eyes turn to disappointment, to disillusion—because he couldn't do it, couldn't give them what they had every right to.

For a few brief days Jess had thought it might work. He'd held slender hopes that he and Alison and the girls might really make a family.

Then, at the dance, his dream had begun to unravel. He'd begun to get an idea of what was expected, of what promises he might be asked for, of the dreams he might have to fulfill.

And the weight of being Les Cooper's son had begun to bear down on him. He'd fought it off, loving Alison last night with a desperation that he hoped would banish his fears. And afterward, lying in her arms, holding her in his, for the remainder of the night, he thought he'd succeeded.

But this morning as he'd come around the corner of the barn, he'd seen the truth, standing there on the porch, staring him in the face.

If he married her, if the girls stayed on, he would only have the chance to prove again what he'd proved as a child. He had no doubt that he'd fail them, too.

SHE WAS A FOOL.

A naive, blind, airy-fairy fool. Princesses in fairy stories had better sense than she did. Cows stuck in thickets had better sense than she did.

Alison sat on her bed in the darkness, wrapped her arms around her legs and pressed a hot tear-streaked face against her knees and felt so cold she thought she'd never be warm again.

She should, long ago, have heeded Jess's words.

"I'm not getting married. Ever." He'd told her that twelve years ago. He said it again on the way to Denver.

"I'm not having children ever." He'd been adamant about that, too.

But Alison had turned a deaf ear. She'd been arrogant enough to think she could change him, make him want what she wanted.

The more fool she.

But he had made love to her, she argued with herself. He had shown her a tenderness and a passion that proved how much he cared.

And yet he had turned away.

Why?

Because he was afraid. She'd flung the accusation at him more in anger than in certainty. She'd known it for weeks, had told herself over and over. And she'd thought she could talk him out of that fear.

Again and again she'd told him with words and actions that he didn't have to be afraid.

But she knew now that sometimes words and actions weren't enough—that sometimes even love wasn't enough. She had done everything she could. The choice wasn't hers.

"I HAVE two requests," Alison said to Jess's back.

He'd heard her come into the barn, had sneaked a glance to see who it was, and, finding out, had kept his back turned. He continued brushing down Dodger, getting snow clumps out of his mane. He waited until he heard her footsteps right behind him before he turned.

He hadn't seen her since last night when she'd rounded on him in a fury, nailing him with her fiery blue eyes, her chin out thrust, her cheeks an angry red. Now she looked pale, but composed, her hair pulled back, neat and anchored with a ribbon, her lips almost colorless.

Like a librarian, he thought. Proper and sedate.

She was wild when she had loved him, rosy and passionate. Who would ever believe—?

He shoved away the thought, clenching the brush with one hand, jamming the other into his pocket.

"What requests?" he asked warily.

"There's only a week left until Christmas. I want you not to do anything until after—not talk to Frank, not tell the girls."

"I—"

"You may think it's hypocritical," she went on without giving him a chance to speak. "I don't care. I'm not asking you to lie. Except," she added honestly, a faint grimace accompanying her words, "perhaps by omission. But if you say anything to Frank, he might say something to someone else. Word might get back to the girls. And if you tell them now, that will ruin it all. The girls are looking forward to

Christmas. Planning on it. *Counting on it.*'' She hit the words with obvious emphasis, echoing his own of the night before. ''They've had a hard time this year, a sad time, Jess. They're happy right now, and I don't want it spoiled.''

Her blue eyes were wide and guileless as she stared at him; her chin was determinedly stubborn.

''I don't want to hurt them, damn it. I don't want to spoil it for them, either,'' Jess said gruffly. ''Making their lives miserable isn't the point.''

Alison made a noise that sounded distinctly like a muffled snort.

Jess gritted his teeth. He yanked off his hat and shoved his fingers through his hair. ''The new semester starts the end of January,'' he said harshly. ''There'll be time enough to tell them after the holiday. All right?'' He glared at her.

She met his glare. Her own expression wasn't angry, just sad. ''Thank you.'' She turned on her heel and walked out of the barn.

HE THOUGHT he'd left in time, thought he'd got out by the skin of his teeth.

He'd believed that determination and distance would solve the problem, hoped that if he left the house, kept himself occupied with other things, he wouldn't miss them a bit. He'd had the girls less than two months, for heaven's sake, and Alison for less than three.

But he'd only had to spend a couple of nights alone in his bunk, staring around at the four bleak walls before his gaze would inevitably go to the window. And he would look up at the lights and warmth within the log house, knowing where he wanted to be.

He couldn't go, though.

Wouldn't.

It was more than his life was worth, trying to smile, to pretend that everything was fine.

So he stayed away. Heaven knew, he did have work.

The snow was thick on the ground now, making the feeding more difficult. He and Brian had tried using the tractor Monday and found it next to useless. They'd had to hitch up the old Belgians and use the sled.

Afternoons when Brian went home to help his father, Jess broke ice in the creeks and water holes so thirsty cattle could get a drink. In the evenings, he was bushed, but he had plenty to keep him busy, mucking out the barn, going over the books, mending harness.

And staring out the window up at the house.

Damn it! He shoved away from the window now and strode over to the table, forcing his gaze back to the broken hame strap in his hand. He lay it on the work table and punched the hole, did it carefully and deliberately, trying not to think about what Alison and the girls would be doing.

He'd hardly seen them in the last three days. Waved at them from the barn when they'd waved to him, talked to Dottie once after school when she'd come out to the pasture where he'd been breaking ice.

She'd looked at him curiously, and he'd wondered if she might ask him what was wrong, why he had moved out, but she didn't.

She'd told him about going down to see the horses with Davy Gonzales. She'd told him about a particularly pretty one, a sorrel with a white blaze and four white stockings that Davy's father, Mike, had let her ride.

Her eyes had shone when she'd talked.

He'd listened but he hadn't said much, and finally she'd stopped talking. He finished cutting the ice and he let her ride Dodger as they went together back toward the road. He let her take Dodger in and unsaddle him and brush him down, telling her he had work in the bunkhouse to do.

She'd smiled, but her smile hadn't reached her eyes, and when he turned to go, she'd called after him, "We miss you."

He missed them, too.

Right now the stereo would be playing, with Christmas music no doubt. He knew Alison had several tapes, and since Thanksgiving, they'd been on almost every night. And while they were listening to them, Alison would be baking or reading or making a Christmas gift. Patsy'd be sitting at the kitchen table doing her homework, chewing her pencil while she tried to puzzle out some algebraic equation. Dottie'd be sprawled on the floor, fists propping her chin as she pored over the stud books, dreaming.

And Sue?

Sue would be sitting on the rug in front of the fire, creating a world for her dolls—dreaming up adventures for "Alison and Jess."

Jess's mouth twisted at the thought. If Sue were running the world, she'd do a damn sight better than this.

He settled the rivet in the hole in the leather and let fly with the hammer—and hit his thumb.

"Geez!" He dropped the hammer, shook his hand, popped his thumb into his mouth.

There was a tiny tapping sound at the door.

He stopped dead, still sucking on his thumb, listening, not crediting what he'd heard.

Until it came again.

Tap. Tap, tap.

Alison. It had to be. But why? Jess took his thumb out of his mouth, gave it one more shake and went to answer the door.

"Uncle Jess?" It was Sue, looking up at him, her big brown eyes smiling at him.

He swallowed, pushed the door open wider, let her in. She wore jeans and her bright lime parka, and her dark brown hair was dusted with snow. She was lugging a small red trunk.

"What's this? Are you running away from home?"

"Course not." Sue dumped the trunk on the floor and proceeded to open it. "Alison" and "Jess" and the rest of their universe tumbled out on the floor. "We came to see you." She looked up at him with wide brown eyes. "We thought you might be lonely," she said. "You haven't been coming home."

"I—I've been busy."

"That's what Alison said." Sue sat down cross-legged and began sorting through the dolls and their accessories. "We've been busy, too," she told him, picking up the boy doll. "'Specially Jess."

"Oh, yeah? Feeding cattle, is he?" Jess asked. He should be bundling her up and sending her back to the house. He sat down on the bed and watched her.

"Oh, he always does that," Sue said casually. "He's busier now 'cause it's almost Christmas. He's makin' things special, you see."

Jess looked into her eyes. "Is that what Alison told you?" He'd kill her if she had.

Sue shook her head, the dark bob swinging back and forth. "She doesn't tell me 'bout Jess an' Alison. I know," she said with a child's faith, "because he is."

Jess digested that. "What's he making for Christmas?"

Sue smiled. "I can't tell you. It's a s'prise."

"What would you like him to make for Christmas?" He studied the dolls in her hands, tried to guess what they would need. "Doll furniture? A table? Chairs? A bed?" He supposed he could do that for her, and then she would have them, wherever she was, to remember him.

"I want a swing."

"What?" His head swiveled. He stared at her.

"Doll furniture's okay," Sue said. "But I got lots of nice cloth so they can have sleeping bags and picnics. I want a swing."

"For the dolls, you mean? For... Alison and Jess?"

"Nope. For me."

"But where would you put a swing?" How could she take a *swing*?

"In the yard, silly." And in case he had any doubt where she meant, she pointed back toward the house up the hill.

"A swing is awful big," Jess managed at last.

"Uh-huh. That's what I mean. I always get doll clothes from Patsy, an' Dottie always gives me a book. They give me things I can take when we move." She tilted her head and looked at him solemnly. "We've moved a lot, you see."

Jess saw—saw a child's hope, a child's faith. He shut his eyes.

"Alison said she moved a lot, too. But once, she had a swing. Not a real swing, but a board and two ropes that her grandfather put in an apple tree."

"I remember that tree," Jess said softly, the memory floating back unbidden. "It was a Greening."

"It was up behind the house," Sue went on. "An' once when she came in the spring, it had blossoms on it. An' she said it was the most beautiful thing she ever saw."

"It was," Jess murmured, remembering.

"But it's not there anymore."

"A few years back it got hit by lightning."

Sue nodded. "If I had a swing, she could swing on it. But it wouldn't have blossoms," she added sadly.

"Maybe you could . . . you could draw her some blossoms. Make her a picture. For Christmas."

Sue's face broke into a grin. "Will you help me?"

"Well, I—"

"An' will you help me write a letter to Santa?" She looked at him hopefully. "Mama always used to."

Another memory came winging back, smiting him, causing more pain than Sue could possible know.

Jess felt his throat tighten. He swallowed. "She used to help me, too," he said roughly. "Even when I told her it was stupid." His voice felt as raw as his emotions.

He shouldn't have said the words aloud, shouldn't have infected Sue with his own cynicism.

He needn't have worried.

She reached over and took his hand in hers. "It's not, Uncle Jess," she said in her clear child's voice. "Mama said it's never stupid to believe."

AND LIZZIE would know, Jess thought savagely hours later, pounding his fist on the bunk, glaring at the ceiling in the dark. Lizzie who'd had her life snuffed out on the brink of her dream.

"Damn you, Lizzie," he muttered raggedly, his throat aching, his eyes stinging. "Damn you for doing this to me."

For Sue's words had skewered him, stopped him right where he was, making him remember what he hadn't remembered in years.

He could see his sister now, as clearly as if she were right beside him, her impish ten-year-old face serious for once as she'd come to try to get him to write the letter to St. Nick.

"I don't want to," he'd told her, pushing her away, trying to brush her off.

But she'd just grabbed his arm and hauled him into the house. "Mama says you got to. She needs to know what you want."

"She knows what I want," Jess had said stubbornly, folding his arms across his chest.

Lizzie looked at him sympathetically. She knew what he meant: that he wanted his father to come home. He'd wanted it so desperately and for so long.

She'd put her arm around him. "She can't make him do it, Jess. And neither can you."

"But I want—I need—!" His voice had broken. He sniffled, swiping at shameful tears. It was worse at holidays, when hopes rose, when he told himself, "Maybe this time," and "Just this once."

He wiped his nose on his sleeve, straightened up, rubbed his eyes. "I could be a better dad than him, Lizzie," he'd said at last.

And Lizzie had looked at him with more than ten years' understanding in her deep brown eyes. She'd smiled then, a thin, sad smile. "I know."

Jess didn't remember what he'd written down on the letter to Santa. Lincoln Logs maybe. Or Matchbox cars. His mother had done her best. She always had.

Lizzie had written, "I want a Patsy Cline record and Dottie West's 'Here Comes My Baby.' And Johnny Cash's record 'Bitter Tears.'" Jess pressed his eyes with his fingers now, remembering how the words had looked in Lizzie's loopy, little-girl handwriting.

Then at the bottom she had written, "I want to be a country-western singer."

Her mother had smiled when she'd read it. She'd stood by the kitchen table and stroked a work-roughened hand down her daughter's long dark hair. "Santa can't bring you that, sweetheart," she'd said.

Lizzie had shrugged her irrepressible shrug. "That's okay," she'd said. "I believe in me." And then she'd looked across the table at Jess. "And I believe in you."

ALISON WAS DOING her best.

She was making cut-out cookies and marshmallow fudge, she was tying little red bows so the girls could hang them on the huge tree to fill in the empty spaces after all the ornaments and lights had been used. She was, when the girls were in school, making the Western shirt for Dottie and a funky shirt and jacket for Patsy. She was trying to be upbeat and cheerful and positive.

She was trying not to think about Jess.

She rarely saw him. The night he moved out of the house, he had, physically at least, moved out of her life. She might see him at a distance now and then. She might answer the phone and send one of the girls down to give him a message. But since the day she'd talked to him in the barn, she hadn't seen him face to face.

She'd thought she might when Sue had said she was going down to the bunkhouse. She'd half suspected that he might pick his niece up bodily and bring her home.

But Sue hadn't come right back. Jess hadn't dumped her on the doorstep and stalked away. He'd been perfectly pleasant and glad to see her, according to Sue.

Alison had been glad. But she'd noticed as well that the next day he virtually disappeared.

She'd seen him come back from feeding the cattle in the morning. But instead of retreating to the bunkhouse or heading back out to chop ice, he got in the truck and drove away.

He hadn't come home before she and the girls went to bed that night. Probably, Alison thought bitterly, to avoid a repeat of Sue's visit. The next day he'd done the same.

The day before Christmas, Sue had gone back down there in the afternoon. She'd come back an hour later.

"Was Jess there?" Alison asked casually.

Sue nodded. "He helped me write my letter to Santa."

Oh, dear. "I don't think— You know the North Pole is a very long way," Alison began, envisioning disappointment on Christmas morning. Damn Jess, anyway.

"He said he'd take care of it," Sue said confidently.

Alison hoped to heaven the little girl's confidence wasn't misplaced. But maybe Jess would be able to find in town whatever it was Sue had on her list. And maybe he'd bring it up so that Alison could slip it under the tree before Christmas morning.

Maybe, just for the memory, he could be persuaded to come.

But she wasn't going to ask the girls to invite him. If he didn't want to come, it would just hurt their feelings. And, she thought resignedly, if he refused her, she could always give the girls the excuse that she'd been giving them for the past week: a cowboy's work is never done.

She went down to the bunkhouse that evening after the girls were in bed. He wasn't home. She went back on Christmas Eve afternoon. He still wasn't there.

It occurred to her that he might have been invited out for the evening. It didn't seem likely. She couldn't imagine he'd do it. But she'd certainly been wrong before.

Clouds moved over, low and leaden as the afternoon waned. Inside Dottie built up the fire and turned on the lights. Alison and Patsy began supper preparations.

It started to snow.

HE SAW THE HOUSE like a beacon, the golden glow of its windows signaling to him the minute he came around the bend in the road. The truck slipped and skidded on the turn, and Jess urged it on as if it were some reluctant pony.

"Come on, come on. Don't die on me now."

The drive back from Durango had been murder. The snow had been falling there since early afternoon, and the storm came with him as he moved eastward again, getting heavier and thicker as the day wore on.

He could have stopped any of a dozen places. He had friends along the highway, acquaintances of Nathan's, plenty of people he knew.

But he kept going, driven as much as driving. He had to. He needed to.

At last he wrestled the truck into the yard, pulled up alongside the barn and got out. The snow whipped around him, blotting out the tire tracks, stinging his face. He yanked his hat down to shield it as best he could and moved to unload.

He worked as fast as he could, stowed everything. Then he ducked into the bunkhouse, washed his face and combed his hair, jammed his hat back on his head and made his way through the snow.

He could see them through the windows: Patsy moving across the kitchen with something in her hands, Dottie zipping past, then Sue. He moved closer, watching them. He saw the tree all lit and decorated for the first time. Saw the presents. Saw the stockings. Saw Alison.

And he stopped, couldn't go on.

He loved her so much he ached with it. Loved her so much that he was terrified of failing her.

"I believe in you," Lizzie had told him all those years ago. And she must have, for she'd left him the girls.

"I believe in you," Nathan had said and he'd left Jess half the ranch and a chance with his granddaughter.

"I love you," Alison had said to him time after time. And he'd been afraid.

Hell, he still was afraid.

He could turn around and walk away or he could open the door and go in.

Jess knew the choice was his.

ALISON DIDN'T HEAR him come in. She'd been hanging up a stocking that Kitten had knocked down, she'd heard Sue give a tiny shriek, she'd turned around.

And there he was.

Lean and rangy and every bit as beautiful as she remembered. And she was glad he came at the same time she felt the ache in her heart.

But in spite of her own pain, she was glad for the girls' sake that he'd bothered. It proved he had feelings. It meant that he cared.

He was holding his hat in his hands, crushing the brim, as he looked at her. His face was wind reddened. His hair was tousled. Snow melted on the hems of his jeans, dripping on his socks. He looked down, noticed, bent quickly and nervously to wipe it up.

"I'll do it," Patsy said, just as Alison said, "It doesn't matter," and Dottie said, "We were afraid you wouldn't come."

Jess straightened up, and the look he gave Alison was apologetic. "I didn't know if..." His voice trailed off.

She managed a smile. "We're glad you did."

"We get to open one present apiece tonight, Uncle Jess. But the rest have to wait until morning," Sue told him. "That's what Alison says."

Jess nodded. "Whatever Alison says." His voice sounded hoarse.

"Can we open 'em now, Alison?" Dottie asked her.

Alison looked at Jess. "We've already eaten. But if you're hungry, I can get you some dinner, and we can open them after."

"No. Let's do it now. Please." She heard an urgency in his tone that made her unaccountably angry. Did he want to get out of here that badly?

"Can I...can I give you mine tonight?" He looked from one girl to the next, his gaze finally resting on Alison.

She looked at him stonily. *So you don't have to come back tomorrow, you mean?* she asked him with her eyes. But she turned to the girls to get their response.

They nodded.

"Wait here," he commanded. He went back out on the porch, they heard him open the door again, heard movement, scraping sounds of chairs being moved, a quiet thud. The girls looked at Alison. She shrugged and shook her head.

Jess came back into the living room. "This is for Patsy," he said and he motioned them into the kitchen.

It was there under the bookcase where the rickety desk had been. It was walnut, with a desk-like look to it. Patsy stared. Then she walked slowly forward, her eyes going from the piece of furniture to her uncle and back again. Hesitantly she reached out and touched it, licked her lips, ran her fingers along the edge.

"Is it..." she ventured, then stopped. Her eyes went straight to Jess.

"Lift the edge," he prompted.

She did. The other girls gasped. Alison did, too.

"A sewing machine!" Patsy's eyes were huge and sparkling. She looked at Jess, gulped, then blinked hard and bit down on her lip. "Oh, Uncle Jess!" She crossed the room in a rush, wrapped her arms around him and hugged him.

And Jess hugged her back this time, pressed his face into her hair and whispered, "I love you."

He lifted his gaze and met Alison's. She felt her heart begin to beat more quickly, felt her pulses begin to pound. *What are you doing?* she asked him silently.

She got a faint smile in return.

"Put on your boots," he told them now. "We've got to go outside for the rest."

There was no grumbling about heading out into the blizzard. The girls wrapped up eagerly and followed him out. Jess held the door for them, then led them down to the barn.

"A new tractor?" Dottie guessed, grinning at her uncle.

"Only if you'd rather," Jess said. He led them into the barn, to the stall next to Dodger's. In it stood a sorrel horse with four white stockings and a white blaze.

Dottie's face went as white as the blaze. Her eyes filled with tears. "You don't mean—" She couldn't finish.

Jess handed her the bridle. "He's yours."

Alison just looked at him. "I hope this boarding school has a stable," Alison said to him as he led them from the barn.

"I think she'll be able to find a place for him," Jess said quietly. "I hope so, anyway."

He took them next to the shed behind the barn. He stopped them by the door, hunkered down so that his eyes were on a level with Sue's and said, "You're going to have to use your imagination for this, but I don't know anyone who's got a better one."

Inside there was a pile of lumber, chains, and a thick webbing of rope. He picked up a piece of paper off the top of the pile and handed it to her.

Sue didn't even look at it. She didn't need to. She just beamed up at him, her confidence justified. "My swing."

Her "swing" was going to be rather elaborate, Alison saw from the sketch Sue held in her hands. When it was built, it would have two swings, a climbing rope, a climbing web and, at one end, a ladder and a fireman's pole that would reach a second-story fort.

She looked at Jess. He was looking at Sue. "Santa asked me to take care of it for him," he told the little girl. "It was a lot of lumber to get in a sleigh."

Sue nodded her head.

Jess lifted his gaze and his eyes met Alison's.

"Quite a boarding school," she said. Her voice felt shaky. Her heart was racing. Her palms were damp.

Please, God, she prayed. *I'll try to understand if he only wants the girls. Really I will. But please, God, I love him so.*

Jess reached for her hand and drew her back to the house with him. "Your turn."

She hoped—she prayed—it might be a tiny velvet-covered box. She mounted the steps, feeling as if she were walking a plank and that when she reached the end, she would fall, and only then would she know if she'd reached heaven. Or hell.

She held her breath, willing him into the kitchen, willing him to reach into his pocket.

He stopped on the porch.

She looked around, saw some garden tools, a ball of twine, a gunny-sacked shape. She felt her chin begin to tremble. She clamped her teeth shut tight.

Jess crossed the porch, reached down and picked up the gunnysack. He turned and carried it back to her. It was a little more than half as high as he was.

She looked at the sack, looked at him.

"You're going to have to use your imagination, too," he said. He held it out, motioning for her to slip off the sack.

Her fingers were cold, that's why they fumbled, why they scratched ineffectually before they pulled the sack away.

It looked like a branch, brown and scrawny, poking up out of the soil. There was a small, white plastic tab stuck in the pot. With nervous fingers, Alison picked it up.

"Malus pumila."

"It's an apple tree. A Greening," Jess said hoarsely. "I know it's not much, but it's—" His voice faltered. He stopped.

Her eyes blurred, her mind spun. Not much? It was everything.

It was a promise. It was a sign of hope in the future. A man didn't buy an apple tree or a horse or enough lumber to build a castle unless he was committing himself for years and years.

She looked into his eyes and saw the love she knew she hadn't imagined. She saw fear and worry and, most of all, hope that it would grow and strengthen and bear fruit like his gift to her.

"I love you, Ali," he whispered.

And Alison went into his arms, parka, scarf, apple tree and all.

Jess held her as if he would never let her go, kissed her as if his very life depended on her touch. And Alison felt, for the first time since he'd left, the ice melt around her heart.

"Thank you, Pops," she whispered. And she thought she heard Jess murmur, "Thank you, Nathan. And thank you, Lizzie."

And then they were kissing again.

There was an insistent tug on her jacket. Still holding on to Jess, still wrapped in his arms, she looked down to see Sue looking up.

"What about Uncle Jess's present? We all got one, but he hasn't."

"Yes, I have," Jess said, opening the circle of his arms to draw them all in. But his eyes stayed locked with Alison's as he whispered, "I've got the best present a guy could ever have. Right here."

IT WAS 3:45 in the morning when Jess remembered what he'd forgotten to ask her.

She was curled into the warmth of his body, snuggling against him, and if he lifted his head from the pillow he could see the curve of her lips, as though she smiled.

They hadn't got to bed until past two. There'd been a doll-sized ranch house to build for Sue after the girls had finally gone to bed. And then there'd been their time alone in front of the fire. He'd put it to good use, he remembered with a smile, loving Alison with a thoroughness and an abandon that had left them both limp.

It had been all they could do to climb the stairs with their arms around each other. And they'd fallen asleep at once, still embracing, in Nathan's big feather bed.

Now he sat up, looking down at her in the faint pinkish silver glow cast by the swirling snow outside. He was loath to wake her, knew how exhausted she was, yet knew as well that he couldn't wait.

He touched her cheek, drew a line along her jaw, watched her nose wrinkle, her brow furrow, her eyes open.

"Jess?" She looked at him, her smile fading to worried concern.

"It's all right," he said quickly. "I just . . . just forgot to ask you something."

She sat up, draping the blanket around both of them, huddling close, cocooning them in their own little world. "Oh? What?"

He hesitated, waited for the familiar shaft of fear, then looked right past it into her eyes. "Will you marry me?"

"Marry you? You *forgot* to ask me to marry you?" Alison stared at him wide-eyed.

He ducked his head, sheepish. "It's not like I go around askin'! I've never done it before!"

"And thank heavens for that." She was smiling at him.

"Well," he said, exasperated, after a moment. "Will you?"

She giggled. She started tickling his ribs beneath the covers, pummeling him until he fell back onto the mattress and dragged her on top of him, imprisoning her hands, locking them against his chest.

"What do you think?" she whispered against his lips.

"Um..." He considered it, considered the way her body moved against his, the way her eyes smiled at his, the way her heart beat in a steady rhythm with his. "Yes?" he ventured at last.

"Yes," Alison said. "Oh, yes."

They loved again, then. Slowly and sweetly. With a tenderness and a passion born of years of dreams and need and hope.

Then Alison snuggled in the crook of his arm and lay her head on his shoulder. She pressed a kiss against his chest, whispered, "I love you, Jess. Merry Christmas," and then she slept.

Christmas.

For years it had been a day like any other when he'd done his chores, checked his horses, fed the cattle. And he'd do all that again today, because those things were a part of his life.

But they were no longer all of his life.

Today when he finished, he would come out of the barn and look up toward the house where the warmth of light and love were waiting. And he would hurry.

He would admire the skirt and jacket Alison had made for Patsy, he would talk horses with Dottie, he would see "Alison" and "Jess" settled in their brand-new ranch. He might even be talked into helping them with a little kissing practice, if Sue would let him.

But he'd save the best of his practicing for Alison—for Alison who had made him a believer, who had taught him to love and to risk and to hope, for Alison who had brought him home.

One year later

ANOTHER COWBOY CAME HOME FOR CHRISTMAS

Jess and Alison Cooper
and Patsy, Dottie and Sue
are delighted to announce the birth of
NATHAN PETER
on
December 24

weight: 7 lbs. 9 oz. *length: 21″*

COMING NEXT MONTH

EXTREME JUSTICE Marilyn Tracy

It had been three years since FBI agent John Chandler had saved Kelsey's life. Now she was in danger again—and John's assignment was to guard her with his life. But Kelsey refused to need anyone—including John.

CHRISTMAS EVERY DAY Marie Ferrarella

The final part of a delightful trilogy featuring the Sinclair family.

Nik Sinclair needed a temporary accountant—and fancy-free Sara seemed just right. But Sara was running from something... Life had taught her that nothing wonderful ever lasted—and she knew her feelings for Nik meant it was time to move on...

LADY OF THE NIGHT Emilie Richards

Jane Doe wasn't just another patient. Mystery surrounded her...and Joshua found himself completely entranced with the amnesiac woman whom he called Maggie...

NO RETREAT Marilyn Pappano

He Who Dares

As a child, Riley Cooper had been the troublemaker from the wrong side of town. Now he *was* the law—and he'd just arrested the young son of Liza Davis, the woman who'd once thought herself too good for him...